The Longest Shadow

R.J.Mitchell

Published by Fledgling Press 2013
www.fledglingpress.co.uk

Printed and bound by:
Bell & Bain Limited, Glasgow
ISBN: 9781905916610

Acknowledgements

FIRSTLY, THANKS to you, the reader, whoever you maybe, for without you there would be no point.

As always, thanks to my darling wife Arlene, a lady who has the patience of a saint, and has needed every ounce of it.

Thanks also to my daughter Ava and my mother Margaret for keeping me in check.

Once again my grateful thanks to Clare Cain, CEO at Fledgling Press, for her continuing support of my heartbroken detective, Gus Thoroughgood. Also to Zander, founder of Fledgling, both have given and continue to give hope and opportunity to aspiring Scottish writers.

Next, my gratitude to "the Rusla" (doesn't want to be named), the editor of The Longest Shadow, for keeping me out of the ambulance! (You know what I mean, amigo!)

Gratitude to Graeme Clarke for maintaining my website, www.rjmitchellauthor.co.uk, and for his technical expertise.

Thanks to my Evening Times colleague, Mick Brady, for his excellent cover design. Also to Brian McIntyre, general manager at WH Smith, Argyle Street, for his encouragement and support.

As always, thanks to my old cop chums Kenny "faither" Harvey and SupaMalky for helping me keep it real.

Finally, if I have forgotten anyone, please accept my sincerest apologies. Enjoy!

RJM

1

"WHAT'S YOUR poison, father?" asked the bartender, taking mischievous delight at the prospect of serving strong liquor to a man of the cloth at two o'clock on a Friday afternoon.

The priest placed his bible on the bar and smiled: "Whisky, my son, malt whisky and the best, a drop of your 18-year-old Lagavulin, if you don't mind."

"Sure," replied the barman, turning round to the gantry to survey his extensive collection of malts, before reaching for the bottle of golden brown liquid. He placed it on top of the bar before asking the priest, an impish smile creeping across his features: "Will that be large or small, father?"

From behind the circular rims of the gold-framed glasses, black eyes burned back at the bartender in a way that seemed strangely incompatible with the otherwise benign appearance presented by the clergyman's collar and neat black suit.

"You'd best make that a large one, my son, for I will need all the strength it gives me to be about the Lord's work this day," said the priest.

Taking the glass, he cradled it and enjoyed the sight of

the sunshine piercing through the liquid then took a sip, savouring the peatiness, before swallowing and letting out a slight sigh of approval.

The raven-haired priest spoke, "This golden drop is produced at Lagavulin on the island of Islay. Mmm, powerful, with a peat-smoke aroma. Well-balanced and smooth, yet with a slight sweetness on the palate. Do you know, my son, what Lagavulin means in the Gaelic?"

The bartender, a fresh-faced student by the looks of him, shook his head.

The priest smiled, "Lagavulin is an anglicisation of the Gaelic '*lag a'mhuilin*', meaning 'hollow by the mill'. So you have learned something new today, my son, and for that may you thank the Lord."

He picked up his bible and left the bemused barman at a loss for words, walking out of the Sword Hotel and making his way onto the footpath that would lead him to his intended destination.

As he made the ascent the wind picked up, causing the branches of the trees that lined either side of the small road to rustle with increasing vigour. Staring straight ahead he clutched his bible in his right hand and gave all his thought to the objective that lay before him and the completion of a vow that would bind him to the man he had made it to, for as long as he had breath in him.

Loud blasts from a horn snapped him from his reverie and the priest turned sharply to see a mini-bus full of teenage schoolchildren pulling up just feet behind him. He smiled serenely and, moving to the side of the roadway, beckoned them forward. As he did so, the passenger in the front seat, a middle-aged man with a cigar hanging out the side of his mouth, leaned out his window.

"Apologies, Father. Simon Duncan, Head of History at Wallace High School. I hope we didn't give you a fright?" he said without removing the cigar from his mouth.

"No, my son. On you go and have no concerns on my account."

"There's still quite a climb ahead of you – and then you have 246 steps to make it all the way to the crown and the best damn view in all of Scotland," the teacher cleared his throat as embarrassment at his curse overtook him. "Ah, please forgive me for a second time, Father. Can I give you a lift and make amends?"

"Not at all," said the priest, his Northern Irish accent becoming clear. "I am in need of both the fresh air and the exercise, to be sure. You go on ahead and I'll see you at the crown as you call it. They tell me Wallace's sword is a wonder."

The man laughed, "Indeed it is. Five foot four inches. Almost as big as a man. A windmill of death in the Wallace's hands, Father. No doubt. But safely encased now." The teacher smiled and nodded to the driver to press on before he turned to the priest once again, "Enjoy the climb, Father."

"I will indeed, my son," said the priest, waving the school party off.

After ten minutes walk up a steadily increasing gradient, he finally arrived at the foot of the towering monument to Scotland's greatest freedom fighter. Gazing at the massive sandstone walls he turned to survey the view around him: the meandering River Forth and the slowly rising urban sprawl of the city of Stirling, which once, hundreds of years ago, had dominated the waist of Scotland from behind the stout medieval walls of its intimidating castle.

3

"Hallowed be thy name, thy kingdom come, thy will be done. I will complete my vow to you now at last, Declan," he said under his breath as he turned towards his task.

2

THE VIEW was stunning by any standards and well worth every one of the 246 steps Thoroughgood had had to climb to appreciate it. The Wallace Monument had always held a special place in his heart. The great Scottish hero had, after all, been one of the main figures in the specialist paper he had written at Glasgow University all those years ago. Its title had been "Robert the Bruce and the Wars of Independence", but William Wallace, freedom fighter and Guardian of Scotland, had received almost equal billing in it.

Thoroughgood had in fact been raised in Stirling. Many of his Sunday afternoons had been spent climbing the impressive building with assorted relatives who never ceased to be amazed by this awesome memorial to Victorian architecture.

Gazing around towards Ben Lomond and the Trossachs in the west and on, over the Forth Valley, Stirling and the Ochil Hills to the Pentland Hills in the east, he felt the kind of inward peace that always returned when he visited the sites of his childhood and early teenage years. He smiled as he remembered the time when, aged just ten, he had been ridiculed by some local girls. One of those Sunday afternoon ascents had been made in a kilt at the insistence of his mother and in the company of two young cousins, who had found it hilarious when he had been subjected to a chorus of "kilty, kilty, cold bum!" by the girls.

Down below, in the village of Causewayhead, was the Birds and the Bees Pub where he had enjoyed his first underage pint as a pale, 15-year-old. He would never forget the wicked pleasure it had given him as, dressed in the trademark biker's jacket of his teens, he became the first in his year to be served in a pub at 6.30pm on a Tuesday night. "Pint of IPA please, miss." And a smile crept across his drawn features as he said the words out loud.

So why was he here? The events of the last two years were hard to comprehend when he tried to take stock, but it was at moments like these, with the wind blasting through his black hair, increasingly marbled with grey, that he was able to focus his thoughts with clarity.

It still seemed like a surreal dream to him; Meechan, the crime lord, ripping off the Mossad – hawking their enriched uranium to the mad Imam, Tariq – and paying for his treachery when his life was terminated by a Kidon death squad. Yet he still cringed at the thought of the carnage that would have ensued, had the mad cleric produced and blown a dirty bomb at that Old Firm game.

Meechan's demise had robbed Thoroughgood of the revenge he had craved above all else against the man who had sanctioned the death of Celine, the woman he supposed he would always love.

Thoroughgood knew he had to start looking forward in order to avoid being devoured by torment. Yet, as he drank in the shining vista on that brilliant spring afternoon, his thoughts once again retreated into the past. The opening lines of "The Go Between" by LP Hartley sprang to his mind readily, "The past is a foreign country: they do things differently there." It was God knows how many years since he had first read these words and yet they had seemed to find their way back into his consciousness with a strange regularity ever since.

Thoroughgood's mind seemed to be on a constant loop of childhood memories, interrupted by an occasional fast forward to Celine's face in her final moments – and finally, a vision of Meechan himself quoting from Thoroughgood's grandfather's bible, so sure that he was about to apply the full stop on the DS' own haunted existence.

The wind stung his cheeks, but it was the short sharp blow on his back which felt alarmingly familiar, that snapped his mind back to the here and now. The voice coming from behind him grated in the harsh Northern Irish accent of his nemesis.

"Turn around slowly, copper, and keep both hands at yer side."

But Meechan was dead . . .

3

THOROUGHGOOD TURNED slowly, as he was bid, and for the first time set eyes on the man who had killed Celine.

"O'Driscoll, you fuckin' murderer," he snapped.

The priest took a step back. His bible, Thoroughgood realised with a sinking heart, housed the barrel of a handgun, which remained trained on him.

O'Driscoll smiled. "You are surprised that with a Kidon despatched after him, Declan Aloysius Meechan would not prepare for every eventuality? That he would not make sure he had a gold-plated insurance policy in place that would mean even if he had departed this mortal coil, you would not be far behind, copper?"

Thoroughgood felt all hope of survival draining away from him. He shot a quick glance towards the uppermost level of the monument but there was nothing there to help him. In any case, he knew that even if there had been, there was little he could have done to neutralise the metal barrel trained on him and ready to pump certain death into his body.

Faced with the inevitable, Thoroughgood said, "So, even from the grave I can't escape your friend, or was he your master? Tell me one thing before you pull the trigger? How did she die, O'Driscoll?"

There was a short pause and for the first time in the moments since they had locked eyes, Thoroughgood detected a tinge of emotion. Something akin to a grimace slipped over the assassin's face.

O'Driscoll replied, "You know, right until I clapped eyes on her, in the last few minutes before I brought her life to an end, I couldn't understand why any woman could make a man like Declan Meechan do the things that 'my master', as you so eloquently described him, did. But – I'll give you this – she was a beauty. In the seconds before I pulled the trigger, there was a serenity in her that I have never come across in a woman in this life, nor probably will in the next, whatever awaits me."

"Serenity? That didn't stop you killing her, did it, you cold-blooded bastard," raged Thoroughgood as his self-control slipped. In desperation, before he met his own death, he had to ask the question that had tormented him ever since Celine's murder, "Tell me, O'Driscoll, if you have one piece of humanity in you, what were her last words?"

O'Driscoll's face remained expressionless while his soulless eyes remained locked on Thoroughgood. "For the record, she said nothing, Thoroughgood. Because I did not give her the chance, but I will say this, I did not agree with Meechan's decision to have the woman you both so obviously loved, killed. I do, however, agree completely with his decision to have you terminated."

O'Driscoll pulled the handgun from the bible and raised it level with Thoroughgood's head, "Back up against the wall, your final resting place awaits you."

He gestured with the gun and Thoroughgood shuffled back, until he was pressed against the cold sandstone and prepared to meet his maker.

An evil smile crept across O'Driscoll's face, "What are your last words in this life, Thoroughgood?"

Words would not come to Thoroughgood and in any case he knew they would have been wasted. This was it then, a bullet in the brain from the man who had killed Celine. Meechan laughing at him from beyond the grave.

He locked his eyes on O'Driscoll with all the defiance he could muster, "Get it over with," said Thoroughgood and braced himself for certain death as the cold wind blowing across the crown of the Wallace Monument stung his face.

But now that was not the only noise filling the air 220 feet up, as the chatter of adolescent voices perforated the deadly silence. The school party that had passed O'Driscoll en route to the monument began to spill out onto the building's top floor. Unaware of the drama playing itself out 20 yards away, the first two boys out were only interested in an impromptu kick-about with the ball they had smuggled up the spiral staircase.

Thoroughgood noticed them first and as the sound of their chatter reached his ears O'Driscoll's attention wavered from Thoroughgood as he glanced to his right.

The taller of the two teenagers, a brown-haired lad, grabbed the ball from his ginger-mopped mate and dropping it, aimed a volley at it. The ball headed straight for O'Driscoll as, belatedly, the teenagers spotted the gun in his right hand. Thoroughgood knew his only chance had been conjured up by divine intervention and he threw himself at the priest as the taller teenager shouted, "He's got a gun!"

O'Driscoll cannoned downwards at the impact of Thoroughgood's attack as the DS wrapped both his hands around the killer's wrist and smashed his hand and the gun it held, off the cement floor.

The gun went off, the bullet ricocheting off the sandstone wall behind Thoroughgood. As it did so, the air filled with the shrill of teenage screams and an adult voice shouting, "Get back down the stairs, back everyone!"

As Thoroughgood rammed O'Driscoll's hand and the revolver off the ground, the handgun slid across the cement. O'Driscoll smashed his forehead into Thoroughgood's nose and was showered in crimson for his trouble. The blow stunned Thoroughgood and the assassin threw him back against the sandstone wall, flashing a vicious smile, as he saw that he was now considerably nearer the stray firearm than Thoroughgood. But Thoroughgood was already on his feet and sprinting across the parapet in a desperate attempt to beat O'Driscoll to the firearm.

Just as the assassin wrapped his fingers around its grooved handle, Thoroughgood smashed into him with all the power he could muster, his weight sending both men into the east wall. Thoroughgood rasped, "At last you're mine O'Driscoll, you murderin' scum," as he attempted to force O'Driscoll's hands and the firearm into the air. But before he could move the handgun clear of his body O'Driscoll pulled the trigger and Thoroughgood felt a rasp of cold air as the bullet shot past his right shoulder.

O'Driscoll stared at Thoroughgood's face, expecting the detective to show signs that he had been penetrated by the lead missile. There were none. This time, Thoroughgood slammed his forehead at the assassin's right eye and the impact threw O'Driscoll half over the rampart. Thoroughgood finally broke his adversary's hold on the gun and it fell from his grip.

The sound of the firearm smashing off the sandstone walls of the monument provided a chilling backdrop to their dance with death, underlining just how far the drop from the building's crown was.

His desperation giving him renewed strength, O'Driscoll slammed his left fist into Thoroughgood's jaw, winning just enough breathing space for him to roll along the wall and pull back from the detective. Backing off another couple of yards O'Driscoll tried to recover his breath and as he did so, a feral grin spread across his venomous features.

"Fancy your chances now, copper, eh? Problem is, I always carry a little something for emergencies." O'Driscoll removed a glinting blade from inside his suit. "You have made this messy, Thoroughgood, but it will be all the more enjoyable for that."

O'Driscoll advanced on him, knife in his right hand. Thoroughgood rolled over to his left, simultaneously ripping his jacket off and springing to his feet.

"You've one chance, Thoroughgood, and that is no chance," smiled O'Driscoll. "Declan told me he would have spit you that time up at Tara, but for her intervention. It was then that he knew he had been cuckolded by you and your beautiful whore. That was the moment the die was cast for you and her. Now I am going to finish what Declan started that night, and gut you once and for all, copper."

As the blade sliced towards Thoroughgood's left shoulder, he ducked low to his right, smashed his right

12

hand into O'Driscoll's ribcage while, with his jacket wrapped around his left hand, he grabbed at the blade and tried to wrestle it from the winded O'Driscoll. The knife was forced up into the air – both men grappling for control of it.

Thoroughgood rammed his knee into O'Driscoll's midriff and the killer let out a gasp, but he retained his grip on the blade and backed away. Thoroughgood was now back where he had started, against the sandstone wall.

O'Driscoll advanced for the final time. "I hope you can fly," he taunted and slashed the blade down, filling the air with the hiss of impending death. But as he moved the knife Thoroughgood pounced. With both hands on O'Driscoll's right arm he pulled himself down, clawing the killer with him and pushing both his feet into O'Driscoll's guts. With all his power, Thoroughgood somersaulted the assassin over his head and rolled free.

Readying himself for his assailant's next attack, Thoroughgood's eyes opened wide as the assassin hit the wall and, caught off-balance, toppled over its edge and into the blue horizon, his death scream filling the air. Shaking, the DS made his way to the wall and looked over. There, at the bottom of the monument, lay the inert form of O'Driscoll, the ruby pool beside his smashed skull growing bigger by the second.

Tears welling up in his eyes Thoroughgood whispered into the wind: "At last, Celine, you are avenged." He grabbed the abandoned football and booted it off the roof of the Wallace Monument, into the sky.

It was over.

Still in a daze, and breathing heavily from his exertions he made his way to the staircase. There, Thoroughgood spotted the brown-haired teenager whose accidental intervention had saved him.

Thoroughgood smiled at him, "Nice work, Becks. You saved my bacon, son, and for that you have my eternal gratitude." The teenager was clearly lost for words, but an astonished grin crept across his uncertain features as Thoroughgood extended his right hand with a crumpled £10 note in it, "That should cover the cost of a new ba'."

"Thanks, mister," said the boy.

4

ELIZABETH, LADY Roxburgh, sipped afternoon tea from a bone china teacup and gazed out of the huge bay window of Roxburgh Hall, enjoying the beautiful view of Loch Lomond that she had taken for granted all these years.

Her eyes swept over the immaculately manicured lawns flanking the Hall and down into the bluebell wood as she lost herself in memories of happy days, long since gone. Lady Elizabeth's mind's eye hit replay as she smelled the sweet aroma of flowers and felt the warmth of the sunshine on her face, picturing her beloved William going down on one knee and proposing to her among the bluebells, all those years back.

It was a special place, one that was a sanctuary for her. When Elizabeth needed to escape she would take the short walk down the drive and lose herself in the stillness of the wood, seated on the wooden bench which exactly marked the spot where William had proposed. A special place, she had made it even more special by having William buried there, and now his grave provided Lady Elizabeth with something tangible she could focus on and somewhere she could lose herself in her most treasured memories.

At times she had whispered his name, recalling those golden times, sure she sensed his presence around her. But today she could not hope to hide from the problems of the present. Lady Elizabeth took a deep breath and tried to compose herself. Over afternoon tea, her future and that of her family, all the Roxburgh dynasty had striven for and held dear for over 200 years, would be decided.

The chimes of the grandfather clock situated in the flag-stoned reception hall struck four and she took a deep breath, attempting to quell the tension growing within her as she awaited the arrival of her two sons, Robert and Alexander. Their meeting, to decide exactly what was going to happen to the family-run distillery, situated a few miles north of the village of Strathblane, was moments away.

The whisky business had made the Roxburghs great. The elevation of James Roxburgh to Viscount Lomond in the late 18th century, and the building of Roxburgh Hall in striking baronial style, 1000 yards from the south bank of Loch Lomond, in 200 acres of prime farm land, had seen the Roxburgh's stately home lauded as Scotland's gothic mansion.

It had been a project funded by the fine malt whisky, born from the secrets of Scotland's slowest whisky distillation, which came courtesy of a pure water supply flowing from a nearby hillside spring that had made the Roxburgh's fortune. Settled in these rich and rolling grounds that stretched back from the bonnie banks of the loch itself, the family had prospered into one of Scotland's greatest whisky dynasties.

Lady Elizabeth gazed at the portrait of the second Viscount, Andrew, dominating the mansion's main reception room, staring down in full Highland regalia. It was Andrew who had helped the family's stock rise still further when he had named the hill, providing the most beautiful view of the loch as the 'Queen's View' during one of Queen Victoria's many visits to the area, and so gained royal patronage and Her Majesty as a regular visitor to Roxburgh Hall.

Her golden hair French-combed to a remarkable perfection and smooth alabaster skin masked the fact that Lady Elizabeth was now nearing her 58th year. She sipped her tea and reflected on the family heritage, wondering just what those distant and intimidating ancestors would make of the impasse the family now found themselves in.

The panelled oak door opened and Robert Roxburgh entered the lounge followed by his younger brother Alexander. At 35, his six foot four frame was a powerful reminder of his spell with the Scots Guards. But the burden of maintaining the family empire was now leaving its mark and his face was gaunt and taut from the strain of preserving the distillery he had run ever since his father's death. Determined as he was to avoid the ignominy of becoming the Roxburgh upon whose watch the family's fortune had been ruined, the effort of doing so was taking an evident toll.

"Good afternoon, Mother," said Robert in the clipped public school tones that had been with him ever since his days at Gordonstoun as he sank into the armchair he favoured whenever he was within the great house's main lounge. It was known as the Scott lounge in honour of the great Victorian novelist, Sir Walter Scott, whose regular sojourns at the Hall were said to have inspired him to write his celebrated Waverley novels.

Eyeing his brother with a contempt that was all too obvious, Alexander leaned against the mantle of the huge fireplace, enjoying the warmth of the crackling logs that helped remove the chill of a cold Scottish spring day, before greeting his mother with due deference.

"Hello, Mother. I hope you are prepared for Robert's cunning plan."

Before Lady Elizabeth could speak, Robert's wrath exploded, "Damn it brother, hold your tongue! Mother knows full well the dire straits we are in and it is I, not you, who has found the means to get us through them and safeguard Roxburgh Hall and the future of the Roxburghs! Pull the chord for Macintosh and see if we can get some coffee before we go into the whole business of the merger with the Gwai Lo Cartel."

Lady Elizabeth's raised finger ensured Alexander remained quiet and did as he was bid. She was the matriarch of Roxburgh Hall and had raised the family almost single-handed since William's death, some 20 years previously, from a massive heart attack on a squash court.

At that moment the door opened and a man in an immaculate pin-striped suit and slick, brown hair appeared bearing refreshments and glided over to a large antique coffee table.

His eyes and his words were directed solely at Lady Roxburgh. "Lady Elizabeth, I took the liberty, in the knowledge that Viscount Robert and Master Alexander would be arriving, of having coffee prepared for them. I trust you are happy with your afternoon tea and confectionery?"

"Indeed I am, Macintosh, and thank you, as always, for

your efficiency. I don't know what we would do without you," said Lady Elizabeth.

"Good show, Macintosh, you are a mind reader," added Alexander.

"Thank you, Master Alexander," replied Macintosh, with a precise nod of his head and adding, "If that will be all, my Lady?"

"Yes, Macintosh, you may go," the dowager replied and Macintosh slipped soundlessly out of the room.

Moments later after taking a draught of his black coffee, Robert cut to the chase. "Forgive my brusqueness, mother, but time is of the essence. I have an agreement in principal from the Gwai Lo and quite frankly, I don't see how it can be bettered."

Alexander was far from convinced, "Is it too much to ask you to translate your new chums' nom de plume into the Queen's English, brother?"

Robert's face seemed to turn to stone as he seared his younger sibling with a glare that showed little evidence of any brotherly love. "Gwai Lo can roughly be translated as Ghost Man, little brother. It was originally used as a deprecatory term towards foreigners. The term apparently arose in the 16th century when European sailors appeared in southern China, as they were associated with barbarians. So our new Chinese business partners are not without humour, Alex, you see. If you will just give them a chance."

Alexander remained unimpressed. "So, what is the deal? A couple of million up front and they take over our distillery and then our Chinese associates remove all presence of the Roxburghs from the board which will in turn be filled with our new Oriental friends? Roxburgh

Hall renamed Mandarin Mansion and Mother evicted and shunted into a converted stable?"

Robert took a deep breath as he tried to keep the lid on his mounting anger, but before he could answer his brother's accusations his mother intervened. "Alexander, flippancy and excited accusation does no one any good! I have every confidence that your brother has acted with our best interests at heart." Yet the fact the matriarch of Roxburgh Hall played with her pearls betrayed the concern that was continuing to mount within her.

Robert's gaze shot from his mother back to his younger brother who stood motionless at the side of the fireplace, one hand wrapped around a coffee cup perched on the mantlepiece, but the younger Roxburgh's eyes blazed.

"The terms are as good as we are going to get from anyone out there for a whisky distillery that is in need of considerable overhaul and to wipe out the debt we already owe the bank. Yes, there is an upfront payment, but it is considerably more than the one you mentioned and will help Mother carry out all of the repairs required at the Hall. It will also sustain her and Victoria here in comfort, where the Roxburghs have been since before the Jacobites were begging us for safe haven back in '45, for the foreseeable future," Robert raised his right hand to stop his brother interjecting.

"I will retain the position of managing director and I have even managed to get a place on the board for you, dear little brother, and a suitable salary to go along with it. So you don't need to worry about your ridiculous subscriptions at the Carrick and your continued control over the day-to-day workings of the distillery. On top of that, we will now have Glen Lomond Malt whisky flooding into the Asian market through the Gwai Lo supply outlets.

"I have also had to agree to the production of whisky liqueur which the cartel wants produced specifically for the Asian market. The translation, in Her Majesty's English, for your benefit little brother, being The Dark Ocean, but, pardon the pun, I can swallow that. Yes, there are some forfeit clauses if we fail to make production targets, but these are minimal," Robert smiled reassuringly at his mother before returning a cold gaze to Alexander. "Mother, I promise you the future of the Roxburghs, Roxburgh Hall, our distillery and Glen Lomond Malt Whisky will be safe."

Lady Roxburgh smiled thinly, "Good boy, Robert. I knew we could rely on you," and rose elegantly from the chaise longue and made her regal way over to the bay window overlooking the drive, neatly colonnaded by birch trees.

The brief moment of silence was punctured by Alexander's dissent, "If you believe any of that, you are even more deluded than I thought. This is your fault, Robert, you and the crap tables you have become obsessed with at the River Boat Casino. We will be no more than puppets in our own theatre. You should be ashamed Robert, you have sold us out. A whisky liqueur called The Dark Ocean, funded by Ghost Men? You are taking the piss. You will make the Roxburgh name a laughing stock. Furthermore, just what are the specifics of these production targets you have neatly avoided telling us about?"

As she sighted a horse and rider galloping through

the parkland leading to the house, Lady Elizabeth spoke, although she did not turn to face either of her sons. "Enough! I won't tolerate such language within the Hall, or out of it, for that matter, Alexander. Victoria is on her way, and I will not have the two of you bickering like two schoolboys over this. Alexander, there is no alternative. You will support your brother in this whether you like it or not. Do I make myself clear?"

But Alexander had one final parting shot to aim at his elder brother before he left. "You mark my words, Rob. You will have the bloody curse ringing throughout the Hall and five centuries of history and the Roxburghs on the banks of Loch Lomond wiped out, just as the damned Jacobites threatened." Then the younger Roxburgh son was gone and the crash of the door provided an answer Lady Elizabeth did not want to hear.

The powerful white stallion galloped over the gently undulating parkland leading to the Hall. The beast's thunderous gallop was the perfect combination of sinew and muscle working in complete harmony, mastered as he was by an expert rider who had been his mistress since he was a colt.

Expertly bringing Pegasus to a stop on the white gravel, just below the famous triple level grey granite stairs that provided the imposing entrance to the hall, Victoria, youngest of the Roxburgh siblings, had reined in her mount just as her brother Alexander left the Hall.

"In a hurry, Alex?" she asked.

"Damn it, Victoria! This business with the bloody Chinks will be the end of everything that we hold dear, and all because Robert has frittered away everything that generations of Roxburghs have built up, with a mountain of gambling debts. Father will be turning in his grave," said Alexander.

Victoria tried to sooth him with a radiant smile, "Come on, Alex, it can't be as bad as all that. If it was, do you think mummy would allow it?"

"He might have all the smart answers, but behind them the plain truth is, Robert has sold out our heritage and is about to make a laughing stock of the Glen Lomond brand. But you can ask Mother about that in a moment. Personally, I have had enough of all this for one day. Bye, Vicky." With that Alexander stormed over to his waiting Range Rover.

Victoria flashed a smile at Macintosh, who had appeared in the central section of the triple archway preceding the Hall's imposing oak doorway. The air filled with the sound of gravel being sprayed everywhere as the seething Alexander took his leave.

Brushing past the butler, Robert also made his exit from the Hall, his face tight with suppressed rage and as Victoria's eyes met his, the eldest of the Roxburgh brood waved a hand at her almost dismissively, "Not now, Vicky. It's been a bad day and I need to get back to the distillery." He stopped a foot away from her, running the fingers of his right hand through the golden hair he had inherited from their mother, "Look, I'm sorry Vicky, but the truth is out now and you might not like what Mama has to tell you. He may be our brother, but that temper Alex has is a liability. He just can't help himself, and shooting off at the mouth about that damned Jacobite curse helps no one. Just remember, I may have contributed to the mess we are in, but I did not bring it all about and I believe I have found the remedy to all of the Roxburghs ailments."

Victoria's brown eyes searched his troubled face as she asked, "Just how bad are our ailments, Robbie?"

The childhood term of endearment cut no ice with her eldest brother, "Trust me, Vicky, it will all be fine. I wouldn't let you or Mama down would I, sis? Now, I must get going. I have a lot to iron out before the deal is ready to be signed on the dotted line."

With that, Robert leant over, kissed his sister on the cheek, gave her a reassuring wink for good measure and strode over to his Bentley.

Victoria was joined by Macintosh at the foot of the steps. The butler smiled benignly before greeting her with a slight and deferential nod of his head, "Good afternoon, Miss Victoria, shall I have Pegasus taken down to the stables?"

"That would be kind of you, Macintosh, he'll need a feed and I will be down to see to him shortly, after I have had a chance to talk with Mama. Tell me, how is she?" asked Victoria.

"Lady Elizabeth is bearing up, miss. I think that is the best way to put it," said the inscrutable Macintosh.

His words failed to stop a mounting sense of foreboding enveloping Victoria as she entered Roxburgh Hall.

5

LADY ELIZABETH continued to stare through the window as she heard the lounge door open, heralding the arrival of her only daughter. As she turned slowly towards Victoria, the youngest Roxburgh could see worry written deep in her mother's face, entirely understandable considering just how much stress the Roxburgh matriarch had been under of late.

"Mama, is everything all right?" asked Victoria, removing her riding hat.

"It will be, my darling," said her mother and in an act that was completely at odds with her usual calm self-containment, she wrapped her arms around her daughter and pulled her close. Her head buried in the mohair of her mother's elegant green cardigan, Victoria heard her murmur, "It will be and we shall make it so, Vicky." Again, the use of the shortened form of her Christian name came as a surprise to Victoria.

Her mother slowly pushed her to arms length, keeping a hand on each shoulder and addressed her daughter, "I do not know how much Alexander told you out there on the drive but I have no doubt he had his say on the business deal. Robert has reached agreement with the Chinese consortium, or the Gwai Lo as I should call them. But whatever Alex has said, you must remember that it is the only deal on the table and the only one that will allow the Roxburghs to retain control of the Glen Lomond distillery and keep us here at Roxburgh Hall where we belong."

As she tried to digest the news Victoria said, "If Robert believes the deal will save us and there is no other option, then what alternative do we have, mother, but to support him?"

Lady Roxburgh smiled serenely, "You are right, but I doubt if Alex sees it that way. However, I want us to make the most of this: make a silk purse out of a sow's ear as your father would say. That means we should embrace the Gwai Lo and the launch of The Dark Ocean liqueur on the Asian market."

A frown crept across Victoria's refined features and she sat down on the elegant chaise longue, but her attention remained 100 percent focused on Lady Elizabeth.

"I just wondered if you knew what the English translation of Gwai Lo was, mummy?" enquired Victoria.

At last a smile crept across the dowager's face as she responded, "I believe it means Ghost Man, or Men, in the case of the cartel. Quite amusing really, to do business with ghosts, don't you think, Vicky?"

Victoria was unable to return her mother's smile. "I think it all sounds a bit creepy, but if needs must then so be it."

"Indeed, my darling. We will put our all into making sure that the launch of The Dark Ocean liqueur will be a night to remember, here. This is a show that will, and must, go on and I want every section of Scottish society that matters here," said Lady Roxburgh. Taking a breath, her voice became steelier. "Instead of allowing this business to be seen as a weakness, we will make it into a strength by adding a new dimension and profile to the Glen Lomond brand, and show our new Chinese friends just how valuable the Roxburgh name is, and its connections, can be to them."

Victoria blurted out words she immediately regretted, "What did Robert mean when he said Alex had been running off at the mouth about a Jacobite curse?"

Elizabeth moved across the room and joined her daughter on the golden settee, taking Victoria's right hand in her own, "Mere old wives tales, my dear, and nothing for you to concern yourself with. What we must do is concentrate on what is important. Robert and I will need your help. You'll be aware that I don't exactly approve of some of your social connections, but now is the time we must make the most of them."

Victoria smiled as she realised that at long last her mother was seeking her help for an event that could prove crucial to their family's future, "You know I'd love to help, Mama, in whatever way I can. I'm thinking a marquee on the lawn, Belgian chocolate and champagne fountains, hog and lamb roasts. This could be one of the most memorable social occasions of the Scottish summer. It will be a triumph."

Lady Roxburgh patted her daughter's hand warmly, "I believe you have made some, what shall I call them . . . associations, at some of those fashion events you love so much which may now come into their own?"

Her daughter's face lit up at the prospect of being handed a key role in the launch, "Yes, Mama, I have an idea. I was at a show to promote Vanessa Velvet's new lingerie range last month and I met her at the post launch party afterwards. She's planning to launch a new range of clothing that is, how shall I put it, less risqué than her usual creations. Let me see if I can persuade her to stage the launch here with us. She might be willing to preview it at the Hall and maybe raise money for charity into the bargain."

"Your father will be resting uneasily at the thought of enlisting the services of that brazen woman to help us save our souls. But she has her name and face everywhere and anywhere, and I have no doubt that she will bring media attention with her."

"You're right, Mama. Once she knows the sort of people who'll be there, I think she will find the proposition very attractive. Trust me, Mama, I won't let you down," said Victoria.

Lady Roxburgh knew this was an opportunity she could not deny her daughter, "Yes, Victoria you may pursue your idea. But I expect you to keep me aware of every development about this Velvet woman. Macintosh will oversee all organisational aspects of our, what should I say . . .?"

"Exclusive launch of The Dark Ocean liqueur. Believe me, Mama, it will not be too difficult to get the fashion magazines interested, and I would imagine if we can get enough of the 'landed' along, Hello! magazine might be tempted. After all, they covered the launch and close of the salmon season up on the River Tay, at Kenmore. I can make our launch bigger than that. Trust me on this, Mama."

Victoria's soft brown eyes met her mother's gaze and Lady Roxburgh found herself welling up at just how much her daughter resembled her beloved William. The father whom Victoria had never known and who had never had the chance to see the daughter he had wanted so much, blossoming into a woman her mother was becoming increasingly proud of.

Tears welling up in her eyes, Lady Roxburgh quickly removed the lace handkerchief she kept up her sleeve and dabbed at the corner of her eyes.

Victoria embraced her mother and whispered in her ear, "Don't worry, Mama, we will make sure father is looking down proudly from above with a smile on his face."

"God, I hope so," said Lady Roxburgh as her eyes strayed to the portrait of her late husband William, magnificent in full Master of the Lomond Hounds uniform, then she looked out of the window into the bluebell wood.

'If only you were here now my darling' said Lady Roxburgh softly to herself.

6

THE TRUTH was something he would never have shared with the rest of his family, yet now it had been forced out into the open by Alex, and his mother knew his tawdry secret. Forced to confront the weakness he had striven so hard to hide and which had contributed to the decline in his family fortunes, Robert Roxburgh blanched with shame.

As his Bentley swept through the gates of the Glen Lomond distillery, owned by his family for almost 200 years, the doubt that had been gnawing at him for days seemed to grow with every passing moment. The public face of the Gwai Lo consortium was one of a well-run conglomerate, but under the surface the money trail revealed that the cabal was essentially a money-laundering operation for a notorious branch of the Triad Chinese criminal fraternity.

The popularity of Scottish malt whisky in the Chinese domestic drinks market had made the purchase of the Glen Lomond Distillery particularly attractive to the conglomerate members. The idea of mixing business trips with the pleasure of the golf tours they regularly undertook around Scotland's prize courses – one of which, The Carrick, straddled the shores of Loch Lomond, itself only miles from the grounds of Roxburgh Hall – was particularly appealing.

Roxburgh's disastrous addiction to the tables of Glasgow's casinos had ironically proven his salvation, for it was there, with his wallet empty and his luck broken, that he had met Raymond Cheung. Plausible and generous, and a fellow student of the school of fortune, Cheung had observed Robert's disastrous run at the tables one December night. He had seen Robert's painful embarrassment and bailed him out by slapping down ten grand in rolled notes and dismissing Robert's hollow protests.

Later, Cheung had insisted he buy Roxburgh a whisky at the casino bar. As Roxburgh laughed at the irony of being bought liquor that was none other than one produced by his own distillery, he unloaded the worries under which he and his family were drowning.

It was then that Cheung had mentioned he and his associates might be interested in brokering a deal which would save the whisky dynasty – one that would allow his cabal to introduce a signature whisky liqueur into the Asian market which would in turn elevate the Gwai Lo to a pre-eminent position in their homeland.

Fast forward and Roxburgh now had 48 hours to make his final decision on the deal that was the only one on the table and thus, his sole shot at salvation.

Robert now understood he would be getting in bed with a notorious criminal fraternity, but he also knew that their need for his expertise in marketing the new brand, as well as that of his brother, in maintaining the distillery, was essential to the Gwai Lo and exactly why Cheung was likely to remain happy as a sleeping partner. Further reassurance had soon been provided by the Triad boss that neither himself nor his associates would be seen or heard, other than to check in person that their new venture was in good health, using their golfing tours as a front. Yet despite his understated way, and behind his immaculate manners, Roxburgh knew that should he cross Cheung, his future would be painfully short.

Seated behind his desk in the distillery office, Roxburgh opened the bottom drawer, reaching instinctively for the bottle of 18-year-old malt that would help dull the throbbing headache he had developed since he had left the Hall after his quarrel with Alex and his shaming in front of his mother.

"Damnation," he cursed as he relished the malt and recalled how shaken his mother had been by the whole unsavoury business. It hadn't helped that Vicky had happened to come by, although thankfully she had arrived too late to hear Lady Elizabeth haranguing him. He took another deep slug of the golden liquid and swilled it around his mouth, staring at the black and white photograph on the office wall showing his grandfather Ludovic and the staff of the distillery, taken on the eve of the Second World War.

The old man would never have got himself into a mess like this and would be cursing him from beyond the grave. "Damn the tables!" He cursed his weakness out loud and stared at the fierce burning eyes he shared with his grandfather. Ludovic, the war-time hero and key member of Churchill's post war cabinet. Robert wondered, not for the first time, how he had managed to combine that position while maintaining and expanding the distillery's fortunes. The thought made him queasy with guilt.

He shook his head. He needed fresh air. Opening the office door he stepped out onto the wrought iron staircase and leaned on the railing that encased the landing. The deliciousness of the fresh pine from the towering tree that cast its shadow over his office, assaulted his senses and he filled his lungs with its freshness. But the questions that came with his plan to bail out the business and preserve his family, and all they stood for, would not stop eating away at him.

Could he really trust Cheung and his cabal to honour their word and leave him to run the business as they had said they would? Or would he become the puppet that Alex believed was his fate?

Yet, while he knew the implications of doing business with the Gwai Lo, he also believed that they were hardly likely to ignore the legitimacy of one of the most respected family names in the Scottish whisky industry. A name that commanded respect worldwide; a name that would help gloss over their illegal activities and this new and diverse way of laundering their ill-gotten gains around Europe.

Yet his shame was nauseating. Why had he allowed his gambling debts to get out of hand? As he took another sip of his family's signature malt the question kept rebounding around his head.

Lost in his silent world of self-imposed torture Robert did not hear the footfall on the gravel behind the giant pine tree. A whipcrack sounded out, shattering the silence of the night and smashing into the railing, inches away from his right hand. Before he knew what was happening, a second shot rang out and this time the office window behind him exploded.

"Jesus Christ!" he swore and dropped to his knees, cowering behind the partial cover of the wrought iron railings.

He needed to get inside the office, and quickly. Roxburgh crawled across the landing and opened the door just as two more bullets slammed into it. His breath rasping in short sharp bursts he charged into the office and slammed it shut behind him. Using his military training he forced himself to calm down and consider his options.

From the open desk drawer he removed the military revolver that had been there since his grandfather's days, and checked that the chamber was still filled with ammunition. It was. Dimming the office light to make sure his silhouette was no longer visible to his would-be killer, he cautiously opened the door and made his way onto the landing at a crouch. Aiming the revolver into the night he felt comforted by the weight of the gun in his right hand.

Once again the silence was broken, but this time Roxburgh saw a single headlight illuminate and heard the noise of the motorbike engine rev. Then it was gone in a screech of rubber, obscured by the foliage at the limit of the distillery grounds.

His would-be assassin had gone, but who had wanted him dead? Roxburgh already knew that sleep would not come for him that night.

7

"JESUS H Christ, Thoroughgood! Every time you turn around you must expect the Grim Reaper is keeping you company! It's uncanny, I tell you. Still, at least O'Driscoll's demise should mean the end of Meechan and everything he stood for, once and for all. Er, yes, of course I am glad it was him and not you!" said Detective Superintendent Valentino Tomachek, holding his pipe in one hand and ripping open his desk drawer with the other before scrabbling about for his favoured pipe tobacco.

His attention on his pipe, the room went quiet as Tomachek salivated at his impending moment of sweet satisfaction. Aware that both Thoroughgood and Hardie were subjecting his every move to intense scrutiny, Tomachek looked up and pierced them both with his pale grey eyes.

"You pair of bally buggers! Let me teach you something about this beauty," said Tomachek waving the index finger of his left hand, still clutching said pipe tightly, at the two detectives, "This beauty is a Cairngorm bent. Manufactured by no less than Blakemar of Northampton, a family business which has handcrafted the finest briar pipes since 1890."

Applying a match Tomachek was soon off and puffing. A deep inhalation was followed by the customary billow, but the detective superintendent had not finished extolling the virtues of his not-so-secret passion, "The tobacco of the moment, for your information, dear boys, is MacBaren's Vanilla Cream." Holding his right hand up Tomachek made sure that both his subordinates knew he had far from finished.

Hardie could not help himself, "Correct me if I'm wrong, boss, but I thought you were strictly a walnut man when it came to the pipe, and that nothing beat the Condor moment when it was down to the tobacco?"

Tomachek unplugged the pipe both detectives now knew was called a Cairngorm Bent from the cavern that was his mouth, and jabbed it in Hardie's direction, "Now listen here, Hardie, don't try and get smart with me or I can assure you any chance of that set of stripes you'd sell your dear old mammy for will be long gone."

"All very fascinating," muttered Thoroughgood under his breath and found himself impaled on the end of one of Tomachek's famous stares.

"I heard that, Thoroughgood, and when it comes to your pips read Hardie and stripes," snapped the detective superintendent.

"Apologies, sir," said Thoroughgood, his exasperation showing.

"Yes, yes that's fine. Now let's proceed to the heart of the matter. Your next case, gentlemen, is indeed one which will represent something of a different challenge for you. A departure, of sorts, from the usual mayhem you find yourselves so routinely involved in," Tomachek paused for a billow, and through the smoke Thoroughgood could see his eyes sparkling.

Tomachek proceeded in an orderly fashion, "Gentlemen, we have an increasing problem with a series of specialist robberies in our city, and one that must be brought to an end."

Hardie shot Thoroughgood a quick glance, unable to comprehend how either of them had failed to hear the first thing about these robberies.

"I see I have your attention now, my fine fellows. You are both asking yourselves how can it be that Glasgow's finest don't have a clue about a problem that is bringing terror to a section of the city's business community?"

"Yes, boss," was the best Thoroughgood could do.

"Well, it's all here and printed fresh off the case management system ten minutes back, by the pretty little WPC on secondment to my office, bless her." said Tomachek, a wicked smile playing at the corners of his mouth.

Hardie's patience was first to snap and the veteran DC grabbed the manila casefile, "What kind of robberies, boss?"

"Indeed, my dear Hardie," purred Tomachek agreeably, "I can see you're hungry to get to the meat of it, as always."

Thoroughgood was unsure if the detective superintendent was playing some kind of joke on him and his partner, "Come on, governor, put us out of our misery."

But it was Hardie who provided the moment of enlightenment his gaffer craved, "Butcher shop robberies!" spat out the DC and the disgust in his tone said it all.

Tomachek removed his pipe from his mouth in an

exaggerated gesture. "I'm sorry, dear boys, I really am, but something has to be done about this. It started before Christmas, on Christmas Eve to be precise, when a butchers in Drumchapel was turned over and he lost all his Christmas orders to the tune of ten grand. Bastards even stole his wee boy's BMX bike."

Tomachek took another puff and then continued apace, "The whole problem has got out of hand and we're averaging around one turn a week. We're talking a six figure sum in stolen meat and the chief constable has taken a personal interest in the matter after the bloody Evening Times ran an exposé on the whole business."

"So you want us to take a butchers?" asked Hardie sarcastically.

"Indeed I do, my dear Hardie. It may not have the profile of your previous entanglement, but by God, it is starting to generate a rotten stink with the press. Right now, who else would the chief constable want most on the trail of the butchers shop bandits but our two most celebrated detectives – Messrs Thoroughgood and Hardie. Well, perhaps he wouldn't have been so insistent until today's Evening Times," with that Tomachek whipped out a copy of the city newspaper and shoved it to the other side of his desk.

Thoroughgood impulsively read the headline out loud, "Butcher shop bandits give cops the chop – again."

"Quite so," said Tomachek before continuing, "That bastard Donald Hurry, the Times crime correspondent, has slapped the latest robbery, which just happened to occur at the chief's favourite Bearsden butchers, right on the front page."

"Great. Just bloody great," said Hardie in an

involuntary reaction that was out of his mouth before he could stop it.

"Now look here, Hardie, I can see this has left you less than chuffed but . . ." Tomachek paused and couldn't help the smile behind his pipe developing into a hearty chortle before ploughing on, "I want you to take the long view here, dear boys. Look at this as the opportunity to clinch the promotions you are so desperate for. Your mission is to find these bandits and bring them to justice before it all goes pear-shaped and someone gets seriously hurt. Should you do so, I can promise you shall go to Pitt Street for the next promotion parade," Tomachek took another puff from the Cairngorm Bent, removed it and pointed to the door with the stem, "There's the door, my fine fellows, but before using it make sure the case notes accompany you out of the exit." In a more placatory tone, "Solve this one, lads, and you will have my eternal gratitude and more importantly that of the chief. $E = MC2$ as dear old Uncle Albert put it, eh?"

The two chairs on the opposite side of the desk scraped back and Thoroughgood scooped up the manila casefile and the newspaper en route to the exit.

As they made for the rear yard of Stewart Street City Centre nick they could hear grunts and snorting as the city centre CID relished the news of their latest mission. Just before they reached their car a voice shouted. "Aye, about time you went on a real steak-out, Hardie," before another one added, "Porks of being the old man's pet, Thoroughgood!" Hysterics erupted from all four corners of the yard before another jibe reached their ears, "Make sure you bring home the bacon, Thoroughgood!" Then in unison a chorus of moos burst out.

"Ah, feck off the lot of you!" shouted Hardie as he and Thoroughgood jumped into the Focus and roared out of the yard at speed.

Thoroughgood surveyed his pint of Stella and took a large gulp from the goblet-style glass that had replaced the traditional pint pot he was far more at home with. His quiet contemplation was shattered as Hardie clattered his glass off the chipped enamel table. The Rock was far from heaving with life, which in many ways was ideal after the day they had just had.

"Fuck me, what next? I never thought I'd see the day when we would be chasin' after a team of bleedin' butcher shop bandits. Bloody newspapers! Trust them to get a hold of this. That bastard Hurry has eyes and ears everywhere. Ten to one, if it hadn't made the front page of the Evening Times then old slippery Salmond would never have heard about it in the first place," said Hardie, before adding for good measure, "Never heard the like of it in all my service."

Thoroughgood nodded. "Well, you heard Tomachek. It's always the same when the press get involved, the heat is well and truly on and you know what Salmond is like when he thinks the hacks are havin' a laugh at our expense. Look at this lot," said Thoroughgood holding up the casefile.

"Aye, you should sleep well tonight, Gussy boy! Privileges of rank and all that, mon gaffeur!" said Hardie with a sarcastic wink.

The DC took another slug of his amber nectar before adding, "Listen, what about that promotion the old man was banging on about? Surely you must be due yer pips after taking care of Tariq and his Revolutionary Guards?

40

In fact, never mind your shoulders, I could bloody well do with the set of stripes and £150,000 lump sum that goes with a sergeant's promotion."

Thoroughgood's eyebrows rose, "If I've heard him say 'you'll be up on the next promotion parade' once, it must be half a dozen times since the business with Tariq. To be quite frank, I'm just trying to forget about it all. Put it this way, if we don't catch this mob we have as much chance of getting promotion as Thistle do. On that note, my dear Hardie, I suggest we finish these up and get going. I have a dinner to cook and a set of casenotes to read."

"The big question, Gussy boss, is, will that be a dinner for one or two?" enquired Hardie.

"Mind yer own, faither, is the only answer you're getting. But I can exclusively reveal that the house speciality, chilli, is on the menu. Washed down with a liberal quantity of Rioja," replied Thoroughgood.

8

THIRTY MINUTES later, Thoroughgood was busy in his kitchen. First glass of Campa Viejo half-drunk and Johnnie Walker's Radio Two Drive Time show filling the kitchen. It dawned on Thoroughgood that he was whistling along in time with the track on the radio: "Communication Breakdown" by Led Zeppelin. Taking another mouthful of the Rioja he splashed the rest into the wok. Helping himself to another mouthful of red, he held it in his mouth for a moment, savouring the full-bodied taste.

Rustling up his favourite dish always took him back to his time at Glasgow University. Back then, in his glory days of the late eighties, sharing a flat in Argyle Street, with two other students who were both from Edinburgh, the unlikely trio had taken it in turns to cook on a weekday evening.

Thoroughgood's big night in had always been Monday night. His dish of choice, the old faithful his mother had taught him the previous summer before he had left for the Big Smoke. As the memories of those sweat-soaked nights came rushing back, Thoroughgood smiled wryly as he recalled how his chilli had got hotter with every serving until it had to be washed down with pints of cold water and soaked up with slices of bread.

The three amigos had steadfastly refused to leave an ounce of the dish, such was each student's determination to show that he could clean his plate and not be left to face a torrent of abuse because he had become too hot and bothered to beat Thoroughgood's Chilli Challenge.

The voice in his head interrupted his wayward accompaniment to Led Zeppelin as it interjected, "Robbie and Derek, wonder where they are now?"

Thoroughgood added some extra salt and pepper and replenished his personal supply of Campo Viejo. After a quick stir he decanted the chilli into an ashet, covered with silver foil and shoved the dish in the oven, setting the timer for an hour. He had reading to do and those casenotes would not wait.

Loosening his tie, he plonked his transistor down on top of the chiffonier that acted as his drinks cabinet and let Walker continue to do what he did best: play quality music to a background of warm and friendly chat, occasionally interjected with wry wit. Combined with the sensuous tones of Sally Traffic's bulletins it was, in Thoroughgood's book, the perfect drive-time show to park his backside to.

Flicking his way through the pages of the casenotes, Thoroughgood had to admit he didn't know whether to laugh or cry over his new assignment. Tomorrow, accompanied by Hardie, he would begin the investigation in earnest, but as he flicked through the pile of A4 he could not dispute that the potential for disaster was present.

While the robberies all appeared to have been staged overnight and therefore no outraged owners had been

43

present to put up a struggle, the thought occurred to Thoroughgood that it was more by good luck than judgement that such a confrontation had not happened.

'Supply or demand?' was the question the voice in his head asked.

As he continued to leaf through the casenotes he saw that Tomachek had not been as au fait with the robberies as he'd suggested. Indeed, Thoroughgood had wondered how they could be called robberies when no violence had been perpetrated on any of the victims whose premises had fallen prey to the spate of crimes.

"Butcher left unconscious by armed raiders at city meat market," read Thoroughgood aloud before adding, "Aah, the violence at last," and as he peeled back a few more sheets of A4 he saw that there was indeed more than one victim of violence who may be able to help him.

But the chiming of the timer in the kitchen signalled that the chilli should be cooked to perfection and that left just half an hour before his dinner guest arrived. Hardie had been, of course, right, he was cooking for two.

As he set the table he admitted to himself that there was a certain intimate ambience about it, then put the rice onto boil. That would give him another 20 minutes or so to consider a case that he was beginning to admit to himself may have a lot more to it than was first apparent. He began to pore over the casenotes and realised there was a geographical pattern to the robberies. However, increasingly, his assessment of his newest case was pushed onto the backburner as his musings on his private life took precedence.

His relationship with Vanessa Velvet, the lingerie tycoon, former glamour model and reality TV star had proven a fitful one, borne of convenience and moments of spontaneous passion rather than cemented by any feelings of lasting warmth. Thoroughgood admitted to himself that while he had a lust life, it was far from the love life he craved.

The truth was that the shadow of Celine, the woman he supposed he would always love, would not fade. And the murder of Aisha, the nurse who had come so close to helping him move on, until she had been blown up by mad Imam Tariq's minions, had only heaped fresh guilt on his shoulders and served to reinforce his view that in this life, or the next for that matter, no true happiness would ever come his way.

The kitchen clock chiming 7pm sounded the end of Johnnie Walker and with Thoroughgood's whistle whetted for more Led Zeppelin, he fished out a compilation CD, crowbarred open the broken Marantz CD player with a bottle opener and slammed in the disc. Ironically, Whole Lotta Love was first up and Thoroughgood smiled sardonically to himself and headed back through to his kitchen.

He decanted the rice into a serving dish and sprinkled parsley on top, but his mind continued to assess just what stage his relationship with Vanessa Velvet was at. He was uncomfortable with her celebrity status and the lifestyle that went with it. He had stopped reading certain papers in order to avoid clapping his eyes on the Tweets the press seemed to hang on and publish in equal measure, and he had absolutely banned her from mentioning his presence in her life. But then the media already knew about this, thanks to their night at the opera. He had been desperate to see La Traviata at the Theatre Royal and they had been snapped leaving the building, looking all too cosy together.

It hadn't got to the stage where they were door-stepping him but he'd already had to have a quiet word in the ear of Hardie's favourite reporter, Donald Hurry, who had overstepped the mark when he'd been leaving Stewart Street nick one afternoon.

The question he had to ask himself was 'is it worth the hassle?' The answer he guessed was that, despite Vanessa's front, and she had plenty of it, in more ways than one, she was every bit as lonely as him. Fate, by bizarre chance, had thrown them together, thanks to the crazy Imam Tariq's craving for the notoriety that would have resulted from her execution. The fact that Thoroughgood had saved her and that before they knew the first thing about each other they had been thrown together in a string of intimate moments, had meant their relationship had been unbalanced even before it started.

Thoroughgood spoke out loud, "What chance do we stand?" That was exactly what tonight was all about. An oasis of normality. He wanted to know if they had enough in common to take things further and to decide whether it was worth him breaking his cover as her sleeping partner – so to speak.

As he sipped more Rioja he admitted to himself that he also had to accept he still wasn't sure if he was any more than a 'bit of rough' for Scotland's most famous businesswoman, whose fame had gone into orbit following her kidnap by Tariq.

'Since I've Been Loving You' wafted from the lounge, with Jimmy Page's guitar solo and the precise percussion of the great John Bonham ensuring that Thoroughgood was off and whistling again. He knew it was time to put his cards on the table and, if possible, get Vanessa to do the same. He leaned against the kitchen bunker, put the glass of wine down and joined Page with a moment of air guitar played with eyes shut, his voice joining Robert Plant in claiming 'he had done the best he could'. But who was he talking to? Himself? Celine? Or just the four walls and his own overriding loneliness.

Page's guitar solo went into overdrive and Thoroughgood raced into his lounge, cranked up the volume and jumped onto the arms of his easychair and let rip on his imaginary Gibson SG. The doorbell rang. He had company.

By the time he reached the hall Rock and Roll was filling the air and he opened the door. Waiting impatiently in the close was Vanessa, the trademark shoulder-length blonde locks, previously butchered by the mad Imam, now restored to their full, flowing magnificence.

"Hi, detective sergeant, you thirsty?" she asked, producing a bottle of Barolo, accompanied by a smile that would have saved the Titanic from any iceberg. Before he could answer she leaned forward and kissed him on the lips. Pushing his right hand out to shut the door he managed to negotiate a temporary separation as his senses spun from the smell of her perfume.

"Mmm, I'm hungry," she said and seared him with a look that implied her particular appetite would not be sated by the chilli. In truth, a big part of the problem he had with their relationship was that Vanessa always set the agenda, as she did with everything in her life, and it made Thoroughgood uneasy.

"Brings back memories, Gus, don't you think?" she

asked, leaning close to him and tracing a ruby red nail down his cheek.

He cleared his throat awkwardly, "Yeah, but at least this time we know that Meechan isn't going to come bursting through the door with all guns blazin'!"

She pressed herself up close and personal and he found his back to the wall, as the silk of her blouse created an odd cooling sensation in contrast to the body heat being generated by their proximity.

"Maybe we should finish what Meechan interrupted then, Gus?" she suggested, a flirtatious grin creeping over her face.

He knew it was lame, but he played the only card that came to mind. Laughing out loud Thoroughgood said, "What? And ruin the house speciality? Come on, Vanessa, dinner is about to be served and I can promise you won't be hungry for long. How does chilli con carne sound? That okay with you?"

Before she could argue he took her hand and pulled her into the kitchen. Pouring the remainder of the Campa Viejo into two glasses, he pointed to the kitchen table and for once she did as she was bid and sat down, glass in hand.

Minutes later his pièce de résistance was served and for the next thirty minutes Thoroughgood tried to keep the chat light and general before timing his move to the big issue to coincide with the opening of Vanessa's bottle of Barolo. Clearing his throat then cursing himself for doing so, he found himself beaten to the verbal punch – again.

"Just wondering if there is any other musical accompaniment on the menu than Led Zeppelin, Gus? It's hardly the most romantic backdrop for a meal for two at chez Thoroughgood," said Vanessa.

"Shit! You're right, sorry. Give me a minute. Think I may be able to rustle up something more suitable for you, V."

Her smile was accompanied by a shake of her golden mane, "I don't think so, Gus. This calls for a more gentle touch. You enjoy the Barolo and I will see what you have in that dusty CD tower with all the music you never listen to!"

"Very good," was all Thoroughgood could think of by way of reply.

Moments later the strains of Love and Money's Halleluiah Man struck up and Thoroughgood smiled in approval as Vanessa sat back down at the dining table.

She took the initiative, "So what's eatin' you, Gus? Come on, it's been pretty obvious from the moment I set foot in your flat that you have something on your mind."

She had him on the back foot again and his gaze dropped to the half empty glass of red he was swirling.

"Where are we going, Vanessa? What exactly are we?" The directness of his question caught her off guard.

"Wow, Gus! You aren't about to propose marriage I hope!" She laughed out loud and threw her hair back in that infuriating way that she used to mesmerise her prey, then added, "What you want to know, detective sergeant, I'll bet, is, are you just a bit of rough to me? Would that be right?"

This time Thoroughgood met her liquid-silk gaze and held it, "Exactly," he said and immediately regretted it.

Vanessa put down her glass, "Forgive me if this sounds a bit callous, Gus, but isn't this a relationship of mutual benefit? You might think I'm using you, but as far as I can see, you are not ready to start a meaningful relationship."

49

Thoroughgood spluttered on his wine, "What do you mean?"

"Come on, Gus, how can any woman compete with a ghost? Until you get over Celine then any relationship will be one-dimensional. Maybe as one-dimensional as I suspect you think I am. But can you really be bothered to scratch the surface, Gus? Or is this enough for you?"

Thoroughgood's frown was accompanied by his hand ruffling through his grey-streaked hair, evidence of the emotional toll this last year had taken.

Vanessa had not finished, "Look, you can't have it both ways, Gus. As far as I can see, you want to have your cake and eat it. You won't be seen in public with me, I can't acknowledge that we are in a relationship and yet in private . . ." Vanessa let the word hang in the air before continuing, with Thoroughgood hanging on her every word. "So, you admit that all along you've been eaten up by the thought that I am using you as my bit of rough?" She asked the question with such force that Thoroughgood was taken by surprise. Here was an intensity about her he had not seen previously.

Thoroughgood was lost for words but Vanessa was now in full flow, "Oh, and in case you haven't noticed, I am still trying to extricate myself from the death throes of my second marriage. So you tell me what this relationship is, what you want from it and where it is going, or should I walk out that door right now?"

She stood up suddenly and placed one hand on her hip as she drained the remains of her glass of Barolo.

Thoroughgood took a deep breath, "Look, I'm sorry. Everything you said is right. Bottom line. Maybe it's time I got some professional help," said Thoroughgood and stared into his wine glass once more.

Again Vanessa shocked him, "Then let me help you, Gus. No more skulking about. Let's just see where things go, like two normal people would."

Thoroughgood couldn't help himself, "But that is the problem, V. You just aren't a normal person." Just as he realised what he had said Vanessa burst into laughter and, embarrassed, he did likewise.

Before he knew it she was sitting on his knee and those delicious lips were moving his way once again, "Look, Gus, there are two people in this relationship who are hurting so let's just take it easy, but let's also give it some oxygen. There's a place and a time for plain talking and we've arrived at it. But hey, it's been fun."

Thoroughgood searched her eyes, not sure what she meant but she smiled reassuringly, "It's okay! I have a question for you. I've been invited to the launch of a new whisky liqueur by Lady Elizabeth Roxburgh, through her daughter Victoria and they also want me to put on a charity fashion show. I'd like you to come with me. It's being held up at Loch Lomond, in Roxburgh Hall, and everyone who matters will be there," she paused for effect.

"If you come, that will mean that we . . ." but this time Thoroughgood took the initiative and finished the sentence for her, "Are an item?"

Her smile was mixed with a fleeting hint of insecurity he had never seen before and Thoroughgood realised that at last he was getting close to the real Vanessa Velvet.

"Count me in, doll," he said with a wink as they abandoned themselves to the moment.

9

THE ENGINE of the white Transit groaned as it was put under increasing pressure by the driver's impatient handling of the wheel. The increasingly early daybreak was a problem that had put pressure on their plan, but there was no time for compromise and the lucrative nature of their trade meant that chances had to be taken.

The man in the front passenger seat sat motionless, looking out of his window as an ethereal mist lifted from the hillside on either side of the Stockiemuir Road. On his lap rested a sawn-off shotgun.

From the back of the Transit came two voices, one rough Glaswegian, the other accented in a manner that pointed to the speaker's Eastern European roots, filled the air, "Nervous, Jammy? How you sweat, my friend, when ground outside is still to lose frost?"

"Fuck off, Tomasz, unless you want to find out just how nervous I can get with a crowbar in my hand and a smart-arsed Pole in my face at 5.30 in the bleedin' mornin'."

The exchange in the back of the vehicle at last brought motion to the front passenger's lips, "Shut the fuck up, the pair of you, and listen to me," barked the man with the shotgun. "We have five miles until we reach the farm so let's run through the plan one last time."

The authority in the gang leader's voice brokered no dissent in the ranks of his gang and the driver echoed Drummond's words, "Aye, Joe's right, give it a fuckin' break. The pair of yous have been at it hammer and tongs since we left Glasgow and you are doin' my fuckin' napper in."

Drummond shot his driver a withering sidelong stare. He did not need his authority over his crew reinforced, not even by his number two, but he could understand the irritation experienced by Frankie Grimes. After all, this would be the biggest raid they had mounted yet. With the goods and the cash kept on the premises they could be looking at a six figure haul.

But Drummond was concerned that the spate of robberies they had mounted over the last six months was beginning to attract headlines and that made him edgy. The bickering that had blighted their trip towards the farm outlet underlined the fact he was not the only one feeling the heat. Drummond was determined there would be no fuck-ups because after two more raids he would have the readies to set up a new life on the Costa del Sol as the bar owner he'd always wanted to be. Fuck Glasgow and the constant rain that did his nut in. He wanted sun on his back and senoritas underneath his belly and he had it all planned. Two more raids, three at most and he would be off and the rest of the gang could take a flying fuck to themselves.

"Now, listen to me, you fuckers. This is the biggest job we will have pulled yet. Do it right, clean out the wedge from the safe and we'll be on easy street. Just what all of us wants from this bleedin' business."

"Whit's that, gaffer?" asked the vacant voice of Jammy Gilles.

"A better life for your weans and your missus, surely, Jammy? You want to be jumpin' about in the middle of the night at the arse end of the universe for the rest of your natural? Ya half wit!".

The silence from the rear of the Transit suggested that Jammy – nicknamed thus for his particularly annoying habit of winning virtually every competition he ever entered, via the back of the cereal packets that provided the staple of his diet – did not.

"I thought not," added Drummond. "Right, one more time, here we go. Frankie?" and Drummond turned to his number two.

"Right ye are, boss. I drop Jammy a mile before we come to the farm road turnoff and he gets the transport motor. Then it's down the farm road and you and Tomasz get dropped to make sure the hoose next to the outlet buildings is empty and I smash the motor through the shutters and immobilise the alarm," said Grimes with no emotion.

"Tomasz?" asked Drummond.

"I check house, make sure boss man not playin' hide the sausage with the missus and when we have all clear you follow in, boss. Then locate safe as in drawing my brother Janek supply us with."

"Excellent," said Drummond before continuing, "Once we've found the safe you then leave me and join Frankie and Jammy," Drummond shot Gilles a withering glance to make sure he had his attention from the back of the van. "Then make sure that every prime cut of meat in the place is bagged and deposited in the Luton Jammy will have parked outside. Then what?" demanded Drummond in his grating Glaswegian voice.

This time Gilles spoke up, "Then we get the Transit disengaged from the shutter, douse with petrol and torch the fucker!"

"So, girls, you have been listening," said Drummond with a hint of a smile. He swept his three subordinates with a stare that left them in no doubt his mind was focused on the business in hand.

The transit was now slowing as it reached Jammy's drop off point and as it pulled to a stop Drummond handed out the stocking masks before once again ramming home his message, "Now listen to me, you half wits, this is the biggest one yet and the information we have from Tomasz's Polish fuckin' Christmas tree workers is that the owner and his missus hit the casino on Wednesday night and stay over in Glasgae town. So the whole place should be empty bar a guard dog, and I have brought a wee treat along for him," said Drummond, pulling out a pork chop that radiated a blueish tinge.

Spotting the look of mystification spreading across his gang's faces Drummond added, "Two drops of anti-freeze and Rover's kidneys are crystallised in moments."

Jammy could not help himself, "That wid be a case of Rover and oot then, boss," he said with a wink.

Grimes snarled, "Keep yer mind on the joab, Jammy, or I'll carve ye a nice little Mars bar down the other side of your puss."

"Quiet," hissed Drummond, "The info we have from our Polish friends is that the house is empty, but if it's not, what happens next?"

Tomasz was next, speaking through the stocking mask

55

he peeled back to his forehead, "Tie 'em up and gag 'em, gaffer and maybe, if the bitch is there, we have some fun. My brother, he tell me she was a cow to him and fired him minus last pay packet, how you say boss, a ton light."

Drummond's right hand shot through the space between the vehicle's two front seats and grabbed the Pole's throat, "Listen to me, you Polak bastard! If any harm comes to anyone, the only job you will be up to will be as the new fairy on top of next year's Christmas tree. I am two hauls away from sun, sangria and sex, and you and no other son of a Polish whore is going to stop me gettin' there!" For effect Drummond ripped out the Beretta he had hidden inside his anorak and rammed it under Tomasz's chin, "I'm not sure about you, Pole. You would do well to remember you are only with us because of your connection with our buyers, and the information we got through your brother. You only get one chance with us. Fuck it up and you won't make it back to Glasgow. Understand?"

Tomasz's eyes watered at the pressure of the handgun pushed up under his chin but he managed to nod his head.

Drummond put the gun away as the van pulled to a stop and the bang of the back door confirmed that Jammy had exited, en route to collecting the Luton van, nicely painted up with the markings of a local removal company.

"Let's get ready to rock," said Grimes and they turned down the farm road.

10

JOHNNY BALFRON tossed uncomfortably in his bed as shards of morning light filtered through the bedroom curtains. Propping himself up on one elbow he looked down at Sophie and could not help the smile spreading across his face.

Childhood sweethearts, they had married a year after graduating and devoted their lives to building up the Balfron family business which specialised in supplying the very best game and meat available from the Scottish countryside.

Given that the 150 acres of rich farmland he had inherited from his late father Edward was teeming with wildlife, it had not taken Balfron and his wife long to develop their business into one that produced a seven figure annual turnover. By diversifying into other interests, harvesting the local pine trees to such good effect that the festive season produced a healthy boom period, such was the business done through the sale of the Balfron House Christmas trees, that Johnny Balfron's business couldn't have been better.

Yet still something gnawed at him. That business with the Polish worker and Sophie back at the turn of the year meant the certainty he'd known every day with her since they met 23 years back was now a fragile one. It had been Sophie's idea to tap into the cheap Polish labour market and when it came to farm labouring, Balfron had to admit she had been right. The Poles were punctual, efficient, hard working and polite, and had become immensely popular with the outlet's middle class clientele.

He thought back to the day he had returned early from a banking trip to Glasgow and found Sophie alone in the Christmas grotto with the Polish worker called Janek, colour high in her cheeks, her silky brown hair slightly dishevelled. Sophie had later explained she had been helping to clear the hay from the marquee which they used to feed the goats and other wildlife that were a major attraction for his customer's kids, but something had jarred with Balfron over an explanation that had been a little too laboured. A week later Janek and the three other Polish workers who had been with them for almost a year were dismissed by Sophie. She claimed they had been pilfering the produce.

Watching her sleep peacefully in the increasing morning light, Balfron recognised that the cause of his sleeplessness since that day was that he could no longer trust his wife. The perfect harmony that had previously underpinned their relationship had gone forever. In its place were rows that were becoming more and more acrimonious.

Their regular midweek luxury trip to Glasgow for a show and late supper at the casino, planned for the previous night, had fallen victim to an argument which had become particularly vicious after Balfron, his tongue loosened by too much Malbec, had finally snapped and given voice to his suspicions.

Sophie had dismissed his accusations and stormed off to bed and now here she lay, so beautiful, so peaceful and how he wanted her, ached for the all-consuming happiness he had taken for granted before the episode in the grotto with 'that bastard Pole'. Balfron found himself mouthing the profanity silently.

Drinking in her dark beauty even now, in the first year of her second half-century, she was still a head-turner and Balfron was honest enough to admit to himself that if his prospects had not been quite as bright all these years before, perhaps she would have looked elsewhere. He had also faced up to the fact that she had a roving eye, but until that incident with Janek, Balfron had never had cause to suspect that it had been more than just that.

As Sophie groaned in her sleep, Balfron felt his feelings of suspicion replaced by a more powerful emotion as the passion for the wife he knew would not leave him, until death did them part, surged through his body. As he leant forward and slowly kissed her, drinking in her smell, he heard the coarse sound of a diesel engine growing ever stronger.

Parting from Sophie's luxurious lips, he saw that she had still not fully wakened as he jumped out of bed; peeling back the curtain and looking out onto the red chip drive just as the white transit pulled to a stop.

11

BALFRON WAS immediately hit by a sense of foreboding as his gaze took in the vehicle that had come to a stop 100 yards from his farmhouse. He suddenly remembered an article he had read in the Milngavie and Bearsden Herald which had carried a police warning about butcher's shop robberies. He knew that Balfron Mill wasn't typical of the places that had been hit, the question that now gnawed away at him was, who would want to pitch up before 6am on a Thursday morning, unscheduled and uninvited?

Balfron was now already halfway down the staircase and making for the locked cabinet where he kept his shotguns. He had worked too damned hard and too damned long to make his business the success it had become. He was taking no chances. As he removed the shotgun he heard a sudden bang on the front door. Balfron knew he had been right to take the precaution.

Tomasz levered the crowbar into the door frame just as the transit smashed into the shutters, instantly triggering the alarm. The door gave way under his boot and his shoulder, but as it sprung open the sight that greeted the robber was one that left him blinking in disbelief.

Balfron stood in the hallway, dressed in his silk Paisley pattern pyjamas with a shotgun cocked against his shoulder and two manic eyes spitting fury at the robber. The Pole was immobilised in the doorway, paralysed by fear and shock until Drummond cannoned into his sidekick, and as he did so the movement spooked Balfron and his finger pulled the trigger. Tomasz was lucky that he had started his descent onto the floor before Balfron had fired. Drummond was not so fortunate. He had taken the Pole's place in the doorway and the shotgun blast struck him full on, smashing him back out of the door and onto the cinder.

The Pole was too concerned with his own safety to worry about his gaffer, the sound of whose agony filled the air behind him. Rolling over onto his side Tomasz scrambled through a doorway into a room that proved to be the kitchen. Panting with fear and seething anger the Pole wildly looked around for something he could use as a weapon. Next to the kitchen sink was a knife block and he grabbed the two biggest blades, just as he heard a footfall behind him and a female voice shouting from the floor above, "What the hell is going on, Johnny?"

Tomasz spun round in time to see the silk of Balfron's pyjamas take on an ethereal glow from the early morning sunshine filtering through the kitchen window. The ominous shape of the shotgun being brought to bear in his direction sent him diving for cover behind the kitchen table.

Balfron seethed with a righteous rage and kicked a kitchen chair out of his way before aiming the shotgun, but the Pole had scurried across the floor and under the table. Sheathing the two blades in his belt he rammed upwards, lifting the table up and smashing it into Balfron. For a second time the shotgun went off and this time the blast hit the kitchen ceiling as Balfron was knocked onto his back by the blow from the table. Tomasz stood over him and Balfron's eyes locked into the hate-filled orbs of his assailant.

"Skurwysn!" he spat in his mother tongue and wrapped both his hands around either end of the shotgun before smashing his forehead into Balfron's face.

The blow exploded Balfron's nose and loosened his grip on the shotgun, allowing the Pole to rip it free and throw the gun across the kitchen floor. Tomasz whipped out the two blades bringing them to rest on either side of Balfron's exposed neck.

"Swinia ty spierdolic!" raged Tomasz once more before adding in English, "Yes, you fucked up bastard, now I make you pay." He pulled the blades away from Balfron's neck and for a moment the estate owner thought he would escape with his life. But Tomasz crossed the blades, clamped them on either side of Balfron's neck and ripped them across his skin with all the force he could muster. Geysers of blood shot from the gaping wounds in Balfron's throat and spurted all over the Pole's face.

"Diabel," spat the Pole as Balfron's eyes became permanently vacant.

Sophie Balfron entered the kitchen just in time to see her husband breathing his last.

Tomasz looked up and smiled malevolently before spitting out, "You whore," as he jumped off Balfron's convulsing body and advanced on his wife.

"Fucking slut! You think you have my brother's Polish cock, have your fun with it then throw him aside when you finish? Rip him off and bitch him for thief then get away with it?"

Sophie's eyes were wide with terror and she stammered in shock, "I, I, I . . ." but Tomasz was keen to help. He rammed one of the blades into the kitchen table and gazed at it as it quivered in the pine. He grabbed her dressing gown. Ripping it free to reveal a black silk camisole, Tomasz brought the serrated, bloody edge of the other knife up to her pale skin, "You fuck my brother Janek? Then you call him thief when you tired of Polish cock, no?"

"I don't know what you mean," sobbed Sophie in desperation as her mind replayed her romps in Santa's grotto with the young Polish worker. A bit of fun gone wrong, that had brought her marriage to breaking point before the events she had just witnessed had ended it forever.

With his free hand Tomasz smashed a backward blow across her face that threw her onto the kitchen table, her head resting only inches away from the knife blade. Her eyes strayed to its glinting steel and her mind registered the opportunity to give herself a way out of this hell she had walked into. But as she tried to grab the blade she found the angle she lay at made it impossible to pull the knife free, and hope died within her as Tomasz once more closed on her. Tossing the other blade aside he wrapped both his hands around her wrists, smashing them onto the table.

"You forget how much you like Polish sausage bitch? We call it kielbasa back in Warsaw." Ramming his groin into her, he prised her legs apart as she stuggled with all her might to try and escape the horror that was coming her way.

63

"I'm sorry, so sorry, it was just a bit of fun and then .
. ." She was cut off as the Pole clamped his jaws on her
mouth and began to kiss her with a wanton hunger before
he pulled back and seared her with his hate-filled eyes,
"You are pathetic."

He grabbed the other knife, ripping it free from the
tabletop and pushing its tip into the top of her camisole. A
laugh of chilling cruelty escaped his mouth, "Uśmiech!"
said Tomasz and ripped open her nightdress. Sophie
closed her eyes and prayed in silence.

12

"WHAT THE fuck are you doin'?" screamed Frankie Grimes, as his eyes took in the scene before him.

Tomasz turned round, but continued to pinion Sophie Balfron to the table. "What you think, old man? I take revenge for my brother," he spat.

"Not here you don't, you fuckin' maniac. What do you think that bastard over there is?" demanded Grimes, gesturing towards Balfron's corpse, "A fuckin' mirage? Get the hell off her and get her out of here and into the back of the van. Christ, how much time do you think we have before the cops are out here? The alarm is bound to be hooked up to some alert system. Plus Drummond is bleedin' his guts out at the front of the farmhouse. We need to go, Tomasz, and if you don't get moving now I will personally blow your brains out, you Polish motherfucker." With that Grimes produced a handgun from inside his quilted jacket, took a step forward and pointed the barrel at Tomasz's head.

The Pole got the message. "Okay, okay, I do what you say, Frankie, keep calm, friend." Slowly he pulled himself away from Sophie Balfron and she immediately grabbed the remnants of her night attire close to her and shuffled over to the inert shape of her husband's body.

"Oh, Johnny. Forgive me, please, please forgive me," she pleaded with her husband's corpse.

Grimes had no sympathy for her, "Save your breath bitch, there's no point asking for his forgiveness now."

He whipped out a roll of parcel tape and threw it to Tomasz. "Bind her wrists and tape her mouth. If you are not at the van within five minutes, I will come back here and personally send you to hell. Understand me, Polak?"

Tomasz nodded that he did and with that, Grimes stalked out the farmhouse kitchen.

A moment later he was hunkering down next to Drummond's heaving body and watching the life fade from his leader's eyes as his vital fluids seeped out, over the hands which Drummond had clamped to the shotgun wound. Drummond's wavering gaze met his number two's eyes and he croaked, "I'm fucked, Frankie. Good and proper. You need to get the boys goin' fast." His words and gaze were interrupted as Tomasz dragged Sophie Balfron by her bound hands, her mouth sealed by the tape, out of the farmhouse door behind Grimes. Drummond's eyes returned to Grimes' face. He gasped in agony as the waves of pain racking his body threatened to become too great to sustain.

"You are the man now, Frankie, but watch the Pole. Don't trust him my old friend. A slug in the head is my advice, mate, as soon as."

Grimes shook with emotion. Death was fast approaching for Drummond and they both knew that to take him with the rest of the gang would make life extremely difficult for them.

Drummond knew the score, "You know where to take the boys, Frankie. It's time you put the lights out for me, old friend."

Grimes grimaced involuntarily at the outcome he knew was inevitable, "Come on, Joe, we can get you patched up, mate. You'll see, you're gonna make it through this."

Drummond shook his head with what seemed like his last ounce of energy and gasped, "I'm goin' nowhere, Frankie," he said and his right hand grabbed Grimes' arm. "Finish it, Frankie, now, for Chrissakes," he hissed.

Grimes offered his boss a tortured smile and stood up, moved behind Drummond, placed the handgun against his head and pulled the trigger.

An hour later the Luton van, sporting the motif 'The Chairmen: Furniture Removal Specialists', raced down a tree-lined road with Tomasz behind the wheel and Grimes sitting in the passenger seat. Jammy Gilles stayed in the back of the van with Sophie Balfron and the cargo of stolen cuts of prime meat.

"There it is on the left," said Grimes and he pointed to what looked like a set of derelict prefab buildings.

As Tomasz brought the vehicle to a halt and applied the handbrake, Grimes spoke once again, "Now listen to me, Tomasz. We need some time to get things sorted and this is an old safe house that Joe, me and the boys have used over the years that has remained under the radar. I don't want any more trouble with the Balfron bitch. We need to decide what to do with her and we need to do it quick."

"Okay, you boss now," said Tomasz through a sickly smile, before adding, "Where are we Frankie?"

"This is the old Millearn Hospital. It was used to tend to injured servicemen – sailors from the convoys and also casualties from Clydebank during the Blitz – way back in

1941. Been derelict ever since, except when Joe, me and the boys have needed somewhere to lay low when the heat has been on, and fuck me, it's on now." With that, Grimes vaulted out of the passenger door and ran around the back of the van, opening the shutters and beckoning Gilles and Sophie Balfron out.

Jammy immediately hauled the female to her feet and shoved her out of the vehicle forcing Grimes to catch her while the tape muffled her screams. Grimes held her tight, smelled her femininity as his arms encircled her, the sensation that swept through his body threatened to break his self control. "Do what you are told darlin' and you will make it out of this alive, fuck us about and you're pan breid. Understand me?" rapped Grimes.

Sophie nodded that she did and found herself being dragged by the wrists into one of three whitewashed buildings, one with a roof covering its prefabricated framework of precast concrete, brick and fenestration mill.

Grimes ordered Gilles to take their captive to a side room, "Get her in there and make sure she is secure and then meet me and Tomasz back in the front room, mate, and make it quick."

"Nae bother, Frankie, whatever you say, mate," replied Jammy obediently and disappeared as he was bid, with Sophie Balfron.

Grimes made his way back into the front room, speaking as he went, "Stop fooling about Tomasz, where are you? We have to get this sorted before we try and punt the meat."

The cold steel that rammed against the side of his head was a shock to the system. "We get nothing sorted, Skurwysyn," said Tomasz and squeezed the trigger.

68

Grimes' body collapsed in an inert heap, his head spouting blood and brain from the hole the projectile had left. Tomasz dragged the body over to the window and then hid behind the open door and waited for the footsteps to come.

Jammy had been startled by the shot. He sprinted out of the back room and along the corridor before entering the main reception room at full pelt. As he charged in his attention was immediately hooked by Grimes' body lying crumpled at the window; he failed to see the leg thrust out in his path and went flying over it. As he hit the ground Tomasz jumped on him, grabbing him by the hair and slamming his head into the cold concrete floor. He then pulled him back up until Grimes' skull met the end of the revolver's barrel.

"Sorry Jammy, but your luck just ran out," said Tomasz and a second crack rang out.

Sophie sat shivering in the corner of the cold, damp room. Her ripped nightdress had been covered by an old coat that Jammy Gilles had wrapped round her in an act of kindness at odds with everything she had experienced from the gang since they had torn her world apart. Gagged and bound, she tried to slow her breathing and impose some sense of calm on herself, but the huge sobs that had racked her body since she'd seen her husband murdered in front of her would not stop. For Sophie blamed herself and the stupid infidelity with the good-looking young Pole that had now left her life in ruins. Tormented by guilt and exhausted by her excoriating emotions, she shut her eyes and prayed.

The door burst open. Tomasz stood in the doorway

and looked at her with a rising hunger, knowing that this revenge was not his to take. "Open your eyes bitch, now it's you and me in old building and we have fun, no?" spat the Pole.

Sophie opened her eyes in terror just as the Pole knelt down beside her and ripped the gag from her mouth, "Please, leave me alone, you have everything – my husband is dead, my life is in ruins, what more do you want? Please, just let me go," she begged.

"You go nowhere, Miss Sophie, until Janek come see you. My brother very angry with you. But it is while before he come to have fun, maybe I take mine first . . ." grinned Tomasz. He ran the index finger of his right hand down the side of her tear-stained face, all the while smiling with ravenous intent.

"What you think, Miss Sophie? We have some fun before Janek come?" he asked, his voice dropping to a whisper that only served to increase the terror now engulfing Sophie.

"I beg you, no. Look, I will give you my bank details and you can empty the business accounts, please just let me go," pleaded Sophie.

Tomasz was not interested and his index finger continued its journey to the top of the old coat which Sophie had buttoned up to her neck. Then he started to pop the buttons one by one and Sophie screamed.

"Please . . . keep screaming Miss Sophie . . . I like very much," said Tomasz.

13

HARDIE FLICKED the ash off his Silk Cut and out of the half-open car window; the stiff breeze whistling outside the CID car did its best to blow it back in. He articulated his disgust in trademark fashion, "Aah, fuck off."

Sitting in the passenger seat Thoroughgood enjoyed a scene he had observed a hundred times before – at least – with a wry smile, and offered his colleague some helpful advice.

"Do you need to have that thing hanging out your mouth when you're driving? For crying out loud, don't you ever feel the draft coming in when you are puffing away on those bleedin' cancer sticks? Serves you right, faither! Your dry cleaning bill, if you ever put one of these monstrosities you call a suit in to the dry cleaners, would be astronomical."

Hardie turned his head and stared impassively at his superior officer. Holding the steering wheel with his left hand, he attempted to brush the ash off his lapel and out of the window, only to see it fall down the space between himself and the door.

Thoroughgood was far from amused, "That's great, that is. We'll have Group Two CID reporting us to

Tomachek over this. Correction, reporting you to the old man, unless you get it hoovered up when we get back to Stewart Street."

Hardie belched his disgust at the order and changed the subject. "I reckon it's three miles until we hit the Balfron Mill. You reckon our butcher shop bandits have branched out and maybes got a bit more ambitious with their targets?"

Thoroughgood frowned, intimating that his number two was stating the obvious, "Well, the factory outlet has been emptied of all choice cuts of game and the safe in the farmhouse is blown open and empty. The worrying thing is that we have the owner cold on his kitchen floor with his throat cut ear to ear, and no sign of his missis, Sophie Balfron. But there doesn't seem to be much point in speculating when we are five minutes away, so let's hold our fire on hypothesising until we get to the locus."

With that, Thoroughgood turned to look out of the window and with his mind evidently elsewhere, he missed the twinkle in Hardie's eyes.

The DC's rumbling baritone soon interrupted the silence. "So how did the big dinner date go then, gaffer? Er," he cleared his throat almost apologetically, "if you don't mind me asking?"

Thoroughgood's sea-green eyes rested on his partner's sagging features and seared them. "I was wondering how long it would take you to get round to that, faither, and to be fair, you never disappoint." Thoroughgood stopped and Hardie was left hanging, just as his DS had intended.

"Aw, come on gaffer, in the name of the wee man, put me oot my misery," whined Hardie. Pointing at the road ahead Thoroughgood said, "Ah. That seems to be the turnoff for Balfron Mill. What a pity your little inquisition will have to wait for a while yet, so get your game face on, faither, we have a murder locus to examine."

Thoroughgood, covered from head to toe in a white paper suit, bent over Johnny Balfron's corpse and examined the wounds that had left him bled out on his kitchen floor.

"If it is our mob then they've certainly done a butcher's job on Balfron. Two serrated edge blades, by the looks of it, drawn across his neck at the same time and it's goodnight, Vienna."

Standing in front of one of the uniformed officers guarding the murder scene, Hardie peered over his gaffer's shoulder, his world-weary features looming large from within the paper hood of his anti-contamination suit. "Aye, I pity the milk man. Not exactly what you sign up for when all you want is to deliver the cream of the bottle, is it? Still, at least we've got Balfron identified. What about the ned lying outside pumped full of lead from Balfron's shotgun? At least he got one of the bastards before they did him."

Thoroughgood was making his way back to the front door, when he stopped to pick up something from the tiled floor, just past the kitchen table, and slipped the article into a transparent evidence bag. It was clear the table had been incongruously re-located at an odd angle to the rest of the room's disturbed furnishings, almost certainly as the result of a life and death struggle.

The DS continued out of the kitchen, past the SOCO personnel busy photographing the locus and the uniformed officers now protecting the scene of the crime. He made his way through the hallway and past the remnants of the smashed door, hanging drunkenly from its hinges, which had led the milkman to investigate the inside of the farmhouse upon his arrival with the daily delivery.

The body of the gang member lay propped up against the farmhouse wall, filled with lead. Smouldering in the background, and embedded in what was left of the outlet shop's shutters, was the torched van. Facing Thoroughgood was the paper-clad back of the force pathologist, Doctor Herbert Strange.

"Good morning, Doctor Strange," said Thoroughgood as he attempted to gain the attention of the physician, who most people thought was perfectly named for his vocation. Strange's sandy-coloured mop turned round and his expressionless gaze swept over the detective.

"Not for this fine fwellow, detective sergeant, or have you been pwomoted at last, Fowoughgood?" said Strange, his lisp almost comical, so pronounced was it.

"No need to ask what was the cause of death, Doctor. But what about time of death?" asked Thoroughgood.

"Stwaight to the point Fowoughgood, as always," responded the pathologist in a delivery that had Hardie clearing his throat behind Thoroughgood in an attempt to avoid an involuntary explosion of mirth.

"Aah, Hawdie it's youwself, whewever one goes the other will follow, eh? The body tempewature has dwopped sevewal degwees but rigow mowtis has not set in yet, as it would about fouw houws aftew death.

"Time now is 08.40hrs so we could be talking appwoximately anytime between say 5.30 am and around 6am. That good enough for you, Fowoughgood?"

"Absolutely, Doctor Strange," replied Thoroughgood,

emphasising the pathologist's name but desperate to call him by the term of endearment he was universally known by in the force – Strangelove.

"I believe the shotgun that did for him has alweady been secured as evidence, but then that is your job Fowoughgood. By the way congwats on that job with the tewowist chappy, what was he called again? Ah, Tawiq wasn't it?" asked the good doctor.

By this time Thoroughgood could hear Hardie starting to split at the seams and attempted to stop himself dissolving into a fit of the giggles. "Thank you, Doctor. Detective Constable Hardie is on his way to take charge of it, aren't you Hardie?" said Thoroughgood. Hardie read between the lines and returned into the farmhouse.

Strangelove had not finished. "Any sign of these pips yet, Fowoughgood? Or is there as much chance of the Fistle getting pwomoted as youwself?" asked Strange.

Thoroughgood smiled, more out of politeness than anything else, "Who knows, doc? Anyway, I will leave you to your work and we can liaise later, after the post mortem and identification."

"Good day, detective," said Strange and put Thoroughgood out of his misery.

Making his way over the cinder drive and car park, Thoroughgood examined the tyre tracks leading out of the farm outlet. Soon the sound of foot steps was coming his way and Hardie joined his gaffer. "Interesting, eh, boss? Obviously it's been a team job and they reckoned without Balfron's shotgun, but there are still a few questions to be answered. Not least the identity of neddy boy there."

Thoroughgood turned his attention from the corpse to Hardie. "Yep. SOCO will need to examine these tyre tracks ASAP and I'm assuming we have taken prints off the deceased already?"

"I believe both matters are in hand, gaffer, pardon the pun," replied Hardie.

"So what is the question at the top of your list, Hardie?" asked the DS.

"You saw the photo on the dresser in the hall? Balfron is married and his missus is nowhere to be seen. On top of that, Balfron was taken out and left lying cold on the kitchen floor, but there seems to have been a secondary struggle going on over at the kitchen table," said the DC.

"Very good, Hardie! Next thing you will be having a go at the Telegraph crossword," mocked Thoroughgood before continuing, "Did you notice that the kitchen table also showed signs of having had a sharp implement embedded in it? That it also had blood traces on it that I would wager belong to Balfron? And . . ." he pulled the evidence bag from his suit pocket, "That this piece of silk fabric is, ten to one, from a lady's night attire."

Almost despite himself Hardie's bushy eyebrows shot up. "Obviously, the gang have abducted Balfron's missus?"

"Elementary, my dear Hardie, as the man once said. Clearly they have used two vehicles for the turn. The first to ram the shutters and the second to load the loot and . . . it would appear, Sophie Balfron. So what we now have ourselves here, is both a murder enquiry and an abduction. Butcher shop bandits? I knew it was too good to be feckin' true," groaned the DS.

"Wait 'til the old man hears about this," said Hardie before adding, "By the way, is Vanessa a black silk girl? The missus is strictly Pyjamarama, as dear old Bryan Ferry would call it!"

But Thoroughgood was already striding towards the Focus and although he could not see his lips moving, Hardie could hear Thoroughgood's words drifting back. "We need an ident' on the gang member and then we need a list of associates, pronto. 'Cos right now we have a gang of tooled-up bastards on the loose and in possession of a certain Mrs Balfron, somewhere out in the countryside."

Jumping into the driver's seat Hardie saw that his gaffer was already on the radio set barking out orders. "I want a stop and search posted for any high-sided vehicles, Luton vans or the like, within a twenty mile radius of Balfron Mill, which will take us out of Strathclyde Police territory and into Central Scotland. So please notify our country cousins at Randolphfield. All officers are advised to use extreme caution, suspects within are armed. Can we also please request armed response vehicles are mobilised and sent out on patrol in the area, just in case we need the back-up. Oh, and if we can manage it, can the Force helicopter sweep the area?"

"Anything else while you're at it, Detective Sergeant?" responded a sarcastic female voice coming from the other end of the radio.

"Nope, that should do for now," replied Thoroughgood and replaced the hand-held radio on its holder.

"Why is it that nothing we ever get involved in is simple, gaffer?" asked Hardie.

"'Cos that's the way the man upstairs likes it, faither, and there ain't nothing we can do about it. Now back to Stewart Street, pronto."

14

DETECTIVE SUPERINTENDENT Valentino Tomachek kept his eyes trained on the post mortem report and the previous convictions print-out that charted the life and times of the late Joseph Melville Drummond. Then he looked up, swept Hardie and Thoroughgood with a piercing gaze and said two words, "Bad bastard."

"PC's going back all the way to his days at the Borstal. A real nasty piece of work, and one who specialised in armed robberies like security vans, betting shops, plus a nice little turn back in the nineties on a payroll office at one of the shipyards down in Clydebank. But he's been quiet since he got out of Peterhead two years back. Well, quiet as far as we knew."

Switching his attention to the post mortem report Thoroughgood continued, "Interesting! Although he's been blown away by Balfron's shotgun, it says here that the fatal gunshot wound was a single shot from a .40 calibre handgun to the back of the head. Well, well . . . although the shotgun wound from Balfron's firearm would have been fatal eventually, somebody else put Drummond out his misery."

"Compassion amongst armed robbers. Who would have thought it?" added the DS.

It was Hardie's turn to chip in his tuppence worth, "Aye, he's tasty all right, and so are his associates. Frankie Grimes is his number two on 70 percent of the armed turns and one look at his PC's shows you he probably likes a bit of violence with his Frosties first thing in the morning. Feck me he's a 'cant' as dear old John Thaw used to call 'em in The Sweeney."

Tomachek pointed his briar pipe at the paperwork, freshly printed off from the crime management system, which now sat on Hardie's lap, and asked, "Anyone else in Joe's gang?"

Hardie nodded. "John 'Jammy' Gilles. Safe blower, getaway driver and bog standard number three, I would say, in a good number of their turns. There is a fourth member of the gang, a Billy Nichol, but there is one problem with him, boss."

"Yes?" asked Tomachek, his impatience starting to show.

"He's brown breid, boss," answered Hardie with some relish.

Thoroughgood shifted uncomfortably in his chair, positioned parallel to Hardie and opposite the intimidating desk that now had Tomachek's brogues resting on it. The detective superintendent joined the discussion, "Interesting, indeed. So we have a team who usually operate four up but in this case are one down . . ."

Before Thoroughgood could continue in an orderly fashion, Hardie had interrupted. "Just like one of these bloody crossword riddles you are always bleatin' about in your Torygraph, gaffer." Remembering that his senior officer was also present Hardie quickly added, "Apologies, sir."

"Yes, yes, Hardie. Very witty, no doubt. Get on with our crossword, Thoroughgood," ordered Tomachek.

"Well, boss, we have two vehicles used on the turn so you are obviously talking two drivers. For my money that means that Drummond has gone into the farmhouse first but, even tooled up, would he have gone in alone? The answer to that has got be no."

Hardie could not help himself, "The other thing that backs up DS Thoroughgood's hypothesis is that Drummond never got beyond the door."

"Mmm," said Tomachek, simultaneously billowing out tobacco smoke, "Plus you have the two vehicles outside and both the drivers are probably loading up with the cargo they've come looking for, while Drummond and A N Other have gone into the farmhouse to empty the safe. Sounds like a bally inside job to me," said Tomachek.

"Exactly," agreed Thoroughgood. "I think we can put our money on Gilles and Grimes as two of the gang still at large, but it's the third member we don't have a Scooby about. He's got to be a new kid on the block, so to speak, and that complicates things, big time."

"Never mind complications, Thoroughgood. All I want is a plan of attack from you and I want it now, Detective Sergeant."

Thoroughgood cleared his throat just as there was a knock on the door. It opened and a svelte female shape, that even a police uniform failed to hide, arrived. "Apologies, Detective Superintendent Tomachek, but you wanted the results of the search of the farmhouse and the surrounding area brought to you as soon as they were complete," said the WPC.

Tomachek's attempt at a benign, almost paternal, smile failed to disguise the wolfish intent in his eyes. "Indeed I did, WPC MacDonald."

The WPC leaned over the desk to place the paperwork in front of Tomachek, and this time it was Hardie and Thoroughgood who had their professionalism tested.

"Ah, yes, I should introduce you, WPC, to detectives Thoroughgood and Hardie, as you will no doubt find yourself coming into contact, er, in the professional sense of the word, with them. A couple of reprobates who occasionally find time for the odd bout of good detective work."

"Pleased to meet you, WPC Macdonald," Hardie was first, offering an awkward handshake and receiving a warm smile for his troubles.

Thoroughgood remained motionless in his chair and offered a lukewarm smile, although her dark complexion and ample curves had registered on his radar, before enquiring, "How you doin'?"

"Very well, Detective Sergeant Thoroughgood," replied the WPC, before adding with more than a hint of sarcasm. "Thanks for asking."

She turned to face Tomachek, "If that is all, sir?"

"Yes, Natalie, that will be all for now. Many thanks for this." And with her presence no longer required, MacDonald left the room with three sets of eyes following her rear view out the door.

"Any luck?" asked Hardie as Tomachek scrutinised the search results.

The shaking of the DS's pipe betrayed an agitation in their superior officer that was ominous in the extreme.

"Sweet Christ . . ." were the only two words that

escaped Tomachek's mouth and at that the detective superintendent shoved the paperwork across the desk towards Thoroughgood.

He scanned the information before him, "Our worst nightmare, boss, in my opinion."

Hardie's patience had snapped and he grabbed the paperwork, "Fuck me gently. Gilles and Grimes both found dead at a steading with fatal gunshot wounds. Along with an abandoned Luton van which had clearly been recently stuffed full of prime cuts of meat."

As Tomachek ran his left hand through his grey hair he felt both detectives' eyes upon him. Silence reigned.

Thoroughgood broke it. "So basically, what we have here is a gang member who is completely unknown to us, and for whom we have no means of identification, who has just polished off two off his amigos and is on the run with Sophie Balfron."

Before Thoroughgood could continue, his superior officer interrupted. "What was the calibre of the weapon Gilles and Grimes were ended with? .40 by any chance?"

"Bang on, sir," replied Thoroughgood, immediately realising his unintentional pun.

A slow, one note whistle escaped Hardie's mouth before he articulated the thought that all three shared, "Our mystery man is making Drummond look like a pussy cat."

"He is indeed, Hardie, but what matters now is what you two have planned next. Whatever it is, I suggest you get cracking, detectives, and by that I mean now," demanded Tomachek.

Inclining his head, Thoroughgood pushed back his chair and caught Hardie's glance as he did so. They had work to do, but not a clue where to begin.

15

ROBERT ROXBURGH made his way through the mirrored entrance doors of the Diamond Palace Casino filled with new found resolve that the deal with the Gwai Lo would save himself, his family and the Glen Lomond Distillery. His hopes had been boosted by the phone call he'd taken from his mother, Lady Elizabeth, late the previous night, in which she had underlined her willingness to throw her weight behind the plan. The launching of the new Dark Ocean liqueur at an exclusive event at the Hall was one he felt sure his new Chinese business partners would go for.

Climbing a set of marble steps, he was escorted by a shiny-suited member of the casino staff to a small lift that delivered them to the third floor. The silence in the lift was deafening but the suit, known only to him as Lam, stared relentlessly at Roxburgh, his cruel, dark eyes pulsing with with contempt.

The Triad leader's stillness was unnerving as he remained frozen, gazing out of the third floor window and looking along the River Clyde. Raymond Cheung's hands remained motionless and crossed behind his back. Although Lam had announced Roxburgh's arrival Cheung showed no sign that he had heard a word.

A surge of anger burned through Roxburgh, unused as he was to being made to wait by anyone, but all too acutely aware that he had no choice in the matter. Slowly Cheung turned around and locked a piercing gaze on the man who was about to provide a whole new veneer of legitimacy to his business enterprises. He gestured to the seat opposite his large black desk and Roxburgh sat down as he was bid.

Cheung remained standing, but his failure to extend a handshake of welcome had been noted by his visitor. At last the Triad leader spoke, "Viscount Lomond, how nice of you to find the time to visit my humble establishment," said Cheung without a trace of sarcasm. Briefly he rubbed his fingers along the designer stubble that chequered his face then reached for a set of papers on his desk. "There is no point in wasting time, my dear Roxburgh. Ours will be a marriage of mutual convenience as we have previously discussed at some length," Cheung pushed the papers towards Roxburgh, "there is nothing there that will surprise you, except perhaps the penalty clause."

Roxburgh's eyebrows shot up in surprise, "What penalty clause?" he demanded.

"Come, come, Viscount Roxburgh," said the Oriental, once again fingering his stubble but penetrating Roxburgh with his dark, unreadable eyes before adding, "Do you think that the Gwai Lo will bankroll your business, save your family from financial shame brought upon it by your, shall we call it weakness, without some form of surety?" Cheung steepled the fingers of both hands together and presented a picture of icy composure, garbed in a black suit that had the most luxurious sheen to it. He left his question hanging in the air.

Roxburgh ruffled his immaculate blonde hair before clearing his throat, "There was no mention of a penalty clause in our previous discussion, Raymond. The deal was that you would be a sleeping partner, that I would continue to retain control of the distillery and its produce, in return for the profit division being 70/30 percent in your cabal's favour and of course, the successful launch of the new Dark Ocean signature liqueur."

Cheung smiled wickedly. "But I have, how do you say, had to move the goal posts, my friend. Unfortunately, my bosses back in China are not as generous in their trust of you as I am. So a penalty clause has been inserted, as you will see if you examine the contract."

Roxburgh's eyes flitted across the printed paper and he felt his temperature rise almost feverishly as he searched for the words which would confirm just how much the Gwai Lo had him by the balls.

At last Roxburgh's eyes locked on the clause that underlined how horribly reliant and utterly vulnerable his 'weakness', as Cheung had described it, had made him, and now his family. Despite himself, Roxburgh could not help but read aloud the words that confirmed how much he was risking by climbing into bed with the Ghost Men.

"Should 80 percent of the profit targets fail to be met within the Asian markets, then control of the Lomond Distillery board will cede to the Gwai Lo and the position of Robert Roxburgh will be reduced from managing director to non-executive director. Further control of the day-to-day running of the Lomond Distillery will be ceded from control of Alexander Roxburgh, who will also become a non-executive director."

Roxburgh slapped the papers down on Cheung's desk

and attempted to use his years of military training to retain control of the rage mounting within him, all the while aware that Cheung was continuing to scrutinise him from behind an ice-cold gaze.

The frozen silence was fractured by Cheung. "If I was in your position, my dear Roxburgh, the question that I would be asking myself is what choice I have? Do I need to provide the answer to that question?"

Roxburgh's brilliant, blue eyes blazed with an anger which made Cheung flick a cautionary glance to his bodyguard Lam, who stood just inside the door. In response to the warning, the henchman's right hand slipped inside his jacket, his fingers clamped on the Glock that nestled in his shoulder holster.

However, Robert Roxburgh was a realist. Although his pride was being stripped from him, he knew that there was only one path down which he could proceed if all he held dear was to be preserved. He stood up in an explosion of movement that underlined the athleticism of his earlier years. The detached calm that Cheung seemed to wear like a cloak was ruffled and behind the Viscount, Lam took two steps forward and pulled the Glock halfway out of his jacket.

Roxburgh surprised Cheung for a second time when he offered his right hand across the Triad leader's desk in placatory fashion. "You are right Raymond, of course. But I am also confident that in pooling my expertise in the industry and contacts within the market, and your distributional skills and ability to take our exciting new product to new market places, that the penalty clause will never come into play."

Roxburgh's hand continued to hover in the air above

Cheung's desk for a second until slowly, the Oriental got to his feet and enveloped the Viscount's hand in a tepid grip before his face at last showed some sign of satisfaction. "Excellent," said Cheung as his eyes signalled that Lam could re-holster his pistol. "It will be a pleasure doing business with you, Viscount Roxburgh, and one that I am confident will be to our mutual benefit."

Roxburgh had one further surprise up his sleeve for the Gwai Lo's leader, and from within his sports jacket pocket he removed a small leatherbound flask and quickly popped two miniature silver, leather-encased cups from it, before pouring a dark golden liquid into both vessels. "Would you like a drop of The Dark Ocean?" asked Roxburgh.

Cheung was hooked as the involuntary gasp that came out of his mouth emphasised, "Aah, excellent, Viscount Roxburgh. I am most impressed. You have been very busy."

Roxburgh now seized control. "Dark Ocean is a blend of aged Scotch whiskies and herbs such as anise, cloves and almonds, plus heather honey and citrus fruits. As you can see it has a deep, dark gold colour and of course, the type of distinctive and unique flavour you would expect. If you will, Raymond, take a sip and hold it on your tongue, just for a moment. Let the luxurious, creamy wave of tangerine and honey wash over your taste buds."

The Triad boss took a sip from the handleless cup and let some air escape from within his teeth as his taste buds were tickled.

Roxburgh pressed home his advantage, "Now, place the cup a few inches from your nose and savour the rich and complex aromas. The sweet tang of syrup, herbs, citrus and the subtle hint of whisky will slowly reveal its many attractive virtues.

"Perfectly balanced, it is a taste that lingers long on the palate and one I am sure, that will make the Gwai Lo and the Glen Lomond Distillery a fortune," concluded Roxburgh, delighted with the impact of his product on the Triad boss.

Cheung smiled his appreciation of the liqueur, "I have no doubt that it will, Viscount Roxburgh."

"What we need now, Raymond, is a launch event to capture the imagination of the whisky industry and the relevant sector of the Scottish public. An event, that with the right sort of people present, will allow us to send advance publicity to your homeland that the Dark Ocean signature whisky liqueur is very much appreciated by the type of person they revere, and would like to be associated with through our new and exclusive product."

Re-seated, Cheung kept his eyes locked on Roxburgh, "Indeed. I can see the benefit in that Viscount Roxburgh. What do you have in mind?"

"On Saturday week, within the grounds of Roxburgh Hall, we will host the launch event for Dark Ocean. Already, my family have been busy utilising our contacts to make sure the event will be covered by the right publications, including an exclusive photo shoot with Hello! magazine and naturally, attended by the great and the good as we call them in Scotland." Roxburgh came up for air as he allowed the picture he was painting to take shape in Cheung's mind.

"Furthermore, Vanessa Velvet, the fashion entrepreneur I'm sure you have heard of, has agreed, through her friendship with my younger sister Victoria, to host a charity fashion show at the event."

His confidence growing by the moment as the impact of his words washed over Cheung's features, Roxburgh added, "I hope that is a date that is compatible with your schedule?"

Cheung nodded and reached down to pick up the leather cup. Examining it with interest, the Triad leader fingered the three initials, LVR, which were stitched into the leather in gold thread, and marvelled at its antique nature.

Reading his thoughts, Roxburgh spoke. "Those were my grandfather Ludovic's flask and drinking vessels. Hence the initials, LVR. They accompanied him both on the disastrous invasion of Dieppe in 1942 and the triumph that was D-Day, a couple of years later. So they have an important part in my family's history. I felt it fitting you should have your first taste of the Dark Ocean from a vessel that had accompanied my grandfather on one of the most important days of the Roxburghs' history."

Cheung lifted the leather-encased vessel to his lips and drained the contents. Then he stood up and this time offered his hand to Roxburgh. "You honour me Viscount Roxburgh, and it will not be forgotten."

Roxburgh quickly replenished both vessels and proposed a toast. "The Dark Ocean." They charged their cups and basked in the warmth that spread through them from the liqueur which they both believed would make them a fortune.

16

ROBERT ROXBURGH sat in his office at the Lomond Distillery, the heels of his Sandhurst brogues resting on his huge, mahogany Victorian desk. Also resting on the desk was his grandfather's whisky flask which he was now in the process of draining, using one of the accompanying miniature drinking vessels.

The audience with Cheung had been a triumph and Roxburgh allowed himself a moment to savour his success. He swivelled his chair around and looked into the identical azure eyes of his grandfather, Ludovic, staring down proudly from above, garbed in full military uniform against the stunning backdrop of Loch Lomond.

Raising the vessel in salute to the portrait, Roxburgh's lips moved in a silent toast to the most famous Roxburgh of the dynasty, confident he had saved everything his grandfather had held dear and also, in one fell swoop, turned impending disaster into the advent of a bright new dawn.

With the last drop of Dark Ocean consumed, Roxburgh got to his feet and made his way over to his drinks cabinet, intent on toasting his moment of triumph. He selected the special 1938 bottle of The Roxburgh he knew had been enjoyed by Ludovic himself, all those years before, on the eve of the war. The Roxburgh retained a special place in the cabinet, not just for its value and the famously rich taste which provided notes of fudge, cocoa and burnt sugar, but even more because it connected Roxburgh with the man who had been his biggest influence and whom he had, until this moment, felt he had failed.

His touch somewhat clumsy, he caught the bottle neck on the hand-carved bracket that ran down the side of the cabinet door, but his curse died on his lips as he saw that a secret drawer had sprung open from the bottom ledge of the cabinet. Startled, Robert took a step backward and peered into the drawer. Inside were three small booklets, tied together in royal blue ribbon. He placed the whisky bottle on the top of the cabinet, bent down and pulled the bundle out, making sure there was nothing else in the secret drawer before closing it.

He untied the ribbon, marvelling as he did so that what lay within might be some piece of secret family history that had not seen the light of day in generations. Opening the first booklet in his hands he saw "LVR War Diary Vol. 1, 1939-1940" printed in his grandfather's neat and precise handwriting.

Robert repeated the exercise with the second diary which covered the year 1941. The final booklet, he observed, covered 1944-45, leaving him to draw the obvious conclusion that the diary covering the period 1942-43 was missing.

Picking up the second booklet Robert leafed through some random pages and began to immerse himself in his grandfather's thoughts during the darkest days of the Second World War starting in September 1941 . . . '*Joy of joys, am to be in charge of No1 Combined Training Centre, Inverorchy. PM determined to take the fight to the Hun, KGVI keen to come up to inspect the base. Have three months to get ready for His Majesty, LVR, Sept 01/41'*

Tingling with the excitement of sharing his grandfather's thoughts at the pivotal moment of his life Robert took another sip of The Roxburgh and moved on to the next page . . . *'Meeting with my darling J at the Dorchester. Hear PM is also resident and will need to be careful!! Afternoon tea for two and then mucho fun! LVR, Sept02/41'*

The words hit Robert hard and straight between the eyes. The grandfather he had revered above everyone else as the epitome of family virtue and all that was good, had been having an affair. Not only that, but Ludovic was meeting his squeeze in one of war-time London's most upmarket hotels and not scared about running the gauntlet of a meeting with Churchill himself in the process of having 'tea and mucho fun'.

It was the stuff of scandal given Ludovic's lofty status as Under Secretary for War and his appointment, confirmed in the previous page, as the commander of Churchill's pet project to take the fight back to the Nazis in Europe, after the success of the Battle of Britain.

The entry of Sept 02/41 hinted at scandal that would not have done Churchill's war-time cabinet any good. It would also have called into question the great war-time leader's judgement in appointing Ludovic OIC of the revolutionary No1 Combined Training Centre.

Goodness only knew what revelations lay in the pages ahead. Robert replayed images of his grandfather and grandmother Margaret from his childhood that had always cast the illusion that theirs was the happiest of marriages. Yet here was proof that it was all a sham. Laying all three diaries out on the desk Robert left a space for the missing journal. Questions filled his mind at a dizzying speed. 'Where was it? How had it become separated from the rest of the diaries? Had it fallen into the hands of someone who would use it to harm his family?'

No sooner had the last of these questions faded into his subconscious than a cold and horrible reality dawned on Robert, Viscount Roxburgh. Pulling a sheet of A4 from his desk drawer, a note he'd found shoved under his desk door a couple of mornings earlier, he flattened it and finally took in the contents that, up until this moment, he had failed to comprehend. In nondescript print the threat was now clear and obvious. Only one line long, what had been completely cryptic now began to take on some meaning if, as Robert now suspected, it related to the content of the missing third journal.

'THE OLDEST SIN CASTS THE LONGEST SHADOW.'

He took another sip of the '38 malt and the thought stumbled into his shell-shocked mind that he was clutching at straws – that the missing diary must surely just have become separated from its companions and be resting somewhere in the drinks cabinet. Triggering the secret drawer he ran his hands over the woodwork, but there was nothing else there. Frantically checking for any other secret compartments he repeated the process that had triggered the opening of the compartment, this time on the other side of the cabinet. Nothing happened.

So there was, indeed, only one secret drawer. As he

sat staring at Ludovic's chiselled features he attempted to elicit some clue as to how the events chronicled in these meticulous, but secret diaries, could have unfolded. Robert's imagination began to run riot. Was it possible that whatever was recorded in the missing journal, or perhaps even the other journals, sitting in front of him, was connected to the attempt on his life? He immediately dismissed the notion as ridiculous.

"Get a grip, man," Roxburgh said as he attempted to reassure himself that the incident on the landing outside his office was a burglary or robbery gone wrong.

But he could not help asking himself, "What is the oldest sin?"

He read the single line out loud, "THE OLDEST SIN CASTS THE LONGEST SHADOW." Then Robert Roxburgh cradled his head in his hands.

17

ROBERT WAS brought back to the present when the door to his office was ripped open with such force that it rebounded violently onto the whitewashed wall of the landing outside. The elder Roxburgh swivelled round in his chair and observed the powerful figure of his younger brother, Alexander.

Robert could feel his jaw setting as he awaited the impending verbal broadside. Placing his drink on the desk he massaged either side of his forehead and attempted to meet Alexander's pulsing venom with as much calm as he could muster.

The younger Roxburgh spat, "So, you have returned from your meeting with Cheung and are clearly savouring saving your skin. You sit there beneath the portrait of our grandfather, full of smugness and self-satisfaction while you have mortgaged to the hilt everything we hold dear. Worse still, you have done so with the Triads."

So Alexander was fully aware of the true nature of the Gwai Lo and just what Cheung represented. As discreetly as he could, Robert pushed the diaries into his desk drawer hoping that Alexander's anger would mean they did not register on his consciousness.

"What's wrong big brother? Surely not more of your secrets?" demanded Alexander.

Robert smiled benignly and attempted to divert his interest, "No, they are not my secrets Alex. But let us stick to the subject you are here to talk about. For your information, what I have done is present Raymond Cheung with his first opportunity to sample the new Dark Ocean liqueur and tantalise him with the plans for its launch, left him tickled and whelping with joy like a freshly born puppy on his back, little brother.

"Cheung's eyes have been opened to the full extent of the possibilities that are open to him through his partnership with the house of Roxburgh, Alex. The prospect of having the Dark Ocean launch splashed over the pages of Hello! which Vicky has arranged, plus the charity fashion show planned with Vanessa Velvet, had him drooling."

But Alexander would have none of it, "Don't feed me your bullshit, Robert. Tell me about the penalty clause, which I believe, is the sword of Damocles hovering above every deal done with the Triads."

Robert knew that his options were limited and he tried to stall, "Look, Alex, join me over a glass of the '38 to mark the bright new future that the Ghost Men have just guaranteed us, just as I am sure grandfather would have," he said.

Alexander eyed his grandfather's flask and drinking vessels and exploded, "You bastard! You've clinched the deal by supping from grandfather's flask with a jumped-up Chinese gangster. You make me sick. If you think I will denigrate grandfather's malt by toasting your sordid deal with these Oriental hoodlums then you are off your head, man."

He stormed over to the drinks cabinet and helped himself to a large glass of the 18-year-old malt that was usually Robert's favoured refreshment. Turning round to face his elder brother he took a slug and washed it around his mouth, enjoying its distinct taste and swallowing abruptly.

"Come on, Alex, sit down and let's get this all in perspective once and for all," said Robert. "I will be honest with you. There is indeed a penalty clause, but it is so lenient it is not remotely a threat and never will be."

Alex slotted himself into the leather chair and said, "At last! The truth will out. So come on big brother, are we to be homeless and potless within a year?"

Robert smiled, "No, we are not. All we need to do is hit 80 percent of the profit target, year in and year out, and everyone is happy and we are safe. Come on, Alex, you know the potential for a new liqueur in the Asian market is massive and you also now know the type of clout that the Triads have over there. It may be a deal with the devil, but for us it's one made in heaven."

The only sound that came from the other side of the mahogany desk was the increasing rasping of Alexander's breathing.

Robert became concerned, "Are you okay, old man?"

"Just a bit hot under the collar," said Alexander and loosened his tie. "I have hardly slept in the last month because of all this . . ." he stopped mid sentence and his hands shot up to his throat as he gasped violently for air, then pitched forward off the seat and crashed to the floor.

Robert sprinted around the desk and cradled his younger brother's head in his arms: "Alex, c'mon old boy, you just got a bit worked up . . ."

Alexander's body gave a violent convulsion as it jerked in Robert's arms and staring wildly down at him, Robert could see the fear in his brother's eyes. Feeling utterly helpless he tried to reassure him that he would be fine while at the same time trying not to let his desperation become apparent to Alexander.

Placing his hand on Alex's forehead he felt the cold clamminess that had broken over his skin, and as his younger brother's eyes began to take on an increasingly glazed look his body was racked by another violent spasm. "C'mon Alex fight it, it's going to be okay!" he shouted, but already the life was draining from Alex and Robert found himself enveloped in panic. A panic that he was losing his little brother and it was his fault.

With one final violent shudder Alex's eyes turned up in a frozen, glazed stare just as a rattle escaped his throat. Gazing down at his younger brother, Robert Roxburgh stared in disbelief at the uncomprehending horror that had just unfolded in front of him. As he did so he noticed the strange, sweet but bitter scent from Alex's mouth which was totally at odds with the aroma of the 18 year old malt he had just drunk. His complexion was almost cherry-red in colour.

Laying his younger brother down, Robert's eyes remained locked on Alex's now permanently vacant eyes, and felt moisture fill his own. Trembling with grief he tried to coordinate his fingers in a bid to punch 999 on the office phone.

He did not know what else to do.

18

THOROUGHGOOD AND Hardie sat in silence in the estate office at Balfron Mill as they examined the staff records and every bit of paperwork they could get their hands on, relating to the business and its employees. The process of interviewing the staff had been exhaustive and frustrating in almost equal measure, and both detectives had no doubt that there was something they had been kept in the dark about. Something they couldn't quite put their finger on.

So far there had been no sign of Sophie Balfron or her abductor, but Thoroughgood remained confident that although 48 hours had passed since the armed raid, the murder of her husband and her own abduction, there was a missing piece of jigsaw that would help them see the big picture – if only they could locate it.

"Look, gaffer, there is something we aren't being told and, for my money, the best way to get it is from one of the farm labourers. I've spoken to them all, but there's a boy by the name of Billy Carson and he's as nervous as a kitten. If you don't mind I'd like to bring him back in for a second bite at the cherry." said Hardie as he tapped the end of a Silk Cut on the office desk.

Thoroughgood remained still in the seat that had once been filled by the late Johnny Balfron himself and, as Hardie had drawn to a close, the DS' eyes looked up from the list of employees and the notes he had made pertaining to each one.

"Yep, that sounds good. I'd wager a pint that something happened around Christmas that left a bad smell lingering around Balfron Mill. I think it had something to do with the Poles. The employment register says three of them were made surplus to requirements, slap bang in the middle of the busiest part of the year, with Christmas trees virtually running out of the door by themselves. It doesn't make sense, and your boy Carson would have been working alongside them. Bring him in."

Moments later Hardie re-appeared at the office door and beckoned in a ginger-haired male. "Billy Carson, gaffer, at your pleasure," said the DC, giving the reluctant witness a prod in the small of the back to propel him into the estate office and towards the empty chair.

Thoroughgood remained seated at the other side of the desk and trained his gaze on the new arrival. Carson, he already knew, was 20 years of age and had been employed as farm hand, odd-job man and a variety of other trivial pursuits since he had left school as a 16-year-old.

The DS smiled reassuringly at the new arrival, "Have a seat Billy. I think you may have some information that could help us find Mrs Balfron."

Carson rammed his hands into the pockets of his overalls, the involuntary jerking of his knees betraying his nervousness at the prospect of helping the police with their enquiries.

"Don't know what you mean, boss," was his opening gambit.

From behind him, Hardie's voice begged to differ, "Listen to me son, and listen good," said the DC and for good measure took a step closer to Carson before bending down and speaking into the his right ear. "We don't have time to fuck about, wee man. What we have here is a murder enquiry in which the deceased's missus has been abducted and three of the gang involved in the robbery are also pan breid. But what DS Thoroughgood and I are asking ourselves is, just why Sophie Balfron ain't lying cold, like her old boy, on the slab? We've heard some gossip we think you know plenty about and which we believe could be a big help to this enquiry. Bottom line, sonny, is that you spill what you know or . . ." Hardie paused and placed a not so reassuring hand on Carson's left shoulder, "You'll be heading for Stewart Street nick and the Bar-L for attempting to pervert the course of justice and hindering a murder enquiry. That plain enough for you, son?"

Carson's eyes had remained staring at his dancing knees all through the Hardie monologue, but at last his gaze rose and he found it impossible to avoid the scrutiny of Thoroughgood's piercing green eyes. Still he remained silent.

Thoroughgood leaned back in his chair, "Look, Billy, I'll make it easy for you. There was a group of three Polish workers here, grafting alongside you before Christmas, helping with the Christmas trees and all of a sudden, a week before Santa hitches up Rudolph to his sleigh, they get binned and there isn't a word of explanation in the employment records.

"But there's more to it, isn't there, Billy boy, than just a bunch of Poles getting the boot for being lazy buggers?

101

'Cos the short and curlies of it is that Poles don't do lazy, do they, pal? So why boot your best grafters out on their tattered arses when the Christmas tree harvest is going into meltdown?"

"How wid I know, boss?" whined Carson, unconvincingly.

This time Hardie whispered sweet nothings into the farmhand's left ear. "But that's just it, wee man, you do know and you know plenty. Now spill."

Thoroughgood, spotting Carson clenching his jaw, decided to offer him some help with his bout of selective amnesia. "Look, Billy, rumour has it that one of your Polish pals was proving very popular with Mrs Balfron. The smart money is on her old man finding out and applying his size 10s to our friends from Eastern Europe tout suite in order to end their mutual admiration society. That about right, Billy boy?" A furtive movement of Carson's eyes indicated that Thoroughgood was onto the truth and the DS was not about to let go.

"Okay, son, here we go," he added. "We have three Polish labourers one minute, enjoying loads of overtime at the peak of the Christmas tree harvest and the next minute, five days before the glorious 25th they are all axed, but two of them turn up at the Smithycroft Farm down the road and the other . . ." Thoroughgood glanced at the employment record and continued, "a Janek Boniek, aged 23, disappears off the face of the earth. You know what that is telling me, son?" asked Thoroughgood, amiably enough.

"Don't know what you're on aboot, boss," muttered Carson.

His rebuttal broke the banks that had been damming Hardie's mounting rage, and the DC administered a stinging slap with his right hand, across the top of Carson's ginger nut. Hardie grabbed him by the shoulder and rapidly spun him around on the swivel chair so that he revolved a full 360 degrees, twice, before coming face-to-face with both detectives again. The DC parked his over-ample derrière on the edge of the desk and smashed his handcuffs down on the wooden surface. Carson jumped out of his seat at the impact.

"Okay, wee man, hold them out and we can get you cuffed and in the Stewart Street taxi," raged Hardie.

"All right, all right, for fuck's sake. I'll tell you what I know." Carson had at last got the message.

"Good boy," said Thoroughgood.

19

HARDIE PARKED the Focus just off the main road, and both he and Thoroughgood trained their eyes on the turnoff that led to Smithycroft Farm and considered their next move. The moment's silence was soon perforated by the DS, "I've texted Morse to see if he can come up with any dirt on Boniek, and given him the address from the employment records. The wee man has been a bit quiet on the information front of late, and it's time he sang for his supper."

"Mmm, funny I was just thinking – it's been a while since we had heard from wee droopy. I guess, given how close he was to Celine, it doesn't exactly bring back happy memories for you when you have to deal with him. But if anyone's going to know anything about some crazy Pole, the wee man has his ear to the ground as good as there is," concluded Hardie.

"There's no point in denying it, mate. You're bang on regarding Morse, but needs must and he is just too good at what he does to leave him lying redundant," admitted Thoroughgood.

Keen to inject some levity into the conversation, Hardie tried to change the subject. "Just wonderin', gaffer, are you ever intending to replace the RX-8? I mean a bird like Vanessa must surely be accustomed to be driven in some style?"

Thoroughgood turned to his subordinate, but surprisingly there was a smile in his eyes. "The answer to that particular source of mirth is a Mini Cooper, and I plan to pick her up at the weekend. If that is okay with you, Hardie?"

Hardie threatened to spontaneously combust, such was the explosion of laughter that shook him, but after recovering his composure he continued on his line of enquiry. "Jeez! A Mini Cooper eh . . . bit of a hairdresser's motor, if you don't mind me saying. You sure there are enough horses under the hood to pull you out of bed, never mind get her Vanessa-ship down to Buchanan Galleries?" asked the DC with unconcealed glee.

"Your ignorance is staggering, my dear Hardie. We are talking 163 bhp of BMW engine. Tell me, just out of interest, how many miles that reconditioned Vauxhall Cavalier has on the clock . . . second time round?"

This time it was Hardie who found himself on the defensive. "What do you mean second time round? 96 thou', for your information, and every one an honest mile."

"Knight to Bishop's rook, I think you'll find my checkmate, now can we turn our attention to the matter in hand? If you don't mind?" demanded Thoroughgood.

For once Hardie was happy to oblige, "Fair enough. A case of vorsprung deutsch technik you might say!" The frown on Thoroughgood's face indicated the DS' patience had now reached breaking point and Hardie moved swiftly on. "Talk about stating the bleedin' obvious, that

Carson kid doesn't have two braincells to rub together. Boy, was that one hard work. Ah mean, we could just about have dotted the i's and crossed the t's with the information we got from the employment records. Still, for every pile of steaming horseshit we have to wade through, there is always the odd nougat!"

His gaze still on the entry road to the farm, Thoroughgood grunted, "Okay, we would have been coming this way to speak to Tomaszewski and Lewandowski anyway, but it's a plus that we know for sure they're still in contact with Boniek. The questions we need answered are, are they still tight enough with him to be harbouring Boniek? And if so, what does that mean regarding Sophie Balfron? I've asked uniform to check out Boniek's address in the employment records."

"Well, there's only one way to find out," said Hardie, gunning the car into life and heading for the farm road.

At the top of the road lay an imposing whitewashed two storey building that was clearly the Smithycroft farmhouse. To its left lay a series of barns. The sound of cattle coming from one underlined the fact that the main source of revenue came through dairy farming.

"What's the name of the farmer?" asked Hardie as he slowed the Focus to a halt.

"Jimmy Rogers. His old boy was evacuated here from Clydebank during the Blitz and stayed on to help out as a farmhand, and eventually the owner left it to him when he died with no heir. So, friend Jimmy has been here all his days, according to the info I have here. Seems a decent salt-of-the-earth sort with no previous or anything of interest to us."

Thoroughgood's need to consult his notes was now

106

redundant. A burly, red-faced man, sporting a checked shirt and a tweed flat cap, strode up to the Focus just as the DS got out.

"Been expecting you, gentlemen. Jimmy Rogers is the name, I am the owner of Smithycroft Farm," and with that Rogers offered a huge calloused paw to Thoroughgood and proceeded to crunch the DS' right hand in his vice-like grip.

From the other side of the Focus Hardie chimed, "So the jungle drums work loud and clear in Stirlingshire, then!"

"Aye, they do indeed, Detective. I would imagine you are here to talk to my two young Polish friends?" asked Rogers, a question he clearly meant as rhetorical.

"What makes you so sure of that, Mr Rogers?" replied Thoroughgood.

"What went on up at Balfron Mill has been the talk of the 'shire, Detective . . ."

"Thoroughgood. Detective Sergeant Thoroughgood and this is Detective Constable Hardie," replied the DS. "You're very well informed, Mr Rogers. Care to elaborate on what you mean by the talk of the 'shire?" asked Thoroughgood.

"That business between Sophie Balfron and young Boniek. It's not the first time her eye has been caught by a young buck."

Thoroughgood let his stare linger on Rogers for a moment longer. "Look, Mr Rogers, I am sure you are very busy and keen to be about your business. Maybe we will come back to you to confirm a couple of things, but what I really need to know is if you have seen or heard anything that would confirm your two hardworking Poles are still in contact with their countryman, and just exactly where they are right now so we can have a word with them."

Rogers frowned, "Look, I haven't seen or heard anything that would suggest the boys are still in touch with Boniek. But at the same time it wouldn't surprise me if they were, given they are all Poles in a foreign land and all that. But if you are asking me, and I know you ain't, I just don't see Boniek being the type that would harm a fly, never mind commit armed robbery and murder. It just doesn't add up for me."

"With respect, Mr Rogers, it is our job to make it all add up," said Hardie "So, if you don't mind, where are the dynamic duo right now?"

"They're both down in the bottom field, fixing some fencing that got busted in the storm last week," Rogers pointed down the track that led past the side of the barns. The farmer glanced at the skies overhead and added helpfully, "Best hurry if you want a chat with 'em, don't think rain is far away."

"Ever heard of a mobile, Mr Rogers?" asked Hardie, dripping sarcasm.

"No reception in certain parts round here, Detective," replied Rogers, almost as sarcastically.

Before Hardie could answer, Thoroughgood did so for him, "Thank you," said the DS and began heading down the track.

"Oh, Detectives," called Rogers from behind their retreating backs, "I've got a couple pairs extra gumboots for you, might be an idea, what with the fields being waterlogged and that."

Thoroughgood turned round. "I'm not planning on leaving the track, mate, but thanks for the offer."

"Suit yourselves, Detectives," said Rogers smugly, and they did.

After they had walked for about 600 yards down an increasingly muddy track, which descended into a gulley, initially hidden from view, the noise of hammering became loud and clear.

"Sounds like our Polish, whatever you called them, are busy, gaffer."

"Przyjaciel is the Polish for 'friend', Hardie. But unlike us they got here via transport, by the looks of these fresh tracks."

"Aye, well, by the time we get there they're gonnae have a right laugh at us Gus, feck' sake, my suede penny loafers are ruined and look at the state of my troosers," moaned Hardie.

"Maybe that will encourage you to take a trip to Slaters sometime this century, then!" said Thoroughgood as the source of the hammering finally came into view.

Tomaszewski and Lewandowski were so engrossed in battering fence poles into the ground that they did not notice the detectives until they were within 15 feet of them.

"For fuck's sake that's it! Cowshit all over my loafers, how in the name of the wee man am I supposed to get that cleaned off brown suede without ruining the buggers?" exclaimed Hardie.

"Maybe you should have had the boots, my friend," said the taller of the two overall-clad men, in an unmistakeably accented delivery, while his dark-haired mate, who was holding the post up, let rip with a chuckle.

Hardie said not a word but the look on his face made it plain that he was far from happy.

109

"So, which one of you is Tomaszewski and which is Lewandowski, my prize przyjaciels?" asked Thoroughgood, pausing a couple of feet from the taller man, who had now brought the mallet he had been using into a semi-defensive position in front of his midriff.

"Gratulujes! I guess that makes you detective," said the one with black hair as he leaned over the post that had been half-hammered into the ground by his mate, adding, "Why you want to know . . . przyjaciel?"

Thoroughgood took a step forward until he was less than a foot away from the man and, whipping out his warrant card he rammed it into his face, "Listen to me, smart arse. I ask the questions and you provide the answers and, if you do, everything will be just fine. Comprendez?"

Black hair remained frozen, his chin resting on his knuckles which remained on top of the post, and the silence was broken by one word, "Culik." Thoroughgood turned just in time to see the big Pole swinging the giant mallet down towards his head.

20

THE MALLET slashed down just wide of Thoroughgood's head and he could feel it whistling through the air before it smashed into the post which had previously been propping up a head of black hair.

While Thoroughgood remained motionless in shock, Hardie was not about to pass up the opportunity for retribution. With all of his weight forward, the larger of the two Poles had left his right flank unguarded and Hardie took a step forward and smashed a fist into his midriff with everything behind it.

Black hair lunged towards the DC, only to have his legs taken from him by Thoroughgood's right foot. As he hit the deck, the DS landed on top of him, grabbing his hair in his right hand, ramming the man's face into the mud and slamming his right knee into the small of his back. "Kurwa!" he spat.

His friend, winded by Hardie, had dropped to one knee, wincing and breathing heavily, but still clutching the mallet menacingly. Hardie held his distance and tried to parley.

"Listen, mate, I think we got off on the wrong foot with you boys. Let's just have a wee chat before we end up calling for the seventh cavalry and you two find yourselves in custody and taking the first steps back to Mother Polska," he said curtly.

The big man still had vengeance in his eyes, but decided to offer an olive branch. "Okay, boss. What you want to know?"

Hardie offered his hand to the Pole, "Your name would be a start, big fella."

The Pole took Hardie's right hand and, in pulling himself to his feet, almost toppled Hardie off his, but a smile flashed across his craggy features. "My name is Robert Tomaszewski and friend over there is Artur Lewandowski."

The outbreak of peace was enough to persuade Thoroughgood to release the pressure of his right knee on Lewandowski's back, and slowly he pulled him backward by the wrists.

"Easy, fella – our dry cleaning bill is going to be bad enough without any more WWF moves," quipped Thoroughgood.

Black hair regained his feet and turned to face the DS, but remained poker-faced, "I am Artur Lewandowski. So what you want, detective?" he spat, with some venom in his accented English.

"Oh, I think you know exactly what we are after, my friend, or rather, who we are after. Where is Jan Boniek?" asked Thoroughgood.

"How we know, detective? We have no seen him since he lost us jobs at Balfron Mill at Christmas," said Lewandowski.

Before Thoroughgood could continue his line of questioning Hardie interjected, "C'mon mate, we aren't going to buy that. We've got a witness at the Mill says he's sure you're still in touch with him, and your gaffer Mr Rogers seems to think that is the case too. Listen pal – the bottom line is, Boniek is gonnae drown in a sea of shit of his own creation and if you don't help us you'll find yourselves without a paddle, and going under with him."

At this, the two Poles exchanged nervous glances and began a heated discussion in their impenetrable mother tongue.

At length, Tomaszewski addressed the two detectives. "Yes, Detective, you are right, we have been in touch with Jan since we all lost our jobs, but not how you think. He stay in Glasgow, in place called Maryhill."

Hardie could not help his gnarled features breaking into a smile, "Ah, hairy mill. Where else would you want to stay in our fair city? Your cooperation is greatly appreciated, my Polish friends, and wisely offered."

Relieved, Thoroughgood concluded what had turned into an informal interview with a word of warning. "Listen boys, if this all checks out then I am prepared to forget about our little altercation today. If it doesn't, then you have my word we will be back and your spell in Scotland will be over. Do you understand me?"

"It is understood," said Lewandowski and handed Thoroughgood a piece of paper on which he had quickly scrawled the address where Boniek could be found.

The journey back to Glasgow was spent dissecting their meeting with the Poles. The address in Maryhill had in fact turned out to be in the Possil area, in contradiction to the employment record, which had Boniek housed in Dumbarton Road. Thoroughgood had radioed it in, along with a description of Boniek, for local uniform to make what was their second home address check.

"Hopefully the wooden tops will pick him up, but I still don't think we've got to the bottom of this one, Hardie. What do you reckon, old son?" asked the DS.

Deep in thought, Hardie completed blowing his mouthful of smoke out of the car window and then flicked the remnants of the Silk Cut out of the vehicle. His craggy features remained expressionless as he gripped the steering wheel and pushed the button to close the window.

"Thank gawd for that, do you think we will ever complete a car journey without your window going up and down more times than a whore's drawers?" demanded Thoroughgood.

"Doubt it, with regard to the second of your questions," answered Hardie with a smirk. "With regard to the first, I'd have to say your Polish przyjaciels are telling us nothing like the whole truth. I can't help thinking there is a twist to all of this, but until we get our hands on Boniek, who knows what that is?"

"I dunno, faither. Do you think we should have Section 14'd them? I would be happier if we had them in and detained until the address checks out, or not, as I suspect may be the case."

"Being honest with you, Gus, I'm just glad we got out of there without gettin' the shit kicked out of us. They were tasty all right and I didn't fancy our chances in a catchweight contest. How long do you think it would have taken for the cavalry to arrive? Christ, can you imagine the mess that big fucker would have made of us with that mallet? Nope, gaffer, I have to say that in this particular case, discretion was definitely the better part of valour.

Plus, we would have had to have brought Central Scotland plod in to detain 'em, given this is all on their turf, and do you see these two widos waiting about for that to happen? I'll bell Central Scotland and get them to put a watching brief on our Polish chums," said Hardie.

Thoroughgood's impatience was made clear when he rapped his fist on the vehicle dashboard. "All right, try this one for size, Hardie. Sophie Balfron is abducted from her place while her old man has his throat cut right in front of her. The original idea behind the Balfron turn looks like it is a robbery, but then something goes wrong on the job, not least that the gang leader is left fatally wounded by Balfron in self defence. Then, as the rest of the gang beat a hasty retreat, one of the three remaining amigos blows his mate's head off. Although I don't see the slug that put Drummond out of his misery coming from our mystery man, my guess is it was a mercy killing by one of the others. Yet still Sophie Balfron is nowhere to be seen. You starting to get my drift?"

"So Boniek is the unknown gang member, and he and Sophie are now on the run together as a couple?" asked Hardie.

"Exactly, plus, our Polish pals know exactly what is going on and I'll bet you ten to one they also know where they are holed up. That's why the area searches in Strathclyde and Central Scotland have come up blank. They're being concealed."

"So the address in Possil is a fanny, and one meant to buy them time while they try to get Boniek and Sophie Balfron out of the area?" asked Hardie.

"Elementary, my dear Hardie."

*

115

It had been another 24 hours of dead ends and frustration, and Tomachek was far from happy with the debrief from his two subordinates, "Now listen to me, Thoroughgood, and by that I mean you too, Hardie. This isn't good enough. We have no leads and yet you say you are confident that your two new Polish chums are harbouring Boniek. Well, why the devil haven't you applied for a search warrant and had that bally Smithycroft Farm, or whatever it is called, turned upside down?"

Thoroughgood frowned. "Because, sir, it's in Central Scotlandville and they've dragged their feet about it because Jimmy Rogers is a local councillor out in Hayseed Dixie land. So really it is their call. They have just been off the blower and been made fully aware of our suspicions, but suspicions are all we have right now, hence their reticence."

"Balls and buggery, Thoroughgood, it's not good enough! And the chief is getting impatient for a result of some kind. I tell you, at this rate your pips are at risk, Gus, my boy. Never mind acting DI, you'll be acting out your days at this rate," said Tomachek, jabbing his Cairngorm Bent in the DS' direction.

The beeping of a text alert from inside Thoroughgood's breast pocket caused Tomachek's eyebrows to rise, but before he could say anything Hardie came to the rescue. "Hopefully, it's a tout, boss,"

"I hope for the DS' sake it is."

"Morse," said Thoroughgood with a sigh of relief. "Bingo, he's come up trumps again, boss. Ziggy's Polish Deli, Hyndland Street. Boniek working in back shop bakery. Turn it first thing in morn. Opens 8am,' read Thoroughgood out loud.

"Interesting information, Thoroughgood, don't ya think? Blows your theory about your Polish pals harbouring him out at Smithycroft farm right out of the water," said the detective superintendent.

"Maybe, but at least it's a lead, and a way of eliminating him from our enquiries. But I still think he's mixed up in this somehow."

"Fair enough. Your fellow Morse has never let us down before, especially with all that business regarding Meechan and . . ." Tomachek silently cursed himself for treading on Thoroughgood's private grief.

Thoroughgood shrugged. "Celine was her name and I'm not going to fall to pieces every time you mention her, boss. She's gone now and I'm moving on, hopefully just like this enquiry. We'll arrange for uniform to be on standby to give our mate the phantom Pole a tug early in the morning, and see what we can shake down."

"I suggest you do just that, Detective Sergeant. I will expect Boniek to be brought in on Section 14 detention early tomorrow morning, then. As for Central Scotland plod, let me make a couple of calls there, an old DS of mine made the move to Randolfield in order to make the next two steps up to DCI, and hopefully he can help us out regarding a search of the farm. Now, shut the door on your way out, gentlemen, and no more blind alleys if you don't mind," finished Tomachek.

21

THE MERCEDES SLK 200 slid down the road leading onto the white pebble driveway at the front of Roxburgh Hall and Thoroughgood had to admit the Gothic magnificence of the country house was impressive.

As Vanessa brought the Mercedes to a halt in front of the mansion's looming sheer spires, she turned to Thoroughgood and made sure his pre-match briefing had sunk in, "I don't know how this is going to go, darlin'. The Roxburgh's have just suffered a death in the family. The younger brother, Alexander, collapsed at the beginning of the week and the post mortem hasn't been made public yet. But Victoria, his sister, called me to say that she and Lady Roxburgh would meet me, regardless. I guess that proves how determined they are to make sure the Dark Ocean launch goes through."

Thoroughgood leaned back in his seat and raised his eyebrows sardonically. "The reason for that, Vanessa, is that the elder Roxburgh sibling, Robert, I believe his name is, was up to his neck in debts accrued at the casinos. This launch of their latest whisky is being bankrolled by the Triads, or so the story goes. I would imagine that they are not the most sympathetic of backers."

Vanessa was less than impressed, "I wondered if you knew anything about it. It's all gossip, and I've suffered enough from that to know that if even a fraction of it was true, then the truth itself would be a fairy tale. What matters is that I'm in a position to help the Roxburgh's, although the charity fashion show will also give my clothing range some extra profile. So if you don't mind, can you just let me do the talking, my sweet policeman?"

"Yes, ma'am," was the best a chastised Thoroughgood could offer.

Climbing the lower section of the granite staircase leading up to four impressive pillars at the top, Thoroughgood couldn't help but be impressed by the home of the Roxburghs. Three outrageously ornate arches loomed above them on the top level, where an imposing oak door opened and an immaculately suited man greeted them.

"Good evening, and welcome to Roxburgh Hall. Miss Velvet, if I am not mistaken and . . . friend?" enquired Macintosh in a clipped tone, laced with slight disapproval.

"You are not mistaken," retorted Vanessa icily, while Thoroughgood shifted uncomfortably behind her.

"Lady Elizabeth and Miss Victoria await you in the Scott lounge, Madame and sir. If you would care to follow me?" asked the butler.

Vanessa nodded curtly and they followed his pin-striped back into the flagstoned vestibule.

The first sight that greeted them was that of Lady Elizabeth standing in front of the full-length portrait of the second Viscount, her arms folded across her chest, a fine golden cardigan was slung over her shoulders, matching her immaculate hair. Her smile was weak and the strain of the grief she clearly bore following the loss of her youngest son was etched across her face; it was obvious that this meeting was the last thing she wished to deal with.

Before any awkwardness could develop a light voice spoke from the side of the huge marble fireplace, "Vanessa, I am so glad you could come and this must be, if the magazines are to be believed, your new friend, Detective Sergeant Thoroughgood?" said Victoria Roxburgh.

As Vanessa greeted the youngest Roxburgh with her trademark kiss on either cheek, Thoroughgood hovered awkwardly in the background, aware that Lady Elizabeth was assessing him with an icy gaze. But as Victoria made her way over to him, Thoroughgood's attention was quickly re-focused on the warmth of her smile and silky chestnut hair – the same shade as the eyes that seemed to suck him in.

"Pleased to meet you, miss," he stuttered in a hopelessly awkward attempt at genteel civility, before quickly adding as a guilty afterthought, "May I offer my sincere condolences on your loss."

Her eyes held his for a lingering moment as her radiant smile faded and Thoroughgood saw a tear well up in her eye and run down the side of her cheek before she made an enormous effort to pull herself together with a deep sigh. Automatically, Thoroughgood reached inside the pocket of his jacket and fished out a handkerchief before offering it to Victoria, as the spontaneity of his gesture became enveloped in more awkwardness.

Yet she took it and dabbed at the tears that now began to roll uncontrollably down her sallow cheeks. Again she drew a deep breath and held out her hand in a greeting that was clearly intended to replace the words she did not have the composure to speak. Thoroughgood felt the warmth of her hand as it lingered in his limp grasp and then she spoke to him and everyone else in the room seemed to disappear.

"So, chivalry is not dead!" she said, trying to stifle a sob before continuing her tortured attempt at humorous etiquette, " You are the detective we have to thank for saving us from the mad Imam Tariq. It's nice to meet you, Detective Sergeant Thoroughgood, and thank you for your thoughtfulness," said Victoria alluding to the handkerchief before reluctantly withdrawing her hand from his.

Lady Elizabeth took charge of proceedings, "Thank you for your kind sentiments and thoughtfulness, Mr Thoroughgood. These are very trying times for our family and we miss Alexander terribly, but that is not why we are here. The show must go on, and I am sure you are not interested in the details of a fashion shoot and ladies clothing range launch," she said, her natural authority, clearly fragile, still brooked no argument.

"Macintosh, why don't you show Mr Thoroughgood into the library and make sure he has a dram to help him enjoy the fire," she added briskly.

Thoroughgood was surprised to see that the butler was indeed still present in the doorway, such was the ethereal quality of his presence.

"If you would be so good as to follow me," said Macintosh before, after a slight delay, adding, "Mr Thoroughgood."

The thought slipped through Thoroughgood's mind that the manoeuvre between the dowager and her faithful servant was so slick it must have been one executed a hundred times before to jettison unwelcome visitors. He wished he had not agreed to come in the first place.

Vanessa's blazing eyes caught and held his as he meekly smiled and followed the butler out, but Thoroughgood knew she would be in a rage over having such a polite but firm control placed on her presence, even in such magnificent surroundings. The thought caused him some amusement. He followed the butler into an oak-panelled room that reeked of atmosphere while the crackling of the logs in the fireplace grabbed his attention and assailed his senses with their aromatic delight.

He was immediately attracted to the window to the left of the fire place, affording as it did a fine view over Loch Lomond, and as Thoroughgood drank it in Macintosh's velvet tones percolated through the silence.

"May I take the liberty of pouring you a dram, sir? "The Roxburgh" single malt . . . sir?"

Thoroughgood turned and slowly subjected the butler to a lingering sea green stare that Macintosh met and held.

"You may," said Thoroughgood.

Macintosh poured the whisky into a fine Edinburgh crystal glass and looking up, subjecting Thoroughgood to a sickly smile, "Will that be all . . . sir?"

"I would think so . . . Macintosh," replied Thoroughgood, drawing out the butler's name to convey his dislike for the man.

The butler offered a slight incline of his head and as he left the room the thought crossed Thoroughgood's mind that Macintosh was the type of individual who revelled in the power of knowledge. A knowledge that had banked all of Roxburgh Hall's secrets and one which made him indispensable to the Roxburgh family and they, in turn, vulnerable to him.

As his gaze swept the library shelves his attention landed on a latticed cabinet at the side of the fireplace, which Thoroughood assumed was for the select of the book collection.

Fortunately, the doors were unlocked and as he opened them one cover caught Thoroughgood's gaze. Ivanhoe, immediately stood out to a man who had idolised the central character, Wilfred of Ivanhoe, in Sir Walter Scott's 12th Century epic tale of Saxon England under the yolk of Norman oppression.

The book had clearly been placed in a prominent position and setting his whisky glass down on the mantel of the fireplace, Thoroughgood removed it with care. He opened the book up and saw that it was a first edition; he pondered its worth before marvelling that it had been allowed to rest on the shelf within the cabinet and was not under lock and key.

Carefully, he opened it and was quickly drawn to the handwritten message scrawled on the flyleaf, "To my darling Jill from your own true Ivanhoe!" with the letters LVR printed in block capitals just below, three crosses that came next underlined the terms of endearment followed by the date, 01.12.41.

Thoroughgood moved over to the fire and placed the book on the mantelpiece, took a sip of whisky and began to read the opening lines of the classic that had done more than anything to make him follow his heart and study medieval history at university. He could not help himself, closing his eyes and reciting Pope's Odyssey out loud: *"Thus communed these; while to their lowly dome, The full-fed swine return'd with evening home; Compell'd, reluctant, to the several sties. With din obstreperous, and ungrateful cries."*

As he stopped to take another slurp of the malt, the silence, previously interrupted only by the crackling of logs on the fire, was broken by another voice, a light voice filled with warmth and at the same time, unmistakable sadness, "In that pleasant district of merry England which is watered by the river Don, there extended in ancient times a large forest, covering the greater part of the beautiful hills and vallies which lie between Sheffield and the pleasant town of Doncaster."

Thoroughgood turned round sharply, almost dropping the priceless book in the process, to find Victoria Roxburgh standing three feet away from him. "I am impressed, Mr Thoroughgood, with your knowledge of Ivanhoe. It is not what I would expect of a . . ." As she stalled, Thoroughgood supplied the end to her sentence, "Policeman."

They both smiled spontaneously and Victoria quickly produced his handkerchief, "Thank you so much for your kindness earlier on. If I had known that you were a fan of Ivanhoe I would not have been so pleasantly surprised." With that she offered the handkerchief to Thoroughgood, but he nodded his head at the book in one hand and the whisky glass in the other, "As you can see, I have my hands full and thanks to my mother, no shortage of hankies at home. Please keep it. The main thing is, are you all right?"

"No, to be honest, I am not, although it is much worse for Mama. Alexander's death is being treated as suspicious and we are still waiting for the full result of the post mortem. All of this is happening at the worst possible time for our family, with the launch of The Dark Ocean whisky liqueur and our deal with the Gwai Lo consortium already set in stone. So Mama is right, the show must go on."

"You can always lose yourself in a good book," said Thoroughgood, realising immediately how clumsy his attempt at kindness had been, before adding, "I never get tired of reading Ivanhoe. The story itself is almost as romantic as the message written inside the cover. I guess that must be related to two of your forebears?"

She smiled sweetly and took the book from his outstretched hand, "Yes, it was my grandfather's favourite. He's probably written some soppy message to my grandma Margaret inside."

Thoroughgood's quick glance at the book immediately alerted Victoria that all was not as it seemed, and as she opened the cover she could not help herself reading the handwritten message aloud, *"To my darling Jill from your own true Ivanhoe!"* signed LVR, dated 01.12.42." She choked back a sob before continuing: "Oh dear, how terribly awkward, Mr Thoroughgood. You see, LVR was indeed my grandfather, Ludovic Roxburgh, but I don't, as you will no doubt have guessed by now, have a clue who Jill was."

For the second time that evening the tears began to flow down Victoria's cheeks and Thoroughgood guided her over to the settee and sat her down. "Hey, take it easy. Every family has a skeleton in the closet," he soothed as he handed her the glass of malt, "Take a deep breath and have a sip. Always remember things are rarely as bad as they seem."

Victoria took a gulp and placing the glass on her lap, buried her head on his shoulder and sobbed.

22

HARDIE TOOK a sip of coffee and balanced the cardboard cup at a precarious angle on the dashboard of the Focus, placed the Silk Cut in his mouth and inhaled. Blowing the smoke out the open window, he turned his head towards Thoroughgood, "Jeez, what a mess. The suspicious death of the youngest son, right on the eve of the deal they hope will save them from oblivion, albeit one financed by Triad money. Then a 70-year skeleton bolts out the closet and shatters the squeaky-clean image of dearly beloved grand-pappy. The Roxburghs may be toffs, but I wouldnae want to be in their shoes right now."

"Sure is a mess all right. I'll give you good money the suspicious death is tied up in the whole takeover business. Apparently Alexander was strongly against the Gwai Lo deal and had let Robert know what he thought of him, in no uncertain terms. Thank God we aren't in danger of catching that one, mate."

Hardie winked roguishly and added, "But hey, every cloud has a silver lining, gaffer. You got to meet Victoria Roxburgh and become her knight in shining armour. Man, if she's half as good-looking as the pictures I've seen of her in the papers then she must be some beauty. So who has caught the enquiry?"

"DI Randolph Pigeon, and good luck to him, he'll need it" said Thoroughgood.

"Old Randy Pigeon, eh? I could see him ruffling a few feathers up at the Hall," sniggered Hardie.

Before Thoroughgood could answer his police radio burst into life – the controller advising that uniform attending from Partick Police Station had been held up after a disturbance in the cells.

"Okay, uniform are runnin' late. A slight problem at Partick nick with some maniac kicking off. Seems the early shift are men down with a flu bug and it was all hands on deck after he smacked the duty officer. We might as well get in position and get ready to ruffle a few Polish feathers!" said Thoroughood and with that they both got out of the Focus and walked down the slight incline from the top of Hyndland Road to the bakery.

"0715hrs," said Hardie helpfully, before continuing, "you never know, we might even get our breakfast out of this if we play our cards right. I used to have a great howf up in Balornock, in Broomknowes Road, when I was in uniform. Homemade soup, hot sausage rolls and just about anything a beat cop could ask for. I wouldn't mind nabbing a couple of freshly baked rolls and heading over to the farmer's market and fillin' them with some black puddin'. That would be the dog's bollocks."

"For feck's sake, Hardie, do you ever stop thinking about that stomach of yours? Let's just get our hands on Boniek and see where that takes us," growled Thoroughgood irritably.

As they walked down the footpath a delivery van pulled up outside the bakery. A dark-haired man jumped out and disappeared behind the vehicle before reappearing on the pavement side with a pallet which he quickly carried into the bakery.

"I don't know about you, gaffer, but it wouldn't surprise me if that was our man. Roughly speaking, he fits Boniek's description. I don't think we can afford to wait on uniform any longer." said Hardie.

"Fair enough. He's pretty much a match for Boniek. Why don't we split up and you come round from the roadside of the van and I'll continue down the footpath. And when we have him back at the vehicle we can have a cosy little chat with Mr Janek Boniek," said Thoroughgood before applying a quick pat on Hardie's shoulders, "Take care, faither."

"Roger that," replied the DC, crossing the street towards the farmers' market that was gradually springing to life just across the way, in an area known quaintly as Mansfield Park, little more than an old, blaize football pitch.

Thoroughgood slowed his pace and held back, tight in the doorway of a shop just two up from the bakers, and waited for movement. Within moments he heard whistling coming from the baker's doorway and the dark-haired male they had seen earlier strolled out of the premises, pallet in one hand.

Thoroughgood made his move and jogged towards the vehicle, but as he peered round the back of the van the man turned round, alerted by the footsteps. He clapped venomous grey eyes on Thoroughgood and cursed out loud in his mother tongue, "Skurwysyn!" as he smashed the pallet over Thoroughgood's head, sending him staggering back into a parked Volkswagen. Quickly, Boniek twisted around and made his way towards the driver's door, only to feel Hardie's fierce grip on his right shoulder. Spinning round, he hammered his left fist into the side of the DC's jaw and Hardie sagged onto the side of the van.

The man jumped into the cabin and gunned the engine just as a police vehicle shot down Hyndland Street. Setting the van in motion he attempted to turn it around, just as Hardie seized the driver's door and yanked it open.

"Out of there you bastard!" he shouted, as he tried to grab hold of the steering wheel, but Boniek hissed at him, "Nie, matkojebco," and rammed his elbow into Hardie's face, sending the DC flying through the air before he crash-landed on the road. The delivery van hurtled down to the bottom of Dumbarton Road only to be met head on by a second police vehicle.

Thoroughgood grabbed Hardie and propped him up against the Volkswagen as they watched the van heading straight for the panda car. With a full-on collision pending, the only word that came out Thoroughgood's mouth was, "Shit." But at the last minute the van swerved to the left of the Panda and turned into Dumbarton Road. By this time the air was ablaze with sirens and as the van attempted to shoot along Dumbarton Road, in the direction of Partick Cross, another cop car blocked its way.

"We've got him bottled up, gaffer," said Hardie rubbing the side of his face.

There was only one route Boniek could take to make good his escape and the realisation dawned on Thoroughgood, "Oh no we haven't, he's turnin' left now. Jesus, he's gonnae try and smash his way through the farmers' market!" Thoroughgood sprinted across the street, vaulted onto a car bonnet and used it as a launch pad onto the brick wall that encircled the market, all the time keeping one eye on the delivery van.

The sound of screeching as rubber burned on tarmacadam brought an end to the van's progress along Dumbarton Road and it swerved viciously to the left, heading straight for the market. There was a loud crash as it ploughed through a set of railings and headed straight for the first green and white striped stall, as the early morning customers milling around the stall began to realise the danger they were in.

A thickset middle-aged man threw himself onto the stall table to avoid the vehicle surging straight for him. A woman grabbed her child up in her arms and ran as screams pierced the morning.

As Thoroughgood landed on the blaize surface to the left of a stall selling Highland game, he saw the van shooting straight down the middle of the market with pedestrians diving out of the way like skittles in front of a giant white wrecking ball.

To his horror, an elderly wheelchair-bound lady hadn't heard the ensuing mayhem that was erupting all around – unaware of the certain death that was hurtling towards her as she examined some wild boar salami. Thoroughgood knew he had seconds to save her and threw himself across the five yard gap between himself and the old dear. As he slapped his hands on the back of the wheelchair the elderly woman began to screech, "What the devil . . .?" However, as she was propelled across the gap, the danger that was just about to send her to her maker became apparent and her face was framed in a look of sheer horror as one elongated scream left her mouth.

The van roared by, missing them by a yard as it seared Thoroughgood with a backdraft of hot air. With no control over his own direction of travel the DS careered into a deck chair and smashed a Thermos of piping hot coffee into the air which came down like a thousand minute blistering hot geysers on top of him, as he lost his footing and thudded to the ground. Thoroughgood was not the only one to have his momentum stalled. As he rolled up onto his feet he saw the van shoot through a stall full of hanging bird carcases and eventually come to a halt, embedded in the railings behind it.

The driver's door opened immediately and Boniek jumped out and broke into a sprint, but Thoroughgood had a head start on him and before he gained any real momentum the DS lunged at him, wrapping his arms around his torso and slamming Boniek into the stall's green and white striped tarpaulin roof, now wrapped around the truck.

23

AS THE duo landed on the tarpaulin, Thoroughgood felt his grip start to slip. Boniek broke his right hand free and smashed his fist into Thoroughgood's jaw with crunching power. The blow was enough to knock Thoroughgood onto his back and the Pole attacked viciously.

"Now, I fuck you good, Polijca," he spat and rained a vicious two-fisted barrage down on the DS.

Thoroughgood took a blow on his forearm as he tried to cover up fast, but the hand that followed cracked into the side of his head and he felt his senses reeling. Another punch thudded into his ribs and, as he desperately tried to grab one of the fists of fury that were threatening to beat him to a pulp, he left his head unguarded and Boniek, who was now on top of him, grabbed his jacket and smashed his forehead into Thoroughgood's nose.

The DS cannoned back into the tarpaulin and he could already see, through the bloody mist shrouding his vision, that Boniek was off and running again. Struggling to get to his feet, Thoroughgood found himself less than steady as a shout from his right snapped his attention away from the receding back of the Pole.

"Jeez, Gus! You've taken a bleaching there, mate!" said Hardie, arriving on the scene at the double.

Ignoring Hardie, Thoroughgood's attention was once more on Boniek and the look of horror enveloping his smashed face made Hardie follow suit. "Oh fuck . . . surely not?" said the DC.

Boniek was closing in on a parked ambulance, about 200 yards up from the farmer's market, at the top end of Hyndland Street.

Thoroughgood broke into an unsteady run and Hardie followed suit.

The ambulance driver placed his hands on the top of the vehicle steering wheel and began to drum his fingers in time to the music as the Stereophonics' Dakota blasted over the airwaves. Jimmy Cairns' impatience at the length of time his partner, Senga McVeigh, was taking at the Polish deli down the street, was growing by the minute.

His gaze trained avidly on the view through his windscreen, he was brought back into the real world with a bang as his door was ripped open and a dark haired male snarled, "Out."

"Get tae fuck," spat Cairns in enraged defiance and found the Pole's right fist pounding him in the face for his trouble.

With the ambulance driver temporarily stunned, Boniek grabbed him with both hands and smashed his head off the steering wheel. Then the Pole hauled him out of the cabin, throwing him onto the pavement like some naughty schoolboy. As he did so, a female voice shouted, "You bastard, get out of my wagon!" and already halfway into the vehicle, Boniek felt the driver's door being yanked open again.

Quickly, he rammed the door with his boot, sending

the green-suited ambulance technician flying back and onto the bonnet. He grabbed the door, slammed it shut and gunned the engine, thankful that the key was still snugly in the ignition; engaged gear and slammed his foot on the accelerator as Cairns frantically pulled Senga clear.

Thoroughgood ripped open the Focus' door and jumped into the driver's seat, starting the engine up as Hardie finally reached the police vehicle and, gasping for oxygen, jumped into the passenger side. Both detectives had kept Boniek in view as they had run for the car and now they saw him mount a u-turn with impressive dexterity as the ambulance crew dived clear of their vehicle.

"Bastard's going back up Hyndland Street for Highburgh Road," said Hardie.

"Never mind stating the bleedin' obvious to me, faither, tell it to Control," rapped Thoroughgood as his foot hit the accelerator and the Focus shot off in pursuit.

The ambulance gathered speed as it sped past the Cottiers Bar and Theatre complex for the junction with Highburgh Road, and as it did so Hardie couldn't help himself articulating his dread. "He's got to be taking a left and be heading for Great Western Road, otherwise he'll have to double-back on himself, if he's heading for Byres Road," said the DC.

With Thoroughgood's foot to the floor the Focus locked into the emergency vehicle's slipstream, just in time to see the ambulance's emergency blue light start to flash and the wail of its siren fill the air. As it arrived at the junction it began to turn right.

Thoroughgood's view was restricted as the Focus shot up the narrow road running parallel with Cottiers, but while the ambulance disappeared to the right at the junction, the mayhem the manoeuvre had caused was brought home to both detectives when a bottle green Volvo shot into the fencing directly opposite the junction in its attempt to avoid the emergency vehicle. As the crash of the impact echoed in their ears Hardie gasped, "He's fuckin' mad."

As the CID car edged out of the junction Thoroughgood could see the ambulance surging down the middle of Highburgh Road towards Byres Road, with vehicles on the opposite side of the road swerving crazily to avoid it. As it did so Hardie blurted out an update on its direction of travel, and the accident it had caused, to Control. Now the police vehicle followed in its wake with the blue light attached to its front grill flashing its own warning.

"Fuck me gently, the middle of rush hour and this mad bastard is gonnae ram right through the junction with Byres Road and fuck knows what kind of carnage that will cause," said the DC.

"The punters have a fighting chance with the ambulance siren on and the lights flashing, but it's University Avenue after that and with two pedestrian crossings to negotiate and all these bloody students headin' for their 9am lectures . . ." Thoroughgood's words trailed off as the vehicle hit the junction with Byres Road.

Boniek had not dropped any speed and as he hit the junction the lights miraculously switched to green and, overtaking the waiting vehicles, he sailed through. As he did so the Focus began to close the gap to within 50 yards.

"What next, Gus?"

"Direction of travel update and see if we can get a

Panda with a stinger to set up on his likely route of travel. I'm betting the maniac is heading for Charing Cross and a sharp exit along the M8 East," said Thoroughgood.

As Hardie updated control, the vehicle tore up the hill that was University Avenue. The pedestrian crossing outside the John McIntyre building came into view – it was teeming with students.

"Sweet Jesus," said Thoroughgood.

Boniek seemed to have picked up speed, but despite the sirens and the blue flashing lights warning of the ambulance's approach there was a fatal delay in the message penetrating the minds of the young academics lost in matters of their alma mater.

As realisation began to dawn on those crossing, screams and shouts of warning pierced the air.

For some it was too late.

A knot of four students were caught on the road between the pavement and the central island. The ambulance shot straight at them.

The impending terror grabbed Johnny Franks' attention at the last minute and his scream of, "Get off the road!" had such sheer terror in it that everyone in his group of friends was, at last, aware of the danger they were in. Johnny dived at the girl nearest him. His momentum knocked her off her feet and onto the central reservation. The couple between him and the ambulance were not so lucky.

A sickening thud filled the air as the vehicle's bonnet sent their bodies somersaulting before the young academics landed with two dull thuds. The scene played out in a surreal slow motion that had Franks retching at the sight. The sausage roll and beans he'd just had for breakfast at the Hub now all over the road. The ambulance surged on.

Hardie updated Control, asking for an ambulance to attend the locus immediately as the screams of the students pierced the air.

"There's nothing we can do for them mate," said Thoroughgood as he carefully negotiated the mayhem and continued after the ambulance.

The emergency vehicle had hit the bottom of University Avenue and turned left, heading for Gibson Street. Thoroughgood continued his pursuit.

"Where the fuck is the cavalry?" demanded the DS.

"Got a city centre unit in Woodlands Road," answered Hardie, before adding, "Fuck all good that will do us, we've got to stop him before he takes out any more punters, Gus."

Thoroughgood's eyes remained trained on the ambulance as it hit the lights at the corner of Gibson Street and screeched right. "He's gotta be heading for the M8. Tell Control to get that fuckin' Panda and any other woodentops in the area to block it up. Christ, where are the fuckin' Traffic when you need them?" raged Thoroughgood.

"Probably doing a granddad for a baldy tyre, bunch of bloody jobsworths," answered Hardie.

His foot to the floor, Thoroughgood brought the Focus up alongside the ambulance and yanked down left, ramming the cop car into the side of the ambulance as the roundabout materialised up ahead. The emergency vehicle veered sharply from the impact, but Boniek steadied it and then pulled his steering-wheel hard to the right.

The force of the contact quivered right through

137

the Focus; Boniek flashed a feral smile at Hardie and mouthed "Fuck you," as the cop car cannoned over onto the other side of the road.

Suddenly a cyclist, his eyes wide in sheer terror, appeared in front of the police vehicle.

"Bloody hell!" screeched Hardie.

The cyclist clamped his eyes shut and waited to be turned into mincemeat, but miraculously slipped through a small gap that had opened up between the ambulance and the cop car and made his way unscathed straight down the middle of the road.

Thoroughgood regained control of the Focus to see that the only way he was going to negotiate the roundabout was by going round it on the wrong side. The double decker bus coming his way meant his chances were slim to non-existent.

"Shit!" cursed Hardie as death headed their way.

24

BETWEEN THE double decker and the roundabout lay their only hope. Thoroughgood knew he had just one chance to avoid the bus and he would have to manoeuvre at maximum speed. He rammed his foot to the floor and the car shot into the gap – the filling in a sandwich between the double decker and the edge of the concrete roundabout.

The DS gritted his teeth and clamped the steering wheel with both hands until the whites of his knuckles showed. Hardie shut his eyes and muttered something about gratitude to the big man upstairs if they made it out unscathed. But as the Focus surged into the gap the double decker, its driver's face enveloped in blank shock, had already begun to close in and the sound of metal on metal screeched its agony through the air as sparks shot out from the collision.

The contact was enough to knock the Focus into the edge of the roundabout on its passenger side, and as it hit the kerb the vehicle began to fly as daylight filled the space between the Focus and the road.

"Throw yourself onto your door!" yelled Thoroughgood as he wrestled with the steering wheel.

Hardie did as he was told. The DS cannoned sideways into him to put more force into the impact. It was enough to stop the vehicle tipping any further and they breathed a collective sigh of relief as the thud of the offside tyres hitting the ground allowed them to breathe again.

The run-in with the double decker had cost them vital moments and the ambulance was clear and continuing on its route to Charing Cross. The hum of blades from above told them that the police helicopter had now been mobilised, but Hardie was more interested in ground reinforcements, "Where the fuck is plod?" he snapped just as the sound of sirens in the distance answered his question.

"Get in there! We've got the bastard!" said an elated Hardie.

The cavalry had indeed arrived, and the off ramp to the M8 had been blocked by a Traffic car. Its crew quickly threw down their stinger device in front of the oncoming ambulance, barely glancing at it before sprinting to comparative safety behind their car.

Spotting that the slip road heading in the direction of Sauchiehall Street and Charing Cross had not been completely closed, with only one Panda car in a blocking position, and realising just how futile that was, Sergeant Jim Brough gave the police helicopter full throttle and surged over the ambulance as it fired along Woodlands Road.

Brough turned his machine around and dipped until he was hovering above the lane that would provide Boniek with an escape route out of the bottleneck. Brough's number two, Cammy Thompson, trained his Heckler and Koch out of his side of the chopper as the traffic cops used their loudhailer to order Boniek to stop.

140

The single finger raised by Boniek from the steering wheel was the only reply they got from the Pole. As the ambulance roared out of Woodlands Road, Boniek immediately saw there was no hope of making it onto the motorway and a quick glance to his right confirmed North Street, immediately to his left, was jam-packed with morning traffic. Ahead lay his only hope.

He pressed the accelerator to the floor and raged, "I fuck you all, pigs!"

As the ambulance surged towards the roadway just under the helicopter, Thompson unloaded his H&K. It was a difficult shot given the movement of the chopper, and the burst of gun fire merely polka-dotted the ambulance roof while the vehicle kept coming.

The helicopter continued to hover about 12 feet off the ground and Boniek knew that this gap was the eye of the needle he had to thread the ambulance through, if his hopes of escape were to remain alive.

He gritted his teeth as the ambulance ploughed relentlessly on and the gunfire stopped, Boniek realising the police marksman must be reloading. Just as the ambulance drew under the helicopter there were two loud bangs and the windscreen shattered in front of Boniek, covering him in a hail of glistening glass.

The helicopter's landing stanchions had caught the ambulance at the juncture of its roof and windscreen and as Boniek stared wildly through the remains of the windscreen he could hardly believe what he was seeing.

Brough grappled with the joystick with all his strength as he tried to counter the vicious blow that had sent the flying machine spiralling into a somersault.

He could not right it.

"Jesus Christ!" were the last two words he spoke in this life.

The chopper began to topple and, for a moment, time seemed to stretch, before it dropped out of sight and onto the M8, underneath the Charing Cross flyover.

Reality was resumed with a vengeance by the vicious explosion and giant fireball caused by its disintegration on the roadway beneath, as a cacophony of horns and the screeching and rasping of metal on metal filled the air from below.

Boniek was through the cordon and the ambulance shot up Sauchiehall Street with only one vehicle in pursuit

25

BONIEK VEERED left into Sauchiehall Street leaving behind a backdrop of flame and destruction but Thoroughgood had closed the gap as Hardie continued to broadcast an update on his direction of travel.

Once again the Pole surprised his pursuers by sliding left across the three lanes and, as he passed the Garage nightclub, he swung the ambulance left up Garnet Street.

"Bad move, fucker," said Hardie as the lack of width and the severe gradient of one of the city's smallest streets slowed the ambulance to a crawl before a violent lurch suggested that the Pole had overdone his gear change.

"There's a primary school around the bend, and you know what that could mean," said Thoroughgood.

However, as the ambulance crested the hill it caught a kerb and its lack of momentum brought it to a shuddering stop. The driver's door swung open and Boniek jumped out of the cabin and took to his heels. Thoroughgood rammed on the handbrake and, grabbing the Maglite Torch out of the driver's door holder, did likewise.

"This time you're mine, fucker," spat the DS, bursting into a sprint.

He reached the corner of Renfrew Street just as Boniek

glanced backwards and in doing so, ran straight into a group of green-blazered school kids, knocking two over as he went flying along the pavement. Thoroughgood knew this was his opportunity to catch the Pole and thanked God for all his hours on the squash courts as he closed the gap to within 10 feet. Boniek rolled out of his fall and regained his feet before charging off. The DS knew there was no point in trying to broadcast the direction of the foot chase. He needed every available breath to try and catch his quarry and hoped that Hardie had made it out on foot in time to take in the pursuit and radio in.

Thoroughgood's eyes swept the street scene and he noticed the Glasgow School of Art coming into view to the right of the pavement he was now pounding. So had Boniek. The Pole took the steps two at a time, under its wrought-iron archway and up to its strangely sinister black wooden doors.

As he hit the bottom of the steps, Thoroughgood glanced up at the doorway – and disbelief and horror swept over him simultaneously. Coming out of the doors was Victoria Roxburgh.

Boniek reacted instinctively and grabbed her long brown tresses before spinning her round so that her back was against his chest and a glinting six inch blade of cold steel was pressed against her sallow skin. Victoria Roxburgh screamed.

Thoroughgood drew to a halt on the second bottom step.

"Now, cop, you stay fuckin' back or I slit bitch's throat!" spat Boniek.

Thoroughgood raised his right hand in an open-palmed

gesture of acquiescence, "Okay amigo, you hold all the aces. But where is this gonna get you, Boniek? Janek isn't it?"

The unmistakeable sound of what seemed like a hundred sirens told Boniek his odds of escape had shortened dramatically and for a moment his gaze slid from Thoroughgood and down over the backdrop of Renfrew Street. Thoroughgood eased a foot up on to the third step, but the Pole spotted his opportunism. He jabbed the blade over Victoria's shoulder and straight at Thoroughgood,

"One step more, she bleeds," he barked as he rammed his back into the door and dragged Victoria through the opening.

As they backed into the reception area, Boniek quickly wheeled Victoria round and propelled her to the foot of an imposing stair at the back of the foyer. The security guard at the reception desk interrupted his conversation with a female student as he spotted Boniek holding the blade to Victoria's throat. He jumped up and ran across the foyer just as Thoroughgood raced through the doors.

"Let her go, you nutter!" shouted the guard.

Boniek pushed Victoria Roxburgh onto the steps, turned and buried the blade in the guard's guts before wrenching its bloodied steel back out.

"Chuj ci w dupe," spat the Pole, grabbing Victoria by her hair and dragged her up the steps. She screamed.

Thoroughgood crouched over the security guard and tried to offer him some reassurance, "Hold on in there, mate, help is on its way." Behind him Hardie, newly arrived, could be heard spitting out an assistance request for an ambulance.

Looking up, Thoroughgood saw his neighbour standing above him, "Nice of you to turn up. Can you hold the fort here?" he asked.

"No problem," said Hardie and took hold of the security guard. Thoroughgood pushed his way through the throng of jostling students all trying to get an eyeful of the carnage that had just erupted. Waving his warrant card in front of him he yelled the words, "Police! Out of the way!"

Reaching the first floor, he almost ran into two teenage males. Breathlessly he panted, "Police! Did you see . . ." but before he could finish the sentence the larger of the two teenagers blurted out, "He's got Vicky Roxburgh. They've gone up again."

Thoroughgood smiled his gratitude and as he surged up the stairs he could hear Boniek's gutteral voice coming from above him.

Reaching the top floor Thoroughgood took a moment to regain his breath, the blood pounding in his eardrums as he scanned the area in front of him. A corridor, lined with what appeared to be white neo-classical Greek busts, stretched out before him and the sound of receding footsteps and a female's sobbing told him that Boniek and Victoria were some way down it.

He broke into a slow run, not wanting to sprint in on anything without giving himself the time to react. As he turned a corner he once again came face to face with the Pole and his captive, half-silhouetted in one of several archways.

Just ten feet away Boniek booted over one of the plinth-mounted classical figures and it smashed on the ground between them. "You stay there cop," he snarled, yanking Victoria's hair, forcing an exhausted scream from his hostage.

Thoroughgood played for time, "Come on, Boniek. Is this how you treated Sophie Balfron?"

A look of surprise spread across the Pole's features, "What you mean, skurwysyn?" he demanded.

Thoroughgood took a step forward and his foot crunched on the shattered plaster of the broken bust.

"Get back, pig," raged the Pole, alerted to Thoroughgood's encroachment.

"Listen, mate, we both know there is no way out of this for you. The building is surrounded and it's up to you how you get out of it, either on yer feet or in a pine box, amigo, I don't give a fuck. But let the girl go. She has nothing to do with any of this."

Boniek refused to play ball and tightened his grip around Victoria's neck, dragging her backwards towards a sunlit corridor that seemed to be made entirely of glass.

Thoroughgood's eyes stayed locked on his quarry. "So, the fox is about to enter the hen run."

"Go to hell, scum!" Boniek snarled, and with all his power the Pole shoved Victoria straight at the DS and disappeared into the brilliant sunlight behind him. For the second time since they had met, Thoroughgood found himself holding Victoria as she sobbed into his arms, but while he muttered words of reassurance his eyes had not left his quarry. Boniek had retreated down the glass corridor, immediately aware that he had nowhere to go.

"Listen, Victoria, can you be brave for me? I need to take care of this situation, so can you make your way back down the stairs? Help should be on the way, and most likely you will meet my colleague, Detective Constable

Hardie, on his way up," said Thoroughgood looking into her eyes with all the calm and reassurance he could muster

Victoria's brown eyes locked on his, arresting his gaze for a moment he didn't want to end, "Yeah, take care, Gus," she said.

He smiled at her, took his hands from her shoulders and ran into the sunlight.

26

THE WOODEN floorboards creaked uncomfortably as Thoroughgood stepped forward and his eyes became accustomed to the brilliance of the early morning sunshine piercing the glass that surrounded him on the top floor of the Art School. Boniek was 20 feet away, desperately kicking a door that would not give.

"It's over, Boniek, now tell me what the fuck you have done with Sophie Balfron." Thoroughgood declared as he advanced towards the Pole.

"You think so, pig?" shouted Boniek, and threw himself at Thoroughgood.

The blood-gored blade sparkled in the sunlight as it descended towards Thoroughgood, but the DS met it full on with steel of his own in the shape of the Maglite Torch and sparks flew as torch met knife. Thoroughgood rammed his knee straight into the Pole's groin with all his might.

Boniek doubled over and Thoroughgood smashed his right hand off Boniek's jaw. The rage in the DS gave the blow more force than any he could remember throwing, and the Pole was thrown across the corridor and smashed into the glazed panels encasing it.

As Boniek's body made contact the crack of the impact was instantly followed by the splintering of the wooden frame holding the windows in place and a look of terror engulfed Boniek's face as he realised death beckoned, a hundred feet beneath him.

Thoroughgood threw himself across the floor and grabbed for the Pole's bloodied white coat, as Boniek, desperately grasping at the shattered wooden frame, began to slip through the smashed glazing.

Grabbing the coat with both hands, Thoroughgood held Boniek, suspended half in, half out of the window.

"It's your choice, you piece of shit! I drop you out the window and no-one knows that it wasn't self defence – or you tell me everything, fucker."

Boniek hovered in suspended animation, his life was in the balance but his defiance remained intact. "You drop me, pig? I tell you nothing," and he flashed a feral smile before adding with dripping sarcasm, "Please, no drop me, Mr Policeman."

Although he remained defiant, Boniek's hold on life was becoming increasingly precarious, the weight of his body ripped off one of his coat lapels and he lurched down in a vicious movement. His right hand shot up and Thoroughgood grabbed it with his left, but his grip instantly began to slip.

"Come on, you bastard, help me here," growled Thoroughgood as he transferred his right hand from the remaining coat lapel and locked it onto the Pole's hand.

A voice from behind offered help, "Hold him steady, Gus. I'm almost there," shouted Hardie.

Too late.

The Pole's icy grey eyes remained locked on Thoroughgood as his hand slid through the DS' grip. Thoroughgood tried one last time to get the information he needed,

"Where is she, Boniek? C'mon man – do you want to go to your death with Sophie Balfron's on your conscience?"

"Matkojebco," snarled the Pole and spat in Thoroughgood's face as his hand slipped free and he began his descent into oblivion.

Thoroughgood pushed his way through the cordon of uniform cops and walked down the steps at the entrance of the Art School, still shaking from his encounter with Boniek and its implications.

As he did so his attention was hooked by Victoria Roxburgh sitting in the back of an ambulance, a blanket wrapped around her and Hardie, his notebook out, taking her statement. As he joined them Victoria looked up and smiled.

"I hope DC Hardie is taking good care of you, Miss Roxburgh," said Thoroughgood awkwardly, aware of the crowd of people that had gathered outside the building and were filling the street along with the emergency services vehicles.

"Please, call me Vicky," she said "I'm fine, Detective Sergeant, thanks to you. But what happened to that man? He was a foreigner wasn't he?"

"Polish, as it happens, and I'm afraid he didn't make it. But the main thing is you are okay, Vicky, and that we get you checked out at the Royal. Shock can do funny things to people and you've certainly had one today." smiled Thoroughgood.

"But thanks to you, Detective Sergeant, I still have tomorrow to look forward to," said Victoria Roxburgh.

27

AS HE strode into the main lounge of Roxburgh Hall it occurred to Robert Roxburgh that every time he did so he seemed to be riddled with feelings of guilt and dread. This time, however, neither could compete with the feeling of nausea as he contemplated the task ahead of him.

The result of his younger brother's post mortem was now known and he had persuaded the authorities to keep it private until he had broken the news to his mother and sister, both of whom now awaited him, seated together on one of the room's elegant chaise longues.

Robert sought some comfort from the welcoming warmth of the fire that crackled within the imposing marble fireplace, spreading its warmth throughout the Scott room. Propping his elbow on the mantlepiece, he took a deep breath and delivered his message.

"There is no way to do this, other than to cut straight to the chase, Mama. The post mortem has come back and we now know the cause of Alexander's death," Robert took another gulp of air and continued. "I am sorry to tell you that he was poisoned by a lethal quantity of cyanide which he consumed from a dram of 18-year-old malt in my office."

The initial silence from his mother and sister unsettled Robert, although it was not long before the dam of emotion they were holding in check burst.

"Poisoned? But how can that be, Robert?" demanded Lady Elizabeth, her voice crackling with raw grief.

"Oh no, poor Alex," gasped Victoria.

"It's the truth and all there in black and white in the P.M.," said Robert brandishing a copy of the post mortem report as he confronted one of the grimmest tasks he had faced in his life. For the truth was that the cyanide-laced whisky had not been intended for Alex, and Robert knew this was something that would not escape either his mother or sister for much longer. This was why he had come to the Hall to tell them personally, in an effort to keep some kind of lid on things, make sure that the launch went through and that his family's salvation was completed.

Lady Elizabeth stood up and made her way to the window, staring through the glass at the timeless beauty of Loch Lomond, her emotions in meltdown as she struggled to comprehend the truth about the end of her younger son's life.

It was Victoria who put two and two together and wiping her tears away with a lace handkerchief she took a deep breath and said, "Poisoned by cyanide-laced whisky from the bottle of 18-year-old malt you keep in your office? That can mean only one thing – the poison was intended for you, Robert."

Roxburgh shifted uncomfortably as he sought how best to answer Victoria, "It is the logical assumption and the one the police have already made. I have spent nearly two hours of my time helping them with what Detective Inspector Pigeon called their 'line of enquiry.'"

Slowly, Lady Elizabeth turned to face her surviving children, "What are the police going to do about it, Robert? Alexander has been murdered and now you tell me you were the murderer's original target. It is too much Robert, too much, look at the marquee on the lawn, the fountains, all the equipment already in place and that Velvet woman's people are due to descend on us today. How can we go ahead with the launch? How can I grieve for my youngest son? How can I bury him, knowing that someone out there wants to kill my eldest son and at the same time, go through with this impossible farce?"

Robert strode over to his mother and took her in his arms, "Because, Mama, we have no choice. It is that, or the Hall and everything we hold dear is gone." Gilding the lily he added, "Ultimately, in his final moments, that is something Alex did not want to happen. This has been made all the more painful because we'd reached agreement on the Gwai Lo deal. Alex did not want anyone else in Roxburgh Hall bar us, Mama and he came to see the deal with Cheung as the only realistic way to stop that happening, believe me."

From behind them Victoria spoke up, "What are the police going to do to protect you, Robbie? Do they have any suspects? What about the Triads? If you are dead what would happen with the deal? Would everything be forfeit and they take complete control?"

Robert drew upon all the powers of self-control he had learned from his years in the military. "The detective inspector has promised they will provide me with protection, Vicky. But you have to stop letting your imagination run away with you. Raymond Cheung is a very smart man and he knows that without the Roxburgh name and the tradition and legacy of our house and brand, what he is trying to sell to the Asian market will ring hollow. Cheung is only too well aware that he needs us every bit as much as we need him. We are the respectable front he needs to make the Asian whisky market his own, without us he has nothing and he knows it."

"Are you really so sure of that, Robbie? Poisoning with cyanide? That sounds exactly like something the Triads would get up to if they wanted rid of somebody who was in their way. Alex was against the deal right up until your last conversation with him. Now he has gone, everything will go through smoothly. It is all very convenient that he has been murdered so close to the launch," said Victoria.

Robert gave Victoria a reassuring smile and as he did so, felt his mother's weight leaving him as Lady Elizabeth regained her self-control and sought the comfort of the hearth. He knew that he needed a diversion to take things away from the inconvenient and tragic truth.

"Come on, Vicky, with everything you have been through at the Art School and Alex's death, your emotions are in tumult. Cheung is just too smart to get involved in anything which would make him an obvious suspect for Alex's death. Clearly, the police will want to speak to you. But that will not be for the first time, Vicky, after your run in with that Polish madman. So, Mama, you see, I am not the only Roxburgh who has had more than their share of excitement in recent days."

Robert knew it was the last thing his mother wanted to hear, but also that it was the perfect way to deflect Victoria from any further uncomfortable questions.

"What is this, Vicky?" demanded the dowager.

Vicky pierced her elder brother with a look before answering her mother, "It's nothing, Mama. It was just a case of being in the wrong place at the wrong time as I left the School of Art yesterday. Thankfully, Detective Sergeant Thoroughgood was on hand to, em, take care of the situation."

Turning to her brother she added quickly, "We have not spoken of the most important matter of all, Robbie, and that is, when we will bury Alex?"

Lady Elizabeth fingered her pearls as her emotions finally buckled and her body was wracked by huge sobs before Victoria could draw her close. It was a question that Robert knew they all needed an answer to, and now the findings of the post mortem had been made public, one that must be resolved.

He said, "My proposal is that we dedicate the launch to Alexander and use it to inform everyone who needs to know that his funeral will be early next week, with the date and time to be confirmed once I have reached agreement on the church service with the Reverend Brunton. Of course, Alex will be buried alongside Father in the bluebell wood, but first we need the rest of the t's crossed and the i's dotted."

Lady Elizabeth pulled herself away from Victoria and faced her eldest son, "Yes," she said, "that would be good."

The throaty roar of a high performance sports car punctured the moment. Robert turned round instantly and gasped his shock when he saw who the driver was. "Raymond Cheung."

28

A WAVE of apprehension swept over Roxburgh as he tried to work out how best to deal with his uninvited guest and the impact that the Triad leader was likely to have on his mother and sister.

His predilection for poker got the better of him and Roxburgh attempted a bluff. Turning from the window he smiled warm reassurance and said, "Yes, Raymond Cheung," and looking down at his Rolex, added, "right on time too, 3pm. Now if you give me a minute, Mama, Victoria, I will meet our visitor at the door and save Macintosh the bother."

Roxburgh swivelled on his heels in a manner that would not have been out of place on the parade ground and made his way out into the flag-stoned reception hall, just as Macintosh opened the front door.

Beyond the entrance the Oriental's slightly nasal tones could clearly be heard, "My name is Raymond Cheung and I have come to see Viscount Roxburgh."

A shudder ran through Roxburgh and he prayed that for once Macintosh would not attempt to produce one of his usual condescendingly tepid welcomes.

"You may indeed be Mr Cheung, but is the Viscount expecting you?" inquired the butler.

Materialising at his shoulder, Roxburgh took control, "Indeed he is, Macintosh. Now, if you don't mind, coffee and tea will be taken in the Scott room. Leave Mr Cheung to me," he said crisply before throwing a warm smile in the direction of the Triad leader. Roxburgh observed that Cheung's intimidating bodyguard had thankfully remained in the driver's seat of the white 5 Series BMW.

Macintosh gave a slight nod of the head in the direction of Roxburgh and bade an "Excuse me," before slipping away in the direction of the Hall's kitchens.

"Come in, Raymond," said Roxburgh, offering his hand and administering a warm greeting to Cheung. "I'm sorry, if I had known you would be visiting us I would have made sure of a suitable welcome."

Cheung's dark eyes scrutinised Roxburgh with a searing intensity.

"It is I who am sorry, Viscount Roxburgh, to have arrived unannounced. News of the post mortem is out and as you know, I must make sure our investment has not been undermined. I realise you have suffered personal loss, but the Gwai Lo have too much invested in this, as do you, my dear Viscount Roxburgh, to see it all turn to dust," said Cheung, whose words may have hinted at reassurance and support but whose delivery did precisely the opposite. "The other thing I do not appreciate," he added, "is a visit from the police without forewarning, my dear Viscount. A Detective Inspector Pigeon called at my offices this morning and suggested I would be happy to have seen your brother removed from this life, and the opposition he had to our plans gone with him. I wonder how he came by that information? Forgive me if I have placed extra importance on meeting you all personally to make sure we, how is it the Detective Inspector so sincerely put it? Ah, yes, are 'singing from the same hymn sheet.'"

Cheung's revelation sent a shockwave of uncertainty through Roxburgh as, he recalled that the ruthless Triad leader had warned him to keep his younger brother firmly in line . . . but would Cheung murder Alexander and jeopardise everything? Roxburgh dismissed the thought as a flight of fancy.

"Thank you, Raymond, I can assure you the Roxburghs are made of stern stuff. We have centuries of family history invested in the Hall and in the reputation of our whisky. Nothing will stop us doing all we can to preserve both," said Roxburgh in a slightly rushed manner, betraying the tensions that were engulfing him.

"Precisely," said Cheung. He paused and his next words were edged with menace as he continued, "Which is why I have come to the Hall personally, to meet Lady Elizabeth and your spirited young sister, Victoria, who has become quite the plucky heroine according to the Evening Times. It also had the story that your brother was murdered." With that, Cheung slapped a copy of the paper into Roxburgh's midriff and strode unannounced straight into the Scott room.

Lady Elizabeth remained seated as Cheung glided through the doorway in his silk suit with Roxburgh immediately behind him. "Mama and Vicky, may I introduce you to Raymond Cheung, head of the Gwai Lo in Scotland," stammered Roxburgh trying to provide a veneer of etiquette to Cheung's unexpected arrival.

The Triad leader remained deliberately oblivious to Roxburgh's words and made his way over to the chaise longue where Lady Elizabeth sat, bowing deeply before offering one hand, which she shook in a clearly lukewarm welcome, before he produced, with a flourish, the bouquet of flowers he had held behind his back until that point.

"Lady Elizabeth, may I offer my sincere condolences and those of the Gwai Lo. May I also take the opportunity to offer my unstinting gratitude that you have decided to continue with the joint venture of The Dark Ocean, in these most trying times for you and your family," before adding for good measure, "The tales of your enduring beauty, Lady Elizabeth, have not been exaggerated."

He smiled at Victoria and again, bowed his respect and offered his hand, "I am honoured to have met you, Miss Victoria. It is rare that one so young combines such beauty and courage with the type of innovation and enterprise which Viscount Roxburgh has made me aware will be vital to the launch of our new liqueur."

Victoria met Cheung's flattery with a smile and returned the compliment, "It is we who must thank you, Mr Cheung, for agreeing to doing business with us and putting your faith in the Roxburgh name at such a difficult time. We appreciate the time you have taken to come to the Hall and offer your condolences."

Cheung shook his head courteously before relocating himself with a languid grace to the fireplace that seemed to draw all who entered the Scott room to its warmth.

The Triad leader swept all three of the Roxburgh's with his inscrutable gaze, "I thought it was vital that I came to visit you all, not just to offer my condolences, if you pardon me, my Lady, but so that I may also stress the level of commitment and investment we are putting into the launch of The Dark Ocean and the relaunch of an exclusive edition of 'The Roxburgh' single malt," said Cheung.

"In Beijing we have a 15,000 square foot, four storey building which is in the process of being branded and liveried as the Ludovic Roxburgh House, in honour of your father-in-law, the great war hero. This will act as a club for, what is it you would call them? Ah yes, discerning, that is the word, whisky lovers. It stands in a quiet courtyard just a stone's throw from Tiananmen Square. The Gwai Lo's intention is to burnish the Roxburgh brand, extolling its long tradition and then present exclusive opportunities to enjoy and associate with the excitement of the new Dark Ocean liqueur. Did you know, my Lady," said Cheung, addressing Lady Elizabeth as if they were the only two in the room, "That 80 percent of Chinese millionaires are under 45? They love brands with history, heritage and provenance."

For the first time that afternoon Lady Elizabeth smiled, her composure recovered. "My dear Mr Cheung, I am so glad you came to the Hall and allowed us to see what a skilled businessman you are, and the true level of your commitment to our brand and the Roxburgh name. I must be honest with you, Mr Cheung, you have surprised me on more than one level."

Cheung smiled benignly and nodded before continuing, "There is more," he said, addressing himself to Robert. "I must ask that Stephen Luker, your master blender, be flown out with our party to Beijing, in order to add his personal touch to our launch at Ludovic Roxburgh House. To further whet your whistle, as you might say my dear Viscount," he smiled, "Each bottle of The Dark Ocean and The Roxburgh will have its own wheeled leather trunk, so that it can be rolled tableside in the private dining rooms of our new establishment. A nice touch, I am sure you will agree," Cheung paused and lost himself in the flicker of the flames.

Victoria Roxburgh broke the silence, "Mr Cheung, you have literally taken our breath away with your innovations and belief in the Roxburgh name, and I can assure you that the launch, here at the Hall, won't disappoint you. As you can see the main marquee is already up and Vanessa Velvet's people are due any minute to begin putting things in place for her charity fashion launch. I'm sure that along with The Dark Ocean launch we'll make the pages of Hello! and the Sunday magazines." She continued, "May I say the choice of our grandfather as the name and identity for your Beijing establishment is brilliant,"

The warmth from Cheung's smile was also brilliant as he replied, "But best of all, we have uncovered a painted advertisement from the 1930s, proclaiming the virtues of 'The Roxburgh' that will be the focal point of our first floor and again stress the whole heritage and history of your brand. We believe, with Mr Luker accompanying us, we can teach our customers the art of whisky and to that extent, I think the analogy of blending whisky and blending tea could be vital, particularly, as you will appreciate, in China. Exclusivity through limited editions, accompanied by certificates and personal editions will all play a key part in making a visit to Ludovic Roxburgh House absolutely unique, and a must for our elite Chinese market."

Roxburgh broke into a luminous smile, "This is truly unbelievable Raymond. Together, I have no doubt, the future of the Roxburghs and the Gwai Lo is very bright indeed." With that, he strode over to Cheung and offered him the warmest of handshakes.

Keeping one eye on Lady Elizabeth and her daughter, Cheung afforded himself a smile of satisfaction. The deal was safe. And the death of Alexander Roxburgh was no longer a threat to it.

29

AS THE sleek BMW sped away, down the gravel drive, Roxburgh felt he could breathe once again. His relief was heightened by the sight of his mother climbing the stairs towards her bedroom, but as his thoughts turned to a medicinal dram he was brought back to reality with a jolt. Standing outside the library door was Victoria.

"We need to speak now Robbie," she said urgently, "because there is stuff bubbling away under the surface that is making me feel sick. Can we talk in the library?"

"Of course," said Roxburgh and followed her into the room.

He sat down on the large leather settee and smiled as Victoria handed him a whisky; the smile disappeared when she passed him the copy of Ivanhoe and asked him to read the message scrawled in their grandfather's handwriting.

Roxburgh read aloud, "*To my darling Jill from your own true Ivanhoe!* signed LVR, dated 01.12.42."

"Do you know anything about this?" demanded Victoria.

Roxburgh ran his right hand through his golden hair and at that moment realised he had betrayed his knowledge by doing so. Clearly there was no point in any prevaricating and Robert Roxburgh found himself recalling the moments before his final meeting with his younger, now deceased, brother.

Clearing his throat he began, "Yes, I believe I do, Vicky. There is only one place to start and that is at the beginning," said Roxburgh wincing at his unintended pun. "Shortly before Alex came to my office on that fateful day, and quite by accident, I uncovered a set of war-time journals belonging to our grandfather. In them, it was made quite clear that he was having an affair. He referred to her only as his 'darling J', but we now know she was his girlfriend and she was called Jill. There were four journals in the set, but only three spilled from the secret compartment I accidentally triggered in the drinks cabinet. The diary missing was the one spanning the years 1942-43. Sadly, it was clear from the first two diaries that I have had time to read, that Grandfather was besotted with this woman and that they indulged their mutual passion for each other at the Dorchester in London, at the same time as Churchill was staying there. It's incredible really," concluded the Viscount balefully.

Victoria sat down next to him and he immediately put his arm around her. "I can't believe grandfather would betray Grandma Margaret like that," she murmured.

"Unfortunately there is no doubting that he did, but . . ." Roxburgh hesitated before ploughing on; his need to unburden himself had become too great to hold back. "It's worse than just uncovering grandfather's war-time indiscretions. It is clear that the missing journal has fallen into the hands of someone who intends to use its contents to threaten us and ruin grandfather's reputation, and that of our family. Someone who will stop at nothing to sate their hatred of the Roxburgh family."

"What do you mean Robbie?" Victoria pulled away from her brother.

Roxburgh pulled out the sheet of paper and spread it out on his knees before her, adding, "Obviously, this is a photocopy of the original I handed over to Detective Inspector Pigeon."

Looking down, she read aloud, "THE OLDEST SIN CASTS THE LONGEST SHADOW. I see. Do you think this has anything to do with Alex's murder?"

Roxburgh looked his younger sister straight in the eye and gave her the truth, "Yes, the cyanide was clearly intended for me and it was the second attempt on my life." Before Victoria could speak, he stalled his sister with a raised hand and continued, "Do I think Cheung was behind it? I don't know. I really don't. At first I thought he may have been because he knew of Alexander's opposition to our deal with the Gwai Lo, but the poison was in my whisky bottle and, as I said, clearly intended for me. Then, when he came out to the Hall today and told us about his elaborate plans for the creation of the Ludovic Roxburgh House in Beijing, then I thought it nonsense."

Victoria agreed, "Yes, you are right, Robbie. To have gone to these lengths and to take the time and trouble to seek Mama's blessing, and also to be using grandfather as the focal point of the launch – why would he do all of that if he was trying to have you killed?"

"I don't know, sis'. Other than complete control of the deal, but that would be too obvious, and the fact the police have already spoken to him would back that up. Yet, could it be that his visit earlier was nothing more than a sham, and that the whole deal has been a sham with it. Cheung is a devious man, but while I can see what he would gain by my death, why would he then strive to ruin grandfather's reputation and therefore the history of the Roxburghs, everything that we stand for in the whisky industry, and so undermine the deal?"

Victoria was determined to explore all possibilities, "So, if it is not Cheung and his Ghost Men who are behind it, then who is?"

Roxburgh's face creased into a frown and steepling his hands, he stared in front of him, "I don't have a bloody clue, Vicky, and that is a hell of a problem. But what I intend to do is to head back to the office and read the last of the diaries – see if there are any clues as to what happens in the missing one. I need to get to the bottom of this and I need to do so before the launch."

Victoria looked puzzled, "So you haven't handed the diaries over to the police yet?"

Robert smiled weakly, "Not yet, but I promise you they'll have them the minute I know what is in them."

30

IT WAS early evening before Roxburgh was alone with the diaries. The distillery office was now a crime scene and he had chosen the peace and quiet of the estate boathouse, situated on the shingled beach adjacent to Loch Lomond, which had been one of his favourite hideouts as a boy. Now it was where he hoped to solve the mystery that was threatening to ruin his family at the point of their redemption.

Having completed a run-through of the launch checklist with Victoria, when they had finished their conversation in the library he had walked down the track to the boathouse feeling increasingly proud of his younger sister. The truth was that he had been sceptical of Victoria's ability to coordinate what had appeared to be fanciful plans but now, with the launch almost upon them, he was impressed and surprised by her attention to detail.

Now inside the boathouse, he looked out of the window and recalled the happy days he had spent with Alex, pushing canoes out onto the loch and engaged in imaginary acts of soldiery trying to repeat the heroics of the grandfather who had now betrayed, through his own careless hand, the extent of his personal treachery.

He sliced the seal off a bottle of the 18-year-old with the Guinness pocket knife that his grandfather had handed him as a 10-year-old and remembered how that act of kindness long ago had made him feel 10 feet tall. Roxburgh uncorked the malt, poured a liberal helping and sprinkled some water from the old estate jug that always sat on the desk.

Kicking his heels up onto the splintered desk he took a sip and gazed out into the enveloping gloom, listening to the water lapping onto the shore. He fingered the opening pages of the 1944/45 journal and attempted to return to the life and times of his grandfather.

After scanning his way through half a dozen chapters of little interest, Roxburgh's attention was at last grabbed. *'What a wretch I have become and all for the selfish pursuit of my own happiness at the expense of all I hold dear,' he read. 'How tough these days are when I have so much to burden my conscience.*

'My clarity of thought is not what it should be, with my mind absorbed by matters concerning both the living and the deceased. I have tainted all those I have had to enlist to end this affair, silence her and stop ruin visiting the reputation of the Roxburghs.

'All my thoughts should be on playing my part in the big push against the Hun in Europe and instead they are filled with her voice, her face, her scent. I fear I am haunted and will be forevermore, and the passing of the months and years will do nothing to diminish my guilt. My darling Jill what have I done?' LVR 01/01/44

"Sweet Christ," exploded Robert Roxburgh as the true extent of his grandfather's sins swept over him.

He flipped the journal over, picked up the malt and strode out the office and into the night.

His grandfather's words had confirmed his guilt beyond all doubt. Ludovic Roxburgh had not only been involved in a war-time affair that had seen him take incredibly high risks with both his and his family's reputations as the Second World War neared its climax, but now it seemed certain he had then arranged for his lover to be murdered when it had turned sour.

Robert walked onto the shingled beach staring out across the dead calm of Loch Lomond and replayed the key words from the diary entry over in his mind.

'I have tainted all those I have had to enlist to end this affair, silence her and stop ruin visiting the reputation of the Roxburghs.

'I fear I am haunted and will be for evermore, and the passing of the months and years will do nothing to diminish my guilt. My darling Jill, what have I done?'

"In the name of the Holy rood!" he exploded.

There could be no doubt what that meant. Ludovic had not only had this woman Jill silenced forever, but he had enlisted the help of others and brought all his influence and power to bear in order to do so. Just what had made his grandfather take such drastic action – and who had been complicit in helping him do so?

Roxburgh knew that the answers clearly lay in the third journal which he suspected had fallen into the hands of a person or persons who had tried to poison him but had taken Alex's life instead.

Picking up a stone from the beach, Robert skimmed it out across the dead pool and watched it jump once, twice, thrice, just as his beloved grandfather had taught him when he was a child. The grandfather he now knew was at the centre of a war-time scandal that would have rocked Churchill's government to the core had it been exposed. But it had been covered up for over 70 years by the establishment, then buried in the mists of time and in the pages of a set of journals, long since lost . . . until now.

The next question hit him, "What do I do now?"

He knew that if he made the odious DI Pigeon aware of the diaries and all that was in them, he would bring the entire scandal out into the open and risk ruining the Roxburgh reputation: a reputation the Gwai Lo were setting such great store on to help crack the Asian whisky market. But if he stayed silent, he and his family remained at risk from this vengeful assassin who would remain ready to strike from the shadows as the moment of his greatest triumph and his family's salvation arrived.

Impaled on the horns of his dilemma Robert Roxburgh raised the whisky to his mouth and took another sip and failed to hear the footfall on the shingle behind him.

A voice spoke out of the darkness, "Time to atone, Roxburgh."

Startled, Robert, Viscount Roxburgh, turned as he heard a rush and felt the sting of the cool night air as something heavy slashed towards him and he caught sight of a metallic glint a couple of feet behind him.

The blow connected and Roxburgh crashed onto the beach.

31

"JESUS, THOROUGHGOOD, you look like shit," grated the harsh Glaswegian voice.

Trying to extricate himself from the CID car, Thoroughgood winced at the physical pain he was in without registering the sarcasm that came his way from the shiny dome and bulky figure of Detective Inspector Randolph Pigeon.

The pursuit of Boniek had taken its toll on the DS and the gruelling post-incident debrief he'd had to endure had left his mental battery all but flat. The sleepless night that had followed had been plagued by thoughts of what else he could have done to save the Pole and retrieve the information, locked inside Boniek's head, which would have led them to Sophie Balfron.

Pulling himself to his full height Thoroughgood replied simply, "I'm fucked, pure and simple, Randy."

The crash of a car door shot out across Stewart Street nick car park and was followed by another voice joining the conversation, "All right, Randy? Aye, the way he dropped Boniek reminded me of Alan Rough in his prime!" quipped Hardie.

"No point blaming yourself, Gus. The bastard was gonnae stop at nothing and he didn't care who he injured or killed in the process. Not much help to your investigation though, having the chief suspect slipping through your hands, 100 feet up!" Pigeon sniggered. Laughter from the other side of the Focus confirmed Hardie's approval.

"You're not joking, Randy, but what about things up at the Hall?" retorted Thoroughgood. "I hear the younger Roxburgh son was poisoned but the cyanide was meant for big brother, and, of course, you know that we came across Victoria Roxburgh during the whole business with that bastard Boniek? Sounds like you got enough problems of your own with the Roxburgh enquiry, especially with the Triads involved. Guess they're behind it all?"

Pigeon's eyes narrowed slightly at the dig before he buttoned up his raincoat just as a sharp gust sent a sheet of stinging drizzle over them. "I don't think it is as simple as all that, Detective Sergeant," he said officiously. "Viscount Roxburgh is being a bit economical with the truth, which is why I am seeing him this morning. That is, if my driver can find his way to the motor. But hey – good luck finding a way out of your own dead end," said Pigeon with an insincere wink.

At that, the back door of the police office opened and the flustered form of Pigeon's No 2, DS Harry Bolt – 'Lightning' to his colleagues – emerged from the station. "Sorry, gaffer, misplaced my notebook for a minute," he said by way of an apology and headed straight to the driver's side of the Mondeo that was now propping up the furious Pigeon.

Hardie couldn't help himself, "Aye, good luck, Detective Inspector Pigeon, I'm sure you'll be good as gold with Lightning by your side."

His mirth, and that of Thoroughgood, ended abruptly as the creak of a window opening was followed by a barked command, "Balls and buggery! I might have guessed, Thoroughgood and Hardie engaged in their own personal comedy act, live from the central car park! By Christ, if you two are not in my office in 30 seconds, I will have your baws in my nutcracker," shouted Detective Superintendent Valentino Tomachek.

"Nice one," Pigeon smirked as Thoroughgood and Hardie charged across the yard and in the back door.

"Sit down," barked Tomachek, and Thoroughgood and Hardie immediately did as they were bid. Almost as an afterthought, he added, "How are you anyway Thoroughgood?"

The DS saw no point in glossing over his physical and mental cracks, "I'm cream crackered, gaffer."

"Aye, and no wonder. Look at these," ordered Tomachek as he spread a sheaf of newspapers across his desk.

"Aye, ma boy – if taking care of the mad Imam Tariq and dating that Velvet bitch weren't enough, the mayhem you caused when you chased Boniek through the city centre has made you catnip for the bloody tabloids. By Christ, you made that car chase with Steve McQueen in Bullitt seem like an episode from the Magic Roundabout. Then you go and drop the bastard out a windae 100 feet up, after smashing up one of Rennie Mackintosh's finest pieces of work for good measure. For fuck's sake, Thoroughgood!" Tomachek ranted before taking a drag on his Cairngorm Bent.

He was soon back in the verbal stirrups, "By God,

if Hardie hadn't been there to witness it you could have been on a murder charge, Thoroughgood." Tomachek paused and his eyes narrowed as he surveyed both his officers. Noticing that both men's jaws had stiffened, Tomachek changed tact.

"Anyway, enough of all that. At least we have one less madman to worry about, but by Christ, he wreaked havoc and we're a helicopter and two good coppers down because of Boniek, with sweet FA to show for it.

"Ah, yes, I almost forgot. The bodies of the two dead gang members who were found shot at that farm steading were dumped there. So the steading has been of no evidential value whatsoever to Central Scotland plod. It's just a bugger that this whole business is straddling our area and theirs. It is a pain in the proverbial, having to pick up the blower every time you want to fart just because you are not sure which way the metaphorical wind will blow with Central Plod."

Hardie was first to respond, "That figures. But it also underlines the point that if Boniek was behind it he must have had some kind of help in dumping them."

Thoroughgood took up the verbal baton, "That is not all it confirms, faither. It also means they have a safe house somewhere near and that with Boniek now dead, somebody else is babysitting Sophie Balfron. It's got to be Lewandowski and Tomazsewski."

"I wonder if the news that Boniek won't be hanging around to have his longed-for reunion with Sophie Balfron has percolated through to the Poles?" Hardie mused.

"Of course it will," snapped Tomachek. "The Polish community in Glasgow is a tight one whichever side of the fence it is sitting on, and that's a big problem for us."

Thoroughgood shook his head, "It's an even bigger problem for Sophie Balfron, gaffer, 'cause if they've taken her captive for Boniek to enjoy some sort of sport with her, there's no point in them keeping her alive if they know of his death. Did Group Two CID liaise with Central Plod, as I requested, over the movements of Lewandowski and Tomaszewski?"

"They did, and it has all gone pear-shaped. The farm owner and local councillor, has gone into orbit. He caught our hick cousins dozing behind the wheel when they were supposed to be conducting discreet surveillance. As a result, he ejected them from his land and went straight to the Chief Constable of Central Scotland Constabulary to make a formal complaint. The whole surveillance operation has had to be pared down," revealed Tomachek.

Hardie grimaced. "What a feckin' joke that is. I don't know how many acres old man Rogers has, but he trusts these two Poles far too much in my book. If they wanted to hide something on his land then they would have no bother. They've got to be up to their necks in it, boss. They're our only lead and now we have petty bloody politics turning them into a dead end."

"A fair summary of events Hardie, but it's not going to stop us, or rather you and Thoroughgood, from getting to the bottom of this," said Tomachek.

"Pardon?" said Thoroughgood.

Tomachek removed his pipe from his mouth and jabbed it in the DS' direction, "Indeed. I have had a chat with Chief Constable Rockford and he's more than happy for you and Hardie to go in under the radar, without his official knowledge, that is, and see what you can turn up.

He'll hold the cavalry in check near Rogers' land until you holler for 'em. Time is ticking for Sophie Balfron. This is our only lead and we need to act and not let an old fool get in the way of justice," said Tomachek.

"Bang on, boss," said Thoroughgood, smiling for the first time that day.

32

THEIR MEETING, with a Detective Chief Inspector McLellan, of Central Scotland Police, had been arranged for 14.00hrs, at a location just off the West Highland Way but Hardie had other matters on his mind. As he drove the Ford Focus along the winding road leading through Strathblane, the DC squinted at his watch in a way that Thoroughgood, despite being engrossed in a map, couldn't fail to notice.

"Yes?" enquired the DS without lifting his head from the map.

"I'm bleeding starvin', gaffer, and if memory serves, there's a little place not far away called 'The Aizle' that does the best homemade sausage roll and beans around. It's just gone midday and we're gonnae be way too early for McLellan. What about a quick bit of scran? You never know the next time we'll get the chance of some grub. As the sayin' goes, an army fights better on a full belly."

Ten minutes later, they were seated at a wooden table and bench in the quaint little countryside diner with Hardie barely able to conceal his anticipation for the forthcoming feast. Thoroughgood unfolded the map he had been scrutinising and used the two mugs of Viennese coffee that had already arrived, combined with the salt and pepper pots, to help hold it down flat.

Just then his mobile rang and as he pulled it out to check the caller, Hardie couldn't help himself from second-guessing their identity. "That'll be Vanessa, I bet. Come on, Gus take the mobi outside and give her some chat, man."

Thoroughgood stuffed it back in his pocket and ignored him. "This is a map of Smithycroft Farm, the surrounding land and buildings. I got it emailed over from McLellan and had it printed off before we left Stewart Street."

Shaking his head in disgust at Thoroughgood's intentional snubbing of Vanessa, Hardie's basic instinct got the better of him. He grabbed his coffee and watched in horror as the corner of the map it had been holding down snapped back.

"For cryin'out loud, faither!" snapped Thoroughgood.

Hardie quickly took a gulp, covering the end of his nose in whipped cream before scalding the inside of his mouth with the piping hot coffee that lay below, "Bastard," he yelped.

"Do you mind?" demanded an outraged blue-rinsed woman sitting at the table behind them.

Hardie blushed his embarrassment and apologised in trademark fashion, "Sorry, grandma, keep your wig on."

Not surprisingly, the elderly lady's ire was not cooled, "Anymore from you and I will have the manageress remove you. I have never heard the like! I have been coming here for 20 years and now they start letting Glaswegian hoodlums in."

Her companion echoed her support, "Nothing short of

a disgrace using such language in a family establishment. This is no place for gangsters."

Thoroughgood quickly attempted to pacify the outraged elderly women, "May I apologise for my colleague, ladies. He has had very little sleep and recently had to have one of his dalmatians put down and clearly, he is still struggling to come to terms with it. I can assure you it won't happen again. Can I offer to pick up your bill, by way of an apology?" asked the DS and was met by twin brilliant white grins that seemed incongruous with the vintage of the two ladies.

"That would be most conducive," smiled the formerly outraged female.

Thoroughgood flashed her his most sincere smile, "The pleasure is all mine," and turned his attention back to Hardie. "Now, if you can keep your temper in check, can we get on with it?"

"Recently deceased dalmatian?" enquired the DC in a whisper, raising one overly bushy eyebrow. Thoroughgood produced a pacifying smile, but Hardie had his own line of enquiry to pursue, "By the way, what is happening at Roxburgh Hall with the big launch? Are you still going along for your first public appearance, almost, as Mr Vanessa Velvet? Mind you, if you keep ignoring her calls then you are likely to be the ex-Mr Vanessa Velvet pretty damn soon. Jeez, just think of all that posh totty, and of course, Miss Victoria will be very pleased to renew your acquaintance, I would imagine?"

Thoroughgood smiled sarcastically at his mate before he answered, "Yes, is the one and only answer you are getting, faither, to all three of those questions," and he returned his gaze to the map, gesturing at Hardie to replace his coffee cup back on the unruly corner, as he began to circle a section of the map with his index finger.

"So what do we know so far, Hardie?" he asked.

"The gang have a safe house and somebody, most probably Lewandowski and the other Polish . . ." Hardie quickly pulled himself up before another expletive could escape his mouth and then continued, "er, gang member, have got to be looking after Sophie Balfron."

"Which means?" asked Thoroughgood.

"If they're babysitters then they'll need to make fairly regular journeys to the safe house to check on her. Which might mean they're using some outhouse on the farm land to hide her –unless there's someone else in the picture."

"I think you are 50 percent right, faither. There's no way they're going to be keeping her at the farm, it's just too close to home, but I think you're probably right about someone else, so far unknown to us, and taking personal care of Mrs Balfron."

The DS gaze returned to the map and pointed to a specific area. "Have a look at the Millearn Hospital. Sitting empty and unused for 40 years, on land that is less than a mile away from Smithycroft farm's boundaries. There's even a single track road between it and the farm land. I'd say that would be the perfect place for a gang to hole up and keep Sophie Balfron under wraps."

Hardie let out a slow whistle of admiration, "I think you could be onto something, gaffer. But what about the other member of the gang, the one we don't know about?"

Thoroughgood lifted his coffee to his mouth and despite the map corner shooting back on itself, took a leisurely mouthful before answering, "I got a text from

Morse last night to say that Boniek has a brother by the name of Tomasz." His mobile chimed and as he fished out the Blackberry from his pocket he grinned his delight. "Aah. Perfect timing." The DS brought up a mugshot of a man and shoved the phone across the table at his colleague, just as two piping hot helpings of homemade sausage roll and beans arrived.

"Thanks to Interpol we can now clap eyes on Tomasz Boniek. I think, at last, we know who the organ grinder is, faither," said Thoroughgood.

"He's a nasty-looking piece of work all right. What about the other two – Lewandowski and Tomaszewski?"

"Not a sausage, old son. I think we're talking a couple of aliases in their case, but with a bit of luck McLellan might be able to help there. At least there should be a paper trail back through their employment records. The only problem is, if they've been using forged documents then who knows who the hell they really are? Although, given their comfortable grasp of Polish, at least we know their nationality," replied Thoroughgood.

"So what does that mean with regard to Central plod?"

"It means DCI McLellan and his mates from Central Scotland have become very important men to us, so let's hope they have come prepared for a bun fight! We're gonna need back up all right, but we have two loci to worry about now and no time to waste. So let's get these finished pronto. I'll bell DCI McLellan en route, and we can set the hounds loose."

"Game on," said Hardie, but not before he devoured a huge forkful of sausage roll topped with beans.

33

IF THEY wanted to come and search for his two Poles then by God let them come with a warrant, otherwise they could keep the hell off his land. The truth was that without the Poles, Smithycroft Farm would have been on the verge of going under. Instead, all the essential maintenance that had been required – like the patching up of the hay loft and the replacement of the rotten fencing to keep his dairy herd in – had been carried out efficiently and with a minimum of fuss. It was true what they said about the Poles, they put native Scots to shame with their appetite for hard graft. Jimmy Rogers smiled with satisfaction at his good fortune in snapping them up. He drained the remainder of his breakfast coffee and slammed the empty mug down on his kitchen table. He was still angry at the intrusion of the police on his land and by the implication that Lewandowski and Tomazsewski were somehow involved in this whole business with Sophie Balfron.

The old farmer returned his gaze to the back pages of the Daily Record and immersed himself in the latest Old Firm news, but he was interrupted by a short rap on the door. Rogers eased his once powerful, but now increasingly arthritic, body out of his chair and made his way over to the door before easing it open.

There, standing in the doorway was the intimidating presence of Tomazsewski.

Rogers, smiling, began to thank the labourer for his efforts, "Good morning, Robert . . ." when a huge fist rammed straight into his face.

Rogers was propelled through the air and back against a counter before he sank to the floor in a semi-conscious state. Tomazsewski dragged him to his feet. Rogers groaned in agony at the pain of his fractured jaw, but his farmhand paid no attention and tossed him like a rag doll back onto the chair he had just vacated.

As Rogers began to regain consciousness he saw Lewandowski materialising at his compatriot's shoulder. The awful truth dawned on him. The police had been right and his two hard-working Polish labourers were up to their neck in the Balfron business. As the realisation swept over him and his mouth opened he was given a vicious backhander by Lewandowski. A coarse gag was shoved in his mouth while his arms were tied to the back of the chair and his legs strapped to its front legs.

The pressure of the gag on Rogers' newly broken jaw sent waves of nausea through him and the old man vomited onto the gag. Two trails of bile poured down either side of his face.

"Old pig, you no worry about mess now," said Lewandowski flashing the farmer a pitiless grin. The Pole pulled a handgun out of his boiler suit and placed it against Rogers' head, he stooped down and looked Rogers in the eye, revelling in the fear emanating from the old man, "Do widzenia," he said curtly and pulled the trigger.

Lewandowski asked, "You have emptied the safe and have the orange juice?"

"Of course, brother," replied Tomazsewski. "What about the note for the polijca?"

Fishing through a kitchen drawer Lewandowski murmured, "Nice." With a blade in his hand, he swivelled round, produced a bit of paper, punctured it with the knife then rammed the blade into Rogers' corpse.

"Now we go, big man," and with that the two Poles slammed the farmhouse door shut and jumped into the waiting 4x4.

The first part of the plan was complete. The bait had been set.

The harsh noise of a diesel engine alerted Tomasz to the fact that he had visitors, and a glance out of the derelict hospital window, or what remained of it, confirmed that Lewandowski and Tomazsewski had arrived.

They had made mistakes, and Tomasz found himself berating himself for them. The most obvious had been the failure to destroy the bodies of Grimes and Gilles, and the discovery that his two countrymen were working at the nearby Smithycroft Farm had surely alerted the police to the fact that Sophie Balfron, and whoever had abducted her, must be nearby.

The coppers whom Lewandowski had seen dozing in their car behind a copse of birch trees on Rogers' farmland had been proof of that. The net was closing but it was not closed yet.

The door opened and the hulking frame of Tomazsewski stooped through it, "Greetings, Tomasz!"

"Djien dobri, my friends. Now, tell me, is the old man

silenced and the invitation left for our friend, the polijca?"

"Of course, Tomasz. The bait has been placed," replied Lewandowski.

"Good," snapped Boniek. "Now tell me once again, everything you know of my brother's murder."

Tomazsewski cleared his throat, "As I say yesterday, Tomasz, it was the polijca called Thoroughgood, the one we told you about, who visit us on farm. He tracked Janek to Ziggy's, and then pursue him through streets like dog until he corner him on the rooftops. They say Janek slip through the polijca's hands as he tried to save him. I no believe this. No one else saw it. I say the matkojebco drop Janek to his death."

"Then he must pay with his life," said Boniek. "It is good that we have made a start towards making that payment, my friends. This son of a bitch, he will not let go and he will be back soon, and then we make him fry. Janek will be avenged and at same time we find solution to problem of his bitch. We have the bait and now it is fit for purpose. She is in the back room, Robert. Bring her out and we make preparations for the polijca, then we wait."

As Tomazsewski headed to the rear of the building Boniek smiled wickedly at Lewandowski. "I have something very special for my brother's pretty whore," he said and pointed to the hospital's old reception desk.

Lewandowski's gaze swept the wooden surface and he noticed what appeared to be an archaic military-style field telephone.

"Did you bring the orange juice?" asked Boniek.

"Ya," responded Lewandowski just as the stifled notes of a scream broke the silence.

Boniek laughed out loud and said, "Ah, good. Bitch still has plenty spirit for our fun."

Sophie Balfron, shoved into the reception room by Tomazsewski, slid across the linoleum floor, losing her balance and crashing onto it before coming to rest in a corner, up against a wall, a sobbing, dishevelled heap of humanity.

Boniek grabbed her jaw and forced Sophie to meet his gaze, "I have bad news for you, Miss Sophie, my brother is dead and so there is no reason for me to keep you alive. But don't worry, you are still going to be helpful to us!" He smiled viciously. "Because, my darling, you are going to help us catch the skurwysyn who murdered Janek, and you are going to do so by paying for your part in my brother's death with your life, Dziwka."

Sophie's eyes almost popped in fear.

Reaching down, Boniek grabbed the cloth that was stuffed in her mouth and pulled it free. "Have you anything to say about part you play in my brother's murder, szmata?"

Sophie tried to stifle a sob but failed miserably, "It was only a bit of fun . . . how could I have known it would end like this? I never wanted it to end this way. It was Johnnie – he found out and . . ." but before she could finish the sentence Boniek backhanded her across the floor.

"Shut the bitch up and tie her to the chair in the back. Then we will connect her up and prepare her for purpose," ordered Boniek.

As Tomazsewski wrenched her to her feet Sophie pleaded for her life. She was in no doubt this was what was at stake now. "Please, please, I beg you let me go . . ." but the cloth was viciously stuffed back into her mouth by the giant Pole.

As she was dragged past Boniek he spat in her face, saying, "Don't worry, dziwka, you do not have long now."

As Sophie felt phlegm drip down her face she knew that her hope of escaping had all but slipped away. Whatever Boniek had planned for her, death was certain to be at the end of it.

Boniek picked up the old army field telephone and followed them into the back room.

34

THE RV point was an old car park off the West Highland way and as Thoroughgood and Hardie arrived they guessed that the man resplendent in a dark wool overcoat, and impatiently pacing the dirt surface, was DCI McLellan.

Jumping out of the Focus, Thoroughgood made his way over to McLellan, a small, stocky, dark-haired man, with lively darting green eyes that missed nothing.

"So, you made it . . . at last . . . Detective Sergeant Thoroughgood," commented McLellan.

"I'm sorry we have kept you waiting, DCI McLellan, it's been a hellish couple of days and the bottom line is that food was required. But while we ate we also worked." Thoroughgood showed McLellan his Blackberry screen with Tomasz Boniek's face on it, and continued, "This is our man. One Tomasz Josef Boniek, who, not surprisingly, turns out to be the brother of the now-deceased Janek Boniek. A nasty fucker from Warsaw who has an Interpol warrant to apprehend, for armed robbery and drug running. I think, sir, that all along we've been looking for the wrong brother. The problem was, of course, that we didn't know the other one existed and

Janek was the only lead to Sophie Balfron and what went down at Balfron Mill."

"Indeed," said McLellan before handing the Blackberry back to Thoroughgood and sweeping him with his shrewd gaze, before adding, "But I wouldn't want you to think we have been sitting on our thumbs in Central Scotland, Detective Sergeant. We've discovered that Lewandowski and Tomazsewski augment their money by selling on choice cuts of meat at various outlets across central Scotland. Places that specialise in filtering stolen cuts of high value game into the market. Within the last 48 hours they have made two such attempts to offload a sizeable cargo of game that matches the missing produce from the Balfron Mill robbery.

"So there is no doubt that the Poles are in this up to their necks. Unfortunately, nothing is checking up with their IDs. The employment records at Balfron Farm which had their details and mug shots have mysteriously gone missing and we're trying to have artist's impressions matched by the Polish authorities. But, suffice to say that Lewandowski and Tomazsewski are in fact famous Polish footballers, one of whom is in his dotage and the other a multi-million pound Polish international who also happens to skipper his country. A grand case of identity theft, but hopefully one we can solve today when we bring these murdering scumbags to justice."

"They play nice and dirty, these Polish fuckers," was Hardie's way of introducing himself to McLellan before he regrouped. "Apologies, DCI McLellan. Detective Constable Kenny Hardie at your service."

McLellan offered a tepid handshake and Thoroughgood appraised the assembled ranks of the

Support Unit, ready to ensure Boniek and his team were finally brought to justice. As he did so, he realised that Sophie Balfron's chances of making it out the other side were slim, to say the least.

Surprisingly, McLellan attempted to break the early frost that had enveloped the initial stages of their meeting, "Been a damn problem keeping these bloody West Highland Way characters out of the car park. If you look down the track towards the Beech Tree pub you can see half a dozen of them sitting on their arses watching us. You'd think we're a new spectator sport!"

That brought a rumble of laughter from Hardie, and Thoroughgood smiled dutifully before cutting to the chase, "It looks like the Poles have been acting as fences for the Drummond gang to punt their stolen meat and then, when the gang lose one of their original members, our pal Boniek is the first man to have his hand in the air as their next volunteer. Almost a seamless transition, but one that goes very badly wrong for old Joe Drummond and his boys."

"I'll wager the Poles always planned to take over the gang and their turf, and that Drummond's death gave them the opening to do so a bit quicker than they would have expected," said McLellan.

"Silly bastards," said Hardie. "I bet old Joe would never have dumped the bodies on a farm steading anywhere near anything to do with him or any of his team, if the boot had been on the other foot. That was one big mistake."

"It was indeed, and we have some new information for you, DCI McLellan," said Thoroughgood. "I believe we know the locus where Sophie Balfron is being held captive right now, and ultimately where the gang must be – or at least Tomasz Boniek."

A look of surprise swept over McLellan's features. "Go on," he said.

Thoroughgood whipped out the map and slapped it on the bonnet of McLellan's Vauxhall Vectra. Hardie held the map flat to stop the slight breeze blowing it about and the DS indicated the point he had inked with a big red X, "Millearn Hospital, is where I believe Sophie Balfron is being held."

"The old World War Two prefab, where they once kept German POWs? Yeah, that would be about perfect for them. There have been various rumours over the years that it has been used at different times by the neds, but we never managed to catch anyone on the premises. At one stage there was chat that it was going to be converted into a top end sports and country club, but nothing came of it."

McLellan's gaze swept over the map and he immediately pointed to the old road leading from Smithycroft Farm into the back of the hospital grounds, "Very convenient, it'll probably be no more than a dirt track, but it's a road of sorts leading from old man Rogers' farm straight into the hospital grounds. I'd say you've hit the nail on the head there, DS Thoroughgood. That plus all the activity involving the other two Poles points to the hospital being their safe haven."

"Exactly," said Thoroughgood. "But I have two concerns, boss. The first is obviously Sophie Balfron, but the second is Rogers the farmer. With the greatest of respect, news of your two lads getting caught dozing the other morning will have reached the Poles, probably via Rogers' own mouth. I'm afraid if we don't get him out of there then he could be a gonner."

"I take it you know all about the shitstorm the old prick has kicked up about us encroaching on his land without a warrant?" asked McLellan.

Hardie butted in. "With respect, DCI McLellan, what about our powers under common law to gain entry to premises or land when we suspect that life is under dire and immediate threat? If you ask me, boss, an ace beats a king and we are holding the ace of spades, as dear old Lemmy might say," quipped the DC before raising one of his large bushy eyebrows to underline the point.

McLellan laughed out loud and in so doing drew some puzzled looks from the black-clad members of the support unit who were assembled beside two vans.

"Aye, it's a fair cop, DC Hardie. I guess I can take the bollocking that will await me from the Chief Constable if old man Rogers is sitting playing his banjo in his armchair when we kick down his door," said McLellan.

"How'd you want to play it then, boss?" asked Thoroughgood.

"In light of everything we have discussed, and the new information you have brought to bear, I think we can now dispense with the niceties. I'll get the Support Unit gaffer to throw a cordon round Rogers' farmhouse while we take obs on Millearn Hospital. The question is, who is going to pay their respects to old man Rogers? If you're right, Detective Sergeant, I don't have much doubt his life is in immediate danger," concluded McLellan.

"Don't worry boss, we'll take that on. After all, there's not much point in you running the gauntlet with Rogers if he turns out hale and hearty," replied Thoroughgood. "I take it we can get Kevlar vests from your Support Unit boys?"

"No problem there, have you come tooled up?" asked McLellan.

Hardie patted the breast of his anorak reassuringly in reply. "I'll get the vests, gaffer," he said, heading towards the Support Unit Inspector who was engaged in a game of cards with his men on the bonnet of their van.

McLellan turned to Thoroughgood, "How you gonna play it then, Detective Sergeant? You driving up the farm road or going on foot?"

"On foot. We don't want to send any more warning signals to our Polish pals than we need to. If you ask the support unit boys to form up at the bottom of the farm road and then spread round in an arc to surround it, I'm sure they'll sleepwalk through the usual protocol and be exactly where we need them if the shit hits the fan," said Thoroughgood, just as the Support Services Inspector joined them.

"All right, gentlemen, glad to meet you. Inspector Alan Bell, Central Scotland Support Unit. My boys are ready to go on your word, DCI McLellan," he said briskly.

"Do you think you could spare a couple of your men to conduct a discreet reconnaissance of the outhouses up at the old Millearn Hospital, Inspector? We believe that's ultimately where the gang are holed up and holding Mrs Balfron. But it must be discreet," said Thoroughgood.

"No problem, I've got just the two boys for that job. Leave it with me and I will rendezvous with you at the farm, pronto."

Thoroughgood smiled his gratitude.

Moments later, McLellan drove the two detectives the quarter of a mile to the bottom the farmhouse road and as they clambered out from the CID vehicle reminded them. "I'm on the end of the radio, as is Inspector Bell. No heroics, Detective Sergeant – just get the job done, and old man Rogers out alive if you can, but most importantly, put your own safety first. Good luck, gentlemen."

As McLellan drove off Thoroughgood saw the black-clad support unit officers fan out along the hedgerow that marked the farm boundary with a 'B' road, at a distance of around 50 metres.

One of their number, whom Thoroughgood recognised as Inspector Bell, took a step onto the road and raised a thumb in the air.

"Here we go again," said Hardie and they turned into the farm road and started walking.

35

"WHAT DO you reckon – front or back door, faither?"

"It's gotta be the old pincer movement if you ask me, Gus, which one you want? Bearin' in mind front door entry is for pussies!"

"Okay, okay I'll take the back door . . . as bleedin' usual. Make sure you've got one hand on your insurance policy," added Thoroughgood, nodding to the standard-issue revolvers they both had holstered under their left arms.

"Fine, entry on the whistle?" asked Hardie.

"Of course, but make sure you knock before booting the crap out of the door just in case old man Rogers is still alive and rockin' in his chair! Give me one minute to get in position and check the support unit are ready to go . . . start countin', faither, and I'll see you somewhere in the middle," said Thoroughgood as he began to jog around the farmhouse to the back door.

Once there he unholstered his firearm and dropped it down by his right side, keeping the revolver close to his body, then, whispering into his radio, he confirmed that Bell and his men were in position. "Roger, affirmative," crackled Bell's voice in response.

Thoroughgood placed the radio back in his pocket and gave Hardie the three note whistle used by Glasgow neds as a warning signal, and long since adopted by Hardie and himself as their calling card. Then he approached the back door. Solid oak with an iron handle.

Thoroughgood hit it hard in the traditional seven rap police knock and called out, "Hello, Mr Rogers, Detective Sergeant Thoroughgood, can I have your permission to enter?"

Silence greeted him and Thoroughgood suffered the intuitive sinking feeling he regularly experienced in the pit of his stomach when he was about to embark on an exercise in futility.

'No point hanging about, Gussy boy, let's be havin' you' said the voice in his head as the bang from the front of the farmhouse suggested that Hardie had beaten him to it.

"Old bugger," muttered Thoroughgood as he tried the door handle, which obligingly invited entry unopposed. Pushing the door open Thoroughgood entered the kitchen, his revolver clutched two-handed in front of him.

He needn't have bothered. There, in his kitchen chair, was Jimmy Rogers, impaled on a six inch blade protruding messily from his chest. Thoroughgood's attention was immediately drawn to the piece of paper transfixed by the blade.

He was soon diverted by Hardie's arrival from the corridor at the other side of the kitchen.

"All clear Gus . . ." said Hardie, trailing off as he took in Rogers' smashed skull, the first thing the DC noticed as he approached the deceased farmer from behind his corpse.

"We're too late, then," he said shaking his head.

"For Rogers yes, but maybe not for Sophie Balfron," said Thoroughgood, tugging the piece of paper off the blade and reading aloud.

'IF YOU WANT SOPHIE BALFRON ALIVE THE POLIJCA THOROUGHGOOD COME ALONE. BE THERE 3PM OR SHE DIE.'.

"Fuck me gently," said Hardie.

Thoroughgood winced. "Nasty. Obviously Boniek wants revenge for his brother. Radio up McLellan and Bell and we'll get a parley here ASAP, and decide on the way forward."

Within minutes Thoroughgood and Hardie were in a heated conference with DCI McLellan and Inspector Bell and it was the support unit gaffer who was making his point most forcibly. "There's no way you can go sauntering your way in there, offering yourself up as some sort of human sacrifice for Mrs Balfron's life when the murderin' bastard will most likely kill her anyway, that is if she ain't cold already," said Bell, a pale-faced individual with receding blonde hair.

McLellan attempted to speak, but Bell held up his hand and ploughed on, "You bloody CID types are all the same. Any notion of protocol just goes straight out the windae when the shit hits the fan. Well, let me tell you that protocol, force standing orders and such are drawn up just to cover such eventualities. I am a trained hostage negotiator and this is the time to employ that particular skill. Because, gentlemen, if we don't do it all by the book and it goes pear-shaped then I can tell you every one of our arses will be out the windae without a prayer."

McLellan broke in, "I don't see how we can do anything else, gents. Inspector Bell is correct, I make it 14.41 so we still have time for a parley and, given the Inspector is a trained negotiator, it is more than our careers are worth, to say nothing of Mrs Balfron's life, not to utilise these skills. If it doesn't work then we look at the other option." With that McLellan flicked a quick glance towards Thoroughgood, making it obvious where the last chance saloon was situated.

"They're both right, Gus. We have got to do it by the book, in the first instance at least. Anyways, I reckon your nine lives must be about used up by now, mate, so no point stickin' your head above the parapet if it ain't required," said Hardie.

"Fair enough, but we better get crackin' 'cause I reckon the old hospital is about a mile down that dirt track and we haven't got much time to play with," said Thoroughgood. Bell nodded and headed over to his unit.

Thoroughgood and Hardie took their places alongside McLellan, behind the hastily thrown up cordon, 100 metres from the broken down, whitewashed prefab walls of Millearn Hospital and watched as Bell took several steps forward with a loudspeaker in hand.

"What happens next?" asked Hardie but no one had an answer.

Ten metres in front of the cordon Bell raised the speaker to his mouth and said carefully, "Hello in the hospital. I am Inspector Bell and I have come to talk with you to see if we can find a reasonable way out of this that will stop any more lives being lost."

Bell did not have long to wait for his answer, "Dupek!

You not read note?" shouted a heavily-accented voice from somewhere behind the open window to the left of the front door.

"To whom am I speaking?" asked Bell, employing the classic hostage-negotiation manoeuvre of getting a handle on the opposition while stalling for time.

"Tomasz Boniek is my name and there be no more talking, idiota. Send the skurwysyn Thoroughgood in or Miss Sophie say night, night, for good. It simple – you send him to me and we let Miss Sophie go. You don't and . . ." the Pole let his words taper off, his meaning clear.

Bell attempted to keep the dialogue going, "That can not happen, Boniek, however I am sure we can reach an agreement that will allow us all to walk away from this . . . situation, with no more loss of life."

Bell's hope was a forlorn one and as soon as he had finished speaking, the front door of the hospital was booted open, and two figures emerged, almost melded into one.

Boniek walked two yards out of the door with Sophie Balfron gagged and bound and gripped tightly to his body. A revolver was pressed against the side of her head.

"Listen to me, dupek. Time is 2.51, so that mean you have nine minutes to send murderer Thoroughgood to hospital unarmed or I blow bitch's brains out. Now, no more speaking. Do what I say, kozojeb."

With that, Boniek levelled his revolver and fired. Just yards in front of Bell the dirt exploded and the inspector took a startled step back; he needn't have worried because Boniek was already dragging Sophie Balfron back inside the dilapidated old hospital.

As Bell retreated hastily to the cordon, Hardie was

first to articulate everyone's thoughts, "Well, that worked a feckin' treat."

Joining the three CID officers, Bell said, "It's not good, gents. If my two lads don't come up with something then we have a real problem because I cannot allow a fellow officer to place his life in danger."

McLellan was first to respond, "The problem is, that son of a bitch isn't interested in talking. You heard him, he wants Thoroughgood and if he doesn't get him then Sophie Balfron's life is over in precisely six minutes."

36

THE THREE CID officers watched intently as Bell was debriefed by the two Support Services cops who had returned from their recce of the hospital, then Bell joined the CID men and said, "Okay, gents, we might have something. My lads have stumbled on an old sewage pipe and vent that looks like it's big enough for a man to get into, and will hopefully provide access to the main hospital building where Boniek and his mates are in situ."

"That's it then, Inspector," said Thoroughgood, decisively. "I suggest you select a team and that DC Hardie here accompanies them and they try and make entry via the sewage tunnel." He pushed up the sleeve of his jacket and read out the time, "14.57hrs, time I made my appointment. Good luck, gents, see you on the other side . . . I hope," and with that Thoroughgood offered a handshake to his three colleagues and gave Hardie his handgun.

Hardie couldn't help himself, "Come on Gus, for cryin' out loud. There has to be another way."

"This is the only way," replied Thoroughgood and started to walk. Silence confirmed there was no other alternative.

As he made his way towards the derelict, antiquated building Thoroughgood tried to take in as much detail as he could of the hospital and its surroundings. The sewage tunnel had to be at the north west side of the hospital so if he could somehow free Sophie Balfron that was where his exit strategy must take him. As he passed the spot where Bell had been shot at, he found himself wondering if this was the ticket that had his number on it – over and over again, for sometime his luck had to run out.

The voice in his head helpfully chimed in, 'Faither's right – how many more times are you gonna get lucky, Gussy boy?'

With around 30 yards to go, the door to the hospital opened and the barrel of a shotgun was levelled at him. As he continued to close the gap at a steady walk, he could make out the hulking shape of Tomazsewski and smiled in resignation at the confirmation that Polish birds of a feather did indeed flock together.

The voice in his head once more came to life, 'Big mistake lettin' these two bastards go, you should have had them bang to rights back at the farm and now you're gonna pay.'

Five feet from the doorway the harsh voice that he immediately identified as belonging to Boniek spoke out, "Stop there, Thoroughgood. You have no weapon?"

Thoroughgood strained his eyes into the darkness of the doorway, but all he could see was Tomazsewski. Holding his hands high in the air he said, "I am clean, Boniek, now where is Sophie Balfron?"

"Why don't you come in and find out for yourself, polijca?"

"I am not taking another step until you let her go, Boniek."

"You throw my brother off roof 100 feet up, and now you tell me what to do, jebak? Are you scared of Polish hospitality, my friend? Okay, we stop this bullshit."

"Look Boniek, just get on with it," snapped Thoroughgood, just as Boniek edged back out with Sophie Balfron clamped to him.

"Take three steps forward, ciota, then bitch go free," ordered the Pole. He ripped the gag from Sophie's mouth and pushed her forward, all the time making sure that he remained jammed against her just in case anyone in the cordon of glinting steel surrounding the hospital fancied his chances at a pot shot.

As Sophie drew parallel with Thoroughgood she could not help herself and, through a huge sob, she said, "I'm so sorry." Thoroughgood did his best to smile reassuringly, but his attempt at encouragement foundered as Sophie was propelled past him and Boniek's right hand grabbed him and with the other, rammed the pistol against the side of the DS' head. With the Pole taking cover adroitly behind his body, Thoroughgood was now a human shield.

Boniek shouted down the track to the cordon, "If you want see your friend again, you keep fuck away until we finish." He laughed out loud and pushed the handgun into Thoroughgood's head with renewed vigour.

"Now the fun begin, matkojebco," whispered Boniek into the DS' ear.

Slightly disorientated by the speed at which the Pole had birled him round, Thoroughgood allowed himself a brief moment of satisfaction that, even if he was to pay with his life, he had at least saved Sophie's. Watching her walk away from them, back to safety, he saw Bell break from the cordon and the welcoming smile on the

Inspector's face as he started to walk towards her and, although he couldn't make out the words of comfort he spoke, Thoroughgood could make an educated guess.

From behind him a crack rapped out and Sophie Balfron's head burst like an over-ripe pumpkin and she collapsed on the dirt track.

"Spierdalaj ty glupia Szmata!" shouted Boniek, dragging Thoroughgood backwards into the hospital.

The rage in the DS erupted like a volcano and he rammed his head backwards and into the Pole's face, stunning Boniek. He turned and surged at the Pole, straight into the barrel of the handgun Boniek had levelled against his forehead.

"Another step and I blow your head off like bitch, Thoroughgood," Boniek grabbed the DS, wrapped his arm around his neck and gave a vicious squeeze that left Thoroughgood gasping for air.

As Thoroughgood was rammed through the doorway he connected with an outstretched boot that he presumed belonged to either Tomazsewski or Lewandowski before he lost his balance and landed on the damp, cold floor. He attempted to turn around and regain his balance, but Boniek smashed his pistol off the side of Thoroughgood's head, sending him reeling against the wall where he immediately found himself pinioned by his old friends, Tomazsewski and Lewandowski. Boniek punched the DS in the midriff with all the power he could muster. Thoroughgood convulsed violently and gasped for air.

"Bring him to back room, Robert. Lewandowski, you stay at window . . . just in case polijca try be smart" ordered Boniek.

Semi-conscious and with waves of nausea sweeping

over him, Thoroughgood felt his clothing being ripped off. Then, through the blur, he became aware that he was being strapped into a chair, before what felt like pincers were clamped onto his genitalia.

"Pour liquid over him," snapped Boniek.

Thoroughgood tasted orange juice as he was doused with the liquid from head to toe. The Pole placed what looked like an old army field phone on the rotten old cabinet to the left of him and Thoroughgood saw through his returning vision that the antique appeared connected to the wires which had been clamped onto his privates.

"Boniek, you maniac! What the fuck do you hope to achieve? There's no way you or your mates are going to get out of this one alive. Do you think they will just hang around until you finish your fun with me, you murdering piece of Polish sewage? You've just lost your insurance by blowing Sophie Balfron's brains out. I don't matter, Boniek. I'm just a number, so they won't hang about bleating about me. One way or another you are going to have company any second now." Inwardly, Thoroughgood made a silent prayer to the big man upstairs that this would indeed be the case.

As he opened his eyes he saw Boniek's face loom large and felt the Pole clamp an iron grip on his jaw, "Ty chuju, you think I give fuck? You murdered my brother and the bitch, she fucked him and then spat him out like piece of shit when she have her fun. It pity that Janek no have chance to enjoy revenge on her. You fucked that up, polijca, and then you drop my little brother on his head. Now I have my revenge."

Thoroughgood grimaced as the spittle from Boniek's mouth exploded all over his face, but he forced himself to maintain grace under extreme pressure and tried to keep the Pole talking, "So what delights do you have planned for me, Boniek? Tell me, are your two pals happy that they are gonna be going to their death with their mad boss anytime now?"

Tomazsewski provided the answer with a fist that smashed into the side of Thoroughgood's jaw and sent a tooth flying out of his mouth, "Quiet, polijca, prepare to fry," said the giant Pole and flashed a grin of dripping evil Thoroughgood's way.

Just then, Lewandowski's voice came from the front of the building, "Tomasz – polijca coming!"

For the first time Thoroughgood saw indecision sweep across Boniek's face and he tried to widen the crack into a fissure, "I hope you have an escape route, Boniek, because otherwise you and your two friends are history."

Boniek quickly regained his purpose and shouted a reply back to Lewandowski, "Tell them we talk, and keep them talking." Boniek returned his attention to Thoroughgood and smiled, "Don't worry, pizda, I still have time to finish what you start."

He walked over to the field phone and began to crank it. Thoroughgood instantly began to feel a burning sensation shoot through his body at its most vital part. The agony seared him and he heard a voice he dimly recognised as his own, scream out, "No!"

"Fry, kozojeb!" screamed Boniek.

37

BY THE time Thoroughgood had taken his first steps along the dirt track towards the hospital Bell had already assembled a group of his support unit officers, including the two who had discovered the sewage outlet.

Turning to Hardie, Bell said, "Okay, Detective Constable Hardie, I assume you are armed?" Hardie nodded.

Bell immediately got to the point, "Sergeant Harris is in charge of the storm team you will accompany. Remember that you do everything Chopper says, he is an expert in this kind of thing and if anyone can get Detective Sergeant Thoroughgood out of there alive, it is him. Understood?"

"Absolutely, Inspector," said Hardie and offered his hand, Bell gripped it firmly.

A voice to Hardie's left proved to be Harris identifying himself, "Call me Chopper, DC Hardie, as you will gather, everyone else does, but we can do the introductions en route. All I need you to do is follow my boys, keep tucked in and do what you're told, and hopefully we can get your mate out of there in one piece."

"Roger," said Hardie. He found himself trying to keep

up with Harris and his four man detail as they skirted around the rear of the cordon, which appeared to have been reinforced by fresh arrivals.

Navigating a copse of birches in a crouch, Hardie could see the hospital from behind Harris, who proved to be a body-fit for Arnold Schwarzenegger. There were a myriad of outbuildings at different stages of rack and ruin attached to it.

Harris signalled to his detail to gather round before addressing them, "All right, boys, here we go. The sewage pipeline leading into Loch Lomond is 500 yards to our right, which is towards the north-west of the main building, which in turn is the only part of the hospital still roofed and habitable, and thus the reason our Polish friends are holed up there. From past experience we are either going to come up in the shithouse, or possibly an old kitchen, but that is academic."

Harris took a breath and continued, his group's attention total, "Okay – we have partial cover from the tree line for the next 200 yards approximately and then it's down and dirty on your bellies." Harris paused and winked at Hardie, "Sorry, DC Hardie, I think you've got a visit to the dry cleaners coming up!" That brought an amused murmur from the group. "Gupta, you have the wire-cutters, so when we get to within 30 yards of the pipeline you will be on first. The burn is in a gulley, once we are down in the water we will have all the cover we need to make our entry unobserved. Dickson and Woods, you will provide covering fire if needed, while myself and DC Hardie follow Gupta into the burn. It would appear there are only three members of the gang and I doubt if they have the first clue that there's another point of entry to the building. But we take no chances, boys. All right?"

Harris was met with three staccato replies of, "Yes, Chopper," while Hardie nodded.

"Okay boys on three . . . three," and with that Harris quickly broke into a crouching trot with his men following, their Heckler and Kochs strapped to their black uniformed backs.

As they hit the edge of the treeline Chopper's hand shot up and he pointed left and right to the cover points he expected Woods and Dickson to take up. They did so almost before he had completed the signal and Hardie watched, impressed, as Gupta, a dead-eyed Indian officer, took his position at Chopper's shoulder.

The sergeant waved him on and Gupta hit the dirt and began to effect a fast crawl across the open ground that would have put a rattlesnake to shame. Next, Chopper turned to Hardie,

"Me next on three, then you, just do what I do and we will be up to our necks in shit in jig time." The sergeant flashed Hardie a smile, turned back to watch Gupta making his reptile-like progress across a boggy-looking surface and said, "Three." He hit the deck and started to writhe his way across the opening.

"The missus is gonnae love this," muttered Hardie, gritted his teeth and did likewise.

His anorak wet and soiled, his trousers soaked and stinging through to his legs from the cold damp of the bog, Hardie made it to the top of the bank and swung himself down, only to land in a huge cow pat.

"In the name of the wee man," he groaned as Chopper patted him on the back warmly and said, "Well done, Kenny, isn't it? Aye, appearances can be deceptive, mate."

"Thanks, Chopper," said Hardie, smiling sarcastically.

Two thuds at his back informed Hardie that Woods and Dickson had also arrived in the gulley. It was clear Gupta had done his work with the wire-cutters as the mesh over the entrance to the vent had been cut wide enough to invite a crouched entry. "Entry point clear," he whispered.

"Good work, boys," said Chopper and provided a radio update to Bell, back at the cordon control point.

"Entry ready to be made boss, permission to go in?" asked Harris down the line, then replied, "Roger, boss."

"Lads, I'm in the lead, Gupta you are my number two and then it's you, Dicko. When we make entry into the hospital building the two of you immediately flank me as much as possible. DC Hardie, you are next and Bunny Woods, you cover our rear as usual, wee man. Everyone good?"

"Roger, Chopper," was the chorused reply.

"On three," said Chopper and pulled the radio to his mouth and spoke. "Three," as the Support Unit Sergeant triggered the same manoeuvre at the Cordon control point.

On the command Harris threw himself on his belly into the stinking, ice-cold water and began to crawl up the tunnel. Although the sewage outlet might have been unused for decades, the scurrying noises that came from all around hinted at the identity of its current residents. But with Chopper's Maglite torch lighting up their route they made good progress and squinting beyond Harris' huge shoulders, Hardie saw the tunnel come to a stop as it joined a wall approximately 15 metres further up.

Within moments they were at the juncture of the tunnel with the main hospital building and Chopper broke the momentary silence, "Dicko, you got the sledge hammer?"

"Yes, Chopper," was the answer from beyond the torchlight now glinting the Support Unit gaffer's way.

"Well, what you waiting for, boy?" asked Harris, fingering the brickwork which proved to be flaking, before adding, "Smash me a nice hole, son."

"Done," said Dickson, sending icy drops of water spraying everywhere as he shuffled past the sergeant before folding himself into a crouch that was all the confines of the tunnel would allow him.

"Okay, boys, here we go. Showtime," said Chopper. "My guess is that the sewage tunnel was probably bricked up when the place shut down, God knows when. We should see, once Dicko has smashed us an entry point, that we are going to be in the building itself and our problems are likely to start there because the chances are the noise coming from the sledgehammer will have alerted the Poles. Hopefully, they will have their hands full elsewhere, though. That's 11 minutes we have been on the job, dead. Let's hope we aren't too late."

In the darkness Hardie prayed aloud, "Amen to that."

"This is your final opportunity to save yourselves. Come out unarmed, with Detective Sergeant Thoroughgood unharmed," shouted Bell down the loudhailer. He was shaking in anger and horror at what had become of Sophie Balfron, whose corpse still lay on the cold ground ahead of him.

"What you offer us, Polijca?" asked a voice that Bell immediately realised did not belong to Boniek.

"Come out and throw your arms down. I will give you 30 seconds precisely," warned Bell, looking at his watch as he began a mental countdown.

"Go to hell, skurwysyn!" shouted Lewandowski.

Bell immediately raised his hand. Glancing to either

side of him, to make sure the cordon was ready to mobilise, he lowered it. The momentary silence was shattered by the sounds of boots crunching on the debris covering the ground.

"Forward!" shouted Bell to his men.

38

THOROUGHGOOD DIDN'T know how long he had been drifting in and out of consciousness, but every time his body was jolted by a shockwave he guessed he blacked out. It was clear that Boniek was ramping up the strength of the voltage and the DS knew that the inevitable was not far away.

"Now, dupek, you wish you had been thrown off roof, no?" sneered Boniek.

His concentration was disrupted by the sound of gunfire from the front of the hospital building. As the Pole's attention wavered, Thoroughgood tried to play for time, "Why, Boniek? Please tell me how this all started before you take your revenge."

"Robert, get to the front and help Artur hold the polijca off while I send this murdering gswno to hell," yelled Boniek.

Tomazsewski immediately sprinted off and Boniek turned his malevolent gaze on Thoroughgood, "Have you ever had your heart broken? Because, Thoroughgood, the bitch broke Jan's heart then toss him aside like piece of shit. She had to pay, but you stopped her paying the price Jan wanted from her."

"Yes, I have had my heart broken too, Boniek. So your plan was to abduct her all along . . . but what about the rest of the gang? You meant to wipe them out from the start?" asked Thoroughgood, straining every fibre trying to hear how close Bell's men were getting.

"I know your game. You try keep me talking. You think me idiota?"

A muffled pounding began to reverberate through the hospital and hope once more sprang eternal within Thoroughgood, "An idiot is the last thing I would accuse you of being. Come on, Boniek, satisfy a dying man's curiosity," pleaded Thoroughgood, frantically trying to loosen the bindings that held his wrists to the back of the chair.

Boniek spotted what he was doing, "There is no escape, Thoroughgood, but before you say bye bye to your world of shit . . . I tell you why. Because Joe Drummond was old and finished, he wanted out. Because, polijca, like everything else in your motherfucking country, we Poles do it better."

Boniek moved away from the old army field telephone and lowered his face to within inches of Thoroughgood, "I was listening, jebak . . . so tell me, where is your bitch now? At home with baby dancing on knee, waiting for Daddy come home?"

Thoroughgood felt his control desert him and as his body began to shake uncontrollably, he spat in Boniek's face, "She was murdered, now get on with it you bastard!"

Boniek wiped the spittle from his face and returned to the antique phone. "Too bad, polijca," he sneered, wrapping his right hand around the old phone's crank.

Seeing Thoroughgood's gaze drop to the phone,

Boniek permitted himself one final moment of triumph, "You like? The Nazis, they used to do this in the Warsaw ghetto to torture my grandfather's people. The orange juice is very good conductor, no?"

He called out to his countrymen, "Artur, Robert, you are good?"

"We are good, Tomasz, but we need go now, the Polijca throw smoke bombs," replied Tomazsewski.

"Give them fire and keep them out for 30 seconds, then meet me at the kitchen and we will be gone," shouted Boniek.

At that he glanced over his shoulder and a look of confusion spread across his feral features at the sound of voices reverberating up the corridor leading to the kitchen. They were not Polish.

Thoroughgood knew he had to stall for his life, "You think your grandfather would be proud of you now, Boniek. A war hero who fought the Nazis and probably paid with his life. Now look at the monster his grandson has become. You've become every bit as big a monster as any Nazi, you murdering bastard. You're a disgrace to your countrymen."

Thoroughgood had overdone it and his tirade sent Boniek into a rage that was only going to end with the DS' death.

"Niech cie diabli wezm! Now I fry you last time, Thoroughgood," spat Boniek.

Before the Pole could twitch a sinew, a shout erupted from the front of the building, "Co Kurwa, do kurwy nedzy!" screamed Tomaszewski, his words immediately followed by a torrent of gunfire.

Lewandowski charged into the room, "Polijca

everywhere! Artur is dead, Tomasz. We must go . . .
now!" screamed the Pole.

Boniek looked away from his instrument of torture,
"One moment more . . ."

The door smashed off its hinges and three black-clad
figures burst through the opening. Boniek cranked up the
field phone and Thoroughgood felt the voltage burn him
inside out. Then his lights went out.

"Fuck you!" shouted Harris and let Boniek have it
with the entire contents of his magazine. The whole room
filled with gunfire and Boniek pitched forward across the
phone, riddled with lead.

Lewandowski threw his hands up but before he had
straightened his arms he was cut in two by the crossfire
from Woods' and Dickson's flanking positions. Hardie
charged over to Thoroughgood, pulling the clamps off his
mate's privates and slicing the bindings from his hands,
before tossing his soaking anorak over the DS.

"Fuck me, Gus, that was just way too close for
comfort," he gasped.

The semi-conscious Thoroughgood managed a weak
smile then passed out again.

Thoroughgood sat upright in the back of the ambulance
and discovered he was wearing one of the unit's black
boiler suits. His jaw throbbed and exploration of his
mouth confirmed that he was minus one or possibly two
teeth. The burning sensation from his nether regions sent
waves of nausea through him.

Hardie's haggard face came into focus on the opposite
side of the emergency vehicle and Thoroughgood sensed
that they were, in fact, mobile.

"Jeez, faither, how long have I been out?"

"Best part of an hour, matey, but hey, it beats the permanent vacation that maniac Boniek had planned for you!" replied the DC.

"Aye, I have to admit I thought I was a goner, old pal, but you came through for me as usual, Kenny. Christ, how many times is that you've saved my skin?" asked Thoroughgood, reaching out to grasp his mate's hand.

Hardie was plainly embarrassed by the DS' show of emotionally-charged gratitude, but returned a warm handshake and as he did so, Thoroughgood realised that he was attached to a drip.

Pulling himself together, Hardie replied, "It's gettin' on for a few now, Gus. To be fair, I did have a bit of help this time, mate! You remember that business with Felix Baker? By God, that was nothing compared with what we've just come through. Even the Imam Tariq would struggle to come up with that business with the old army field phone. He must have doused you in orange juice to make extra sure you held the charge. How are the crown jewels, mate?"

"Throbbing is the best way to describe them. But what happened to Sophie Balfron? Did she make it?"

"Sorry, mate, I thought you knew, no surprise if you are concussed, maybe even lobotomised from the balls up," said Hardie, allowing himself a mischievous smirk. "I'm sorry, Gus, they blew her brains out right in front of you. You went through all of that for nothing, mate, but at least those Polish bastards have all said good night Vienna for the last time."

"I guess it's gonna take me a few days to bounce back from this, faither. I'm just glad it's DCI McLellan's show and we did everything we could. I'm fecked, mate. Feel like I could sleep for a week."

"Hey, Gus, if that is what it is going to take, then do it. I would imagine you'll be kept in over night for observations and such, and then we can see about getting you hame, and you can get Vanessa to show the Florence Nightingale in her. Aye, come to think of it, I wouldn't mind seeing VV in a nurse's uniform, all right. You better make sure you don't get too worked up when she gets to work on you mate after your . . . er," as usual, Hardie attempted to stop digging way too late.

Thoroughgood winced as he was jolted back against the side of the ambulance after a bit of turbulence on the road, "Hilarious as always, faither. Listen – I'm not spending a moment longer in the Western than I have to, I can assure you. Plus, there will be statements required tout suite."

"Don't worry about that right now, Gus. Just make sure they are happy with you once they have given you the MOT, and then get home. Get some kip and a bit of TLC from Vanessa, was all I was trying to say, and make sure you take your time getting back to yourself," said Hardie, belatedly attempting to show his caring side.

"Not much chance of that, mate. Vanessa wants me in attendance at the bloody whisky launch at Roxburgh Hall. It might actually be fun to be there and watch old Randy Pigeon jumping about like a kangaroo on fire, trying to make sure his VIPs are all tucked up nice and safe. I daresay he'll get another bloody pip out of it," said Thoroughgood, his energy plainly ebbing.

"If you look at all the shit that McLellan has to deal with, being a member of the brass ain't all that it's cracked up to be, Gus, just remember that. Anyway, why don't you try and get some shut-eye before we get to the Western. Christ, you've earned it mate."

"As you might say, faither, maybes aye, maybes naw," said Thoroughgood and collapsed on the ambulance bench.

39

THOROUGHGOOD WAS woken up by the doorbell ringing repeatedly, someone was clearly very impatient to see him, someone he knew would be Vanessa.

He knew she wouldn't be happy that he had got Hardie to pick him up from the Western and drop him back at his Partickhill Road flat. He guessed she'd probably have loved to play the adoring girlfriend; there to pick up the pieces and bring her hero-cop boyfriend home. A wave of guilt washed over him and the voice in his head spoke up, 'Come on, mate, give her a break. This is all about your problems, not hers. Face it for once.'

The truth was that Thoroughgood didn't feel like much of a hero. The bottom line was that he had failed to save Sophie Balfron and he blamed himself for not having brought Lewandowski and Tomazsewski into custody when he and Hardie had first met them at old man Rogers' farm.

Because of that, reasoned Thoroughgood, both Rogers and Sophie Balfron were dead. Dead, when they should have been very much alive, all because he had failed to huckle the Poles, at the first time of asking. Now he had to contend with Vanessa. He tried to rouse himself from the blanket he lay under, and switched off the tv.

221

He tried to ready himself to face the tirade that was likely to come his way over the text messages he had not returned and his failure to call her; the histrionics that were likely to erupt over him not supporting her ahead of one of the biggest events in her career. He could imagine it all and hesitated at the bedroom door as the thought crept into his head that he would be better returning under the blanket than face Vanessa's ire. A new question arose in his mind, 'What had changed since the meal they had shared, just days before in this very same flat?'

Walking to the front door, Thoroughgood began to realise that his latest brush with death had brought Celine's memory back to life. Yet there was something else that was gnawing away at him – the memory of an encounter with someone who was very much alive, someone almost half his age, someone called Victoria Roxburgh. He realised this had confirmed that his relationship with Vanessa was almost as superficial as the pages of the glossy magazines she loved to play her life out on.

Thoroughgood opened the door. 'Christ, she's hot, Gussy boy' said the voice in his head helpfully, and Vanessa was exactly that. Knee-length black leather boots topped with a brown suede band, tight jeans, and a bubble jacket, then that beautiful, almost flawless, skin and shock of blonde hair. But then, she was one of these women who was always going to have 'it', regardless of what she wore. As his eyes devoured her, Thoroughgood felt a fool for the doubts that had just been surfing through his conscience.

Vanessa spoke. "How are you, Gus? Come to think of it, why is it I am always the last to know how you are?"

Thoroughgood attempted a fudge, "Nice to see you too, Vanessa! I've been better, is probably the best way to describe how I am," and offered her a weak smile. "Are you coming in?"

Vanessa was not interested in the sympathy card, "Do you want me to come in, Gus? Clearly you preferred Hardie's company to mine earlier on. Why didn't you call me to come and get you? For crying out loud, Gus! I didn't even know what had happened to you until I saw Reporting Scotland."

She stepped over the threshold anyway and as Thoroughgood closed the door behind her he found himself enveloped in her arms. She pulled her head away from his and pierced him with her brilliant azure eyes, "What's wrong, Gus? Can't you understand I have been out of my mind worrying about you? Worrying about us? The last time I was here you said all these things that made me believe we had a real chance, and ever since then it seems like you have been doing your best to avoid me. I thought we'd moved on from all our problems, but even that night at the Hall you were strange. I need to know if you are having second thoughts, Gus."

Thoroughgood held her gaze, "Look, can we go into the lounge, 'cos quite frankly I don't know if I can stand up for too much longer."

The guilt that engulfed Vanessa's beautiful features and the hurt mirrored in her eyes pricked Thoroughgood's conscience but his sympathy ploy bought him the space he required. Hand in hand, they walked through to the lounge.

"Fancy a glass of red?" asked Thoroughgood. He took Vanessa's smile as a yes and added, "Why don't you put the telly off and put a CD on? I'll get a bottle out of the kitchen. Malbec, okay?"

Again, a smile that seemed to ooze hurt. He made his way through to the kitchen. He began to wonder just who held the balance of power in their relationship. Vanessa seemed strangely vulnerable. Moments later he returned with two large glasses of red, but instead of sitting down next to Vanessa on the leather Chesterfield settee he elected to claim solace in his favourite armchair. The significance of the manoeuvre was not lost on Vanessa who sat, watching him over the rim of her glass, letting the silence reign. It occurred to him that she had not put on any music after all.

She spoke, "Are you going to tell me what went on at the old hospital, Gus? Is it true what they are saying that Pole did to you?"

Thoroughgood winced at the memory of the pain Boniek's imaginative torture device had dealt him.

"How can I understand you, or get near to you, if you won't let me in on your world and what you have gone through? I thought we had shared so much in the tunnels under the Botanics that we would have something worth fighting for, something special that we could build on. But I'm not sure you want to build on anything, Gus."

Thoroughgood attempted to smile but his mouth wouldn't obey his mind's command, "It's difficult, Vanessa. The problem is that when you come out the other side of the type of shit I have been through these last few days, you just want to shut it all out. I just feel like hiding inside my own four walls 'cos I don't have the energy to do anything else, and that doesn't make me very good company right now."

He knew it wasn't much of an explanation but it was all he could come up with and also pretty much the truth. He was physically and mentally exhausted.

Now it was Vanessa's turn to feel guilty, "I'm sorry, Gus, I'm so sorry. Why don't you let me take care of you tonight? I can order take-away, after all you've got to eat!"

Thoroughgood surprised her with his reply, "What about you, Vanessa? I know how much this launch up at the Hall means to you. It's a helluva opportunity and I would imagine it must have been pretty stressful trying to keep her Ladyship happy. I'm not sure she sees the benefits outweighing the negatives the way that Vicky does."

It was a schoolboy error, the shortening of Victoria Roxburgh's name implying an inappropriate closeness between them. Vanessa seized upon it, "Vicky? I didn't know that you two were on such familiar terms, Gus. But of course, it was you who played her knight in shining armour at the School of Art. Another one of your adventures that you failed to tell me about but then, as I said earlier, you don't text me, never mind return my calls, so why should I expect your little encounter with Victoria Roxburgh to make the cold light of day? The problem is that Vicky, as you like to call her, seems to have fallen under your spell, Gus."

Thoroughgood felt a schoolboy awkwardness give way to mounting anger, "For crying out loud, Vanessa, what do you expect me to do? That crazy bastard Boniek, the first of the brothers bleedin' Grimm, had done me over then led Hardie and myself a merry dance through the streets of Glasgow! And the icing on the cake was

225

that Victoria Roxburgh happened to be coming out of the School Of Art just as he was going in. I don't imagine you would love to have a six inch blade of cold steel held to your throat, or have you forgotten all about the Imam Tariq's hospitality already? Come to think of it, I don't exactly recall you complaining when I got you out of the old tunnels under the Botanics in one piece." Before he could stop himself Thoroughgood over-played his hand, "Maybe I should have left you there."

The contents of Vanessa's glass of red splashed over his face before he had time to blink. She slammed the glass down on the coffee table and jumped to her feet, "Listen to me, you bastard, I know you have been through a lot, although just how much I am not likely to know, as you seem unable to, or refuse to, share it with me, Gus Thoroughgood. But that doesn't give you the right to speak to me like that. You're right, I have a lot on my plate with the Roxburgh launch, but I came here to share it all with you and hoped you'd want to support me this weekend. Hoped that you'd also share what has been going on in your life with me, but that was never going to happen was it, Gus? The reason for that isn't because you are physically and mentally exhausted, it's because you are an emotional screw-up and you know what? If this is the way you treat every woman you get involved with then I am not going to have my name added to the list."

Thoroughgood got to his feet and tried to place his hand on her shoulder but she shook it off furiously, "Don't bother, it's too late, Gus. I haven't got the time or the inclination to waste any more emotion on you."

"Come on, Vanessa, cut me some slack will you? Less than 24 hours ago a madman was trying to turn my balls into a Polish hors d'oeuvre. I just need time and a bit of space to get things sorted in my head."

"You take all the time you need, Gus Thoroughgood," shouted Vanessa, turning on her heels and storming out of the room. Seconds later the slam of the front door confirmed she had gone and this time, thought Thoroughgood, maybe it was for good.

40

THOROUGHGOOD TRUDGED down Hyndland Road in a daze. The encounter with Vanessa had left him both shaken and stirred and, examining what he had left in his life; what he knew he didn't have was any certainty or emotional security.

"Jeez, I need a pint," he muttered to himself. A lukewarm smile swept across his overwrought features at the prospect of meeting up with Hardie for some liquid anaesthetic. After Vanessa had left he'd spent 10 minutes trying to ring her, sent her a text and then realised that was the last thing he should have done, 'Another bleedin' schoolboy mistake, Gus,' said the voice in his head with its usual sympathy.

Desperate for company and a sounding board, his next text had been to Hardie and fortunately, the DC had agreed to meet him for "a shandy" at the Ubiquitous Chip.

As he continued his walk into the stinging rain of the late spring evening, it occurred to him that Hardie supplied just about the only emotional security in his life. Things were that bad. Reaching the crossroads of Byres Road and University Avenue, Thoroughgood stopped for a moment and, looking up towards the university, replayed the pursuit of Janek Boniek, another source of guilt for him.

He asked himself, what had it achieved but more death? The loss of the police helicopter and two good coppers, countless injuries in the pile-up that had ensued on the M8, the death of one of the students and of course, the sight of Boniek, spitting hate at him, slipping through his hands at the top of the Art School.

'Christ, you'll be lucky if you ever get another moment's sleep at this rate,' said his inner voice.

Turning into Ashton Lane Thoroughgood felt so weak he didn't know if he had the energy to make it to the Chip and stopped, leaning against a wall outside the Ashoka Restaurant. Seeing couples, content and radiant in each other's company fuelled his anger; here he was on the verge of yet another doomed relationship – the thought boiled over, "Ah, fuck off," he raged out loud just as a beggar drew up next to him.

"Keep yer hair on, mate, I only asked if you could spare any change. You're all the same, you middle class West End bastards," snapped the beggar from under his filthy woollen hat. As he began to turn away from Thoroughgood, the DS clamped a hand on his shoulder, spun him around and rammed him up against the restaurant window, "Look mate, I'm just half way up shit creek without a paddle right now and I don't need a lecture from the likes of you on the class system. Here . . ." Thoroughgood offered him the contents of his trouser pocket, "Treat yourself to a Special Brew, on me, pal," lobbing three pound coins at the beggar's out-stretched hands and walked off.

'You're losing it, mate,' said his consciousness as he

climbed the steps on shaky legs to the upstairs bar in the Chip.

As he opened the bar door Thoroughgood almost fell over a black and white collie, whose grey-haired master sat, despite the icy wind and stinging rain, in shorts and a t-shirt on the seat just to the right of the entrance. The dog let out a yelp at Thoroughgood's near miss with his front paw.

"Sorry, mate, never saw Rover there," said Thoroughgood, holding up a hand in apology to the owner, whose glazed eyes indicated that he wasn't particularly bothered whether Rover had been given pause for thought or not.

Scanning the bar, Thoroughgood spotted Hardie sitting on slightly raised dais seats at the other side, a pint of Furstenberg just leaving his mouth and a coating of froth on his unruly moustache.

"How you doin'?" asked Hardie indicating that the pint of Guinness next to him was for Thoroughgood. "I thought you could probably do with some building up after all you've been through, mate. You sure you should be out, Gus?"

The DS sat down beside him and unzipped his jacket, "It was either that or I climb the four walls of my lounge, faither."

"How are they?" asked Hardie and when a mystified expression enveloped Thoroughgood's features the DC dropped his gaze towards Thoroughgood's midriff, before adding helpfully, "Yer crown jewels, that is?" he applied his trademark wink and a wolfish grin crept over his face.

"They, as you so delightfully referred to them, are coming along nicely, thanks to the ointment I was so helpfully furnished with by the Western, but before you ask, it will be a while before they resume active service and that is not just because of what they," emphasised Thoroughgood, "have been through."

"Vanessa?" asked Hardie before returning the pint of Furstenberg to his cavernous mouth.

Thoroughgood winced, "Indeed. She just left the flat an hour ago in a helluva strop and you know what? I guess I can't blame her."

Hardie replaced his pint pot on the coaster in front of him and folded his arms, allowing a temporary silence to develop, which usually implied the wheels of his mind were in operation.

Thoroughgood finally took a deep draught of his Guinness and stared balefully towards the bar where he had noticed a sharply-dressed female displaying an enticing view of stockinged leg from a bar stool while engaged in deep conversation with an older man in a Crombie.

"Lawyers," said Hardie, "I've been listening to them moaning about the sheriff court since the missus dropped me off. Decent leg though," concluded the DC before helpfully adding, "but not what you need right now, Gus."

"You're no' jokin', faither. I'm buggered if I know how to play this one, Kenny," said Thoroughgood.

"So what's her problem?" asked Hardie before answering his own question. "She's hacked off that you haven't been replying to her text messages. You haven't been calling her, she doesn't have a clue what is going on in your life and then, to cap it all, you get me to pick you up from hospital and not her?"

"That's just about bang on, mate," admitted the DS.

"But what we need to know right now, Gussy boy, is what is your problem?" asked Hardie, surprising Thoroughgood with his perception.

"Eh?"

"I was talking about this with the missus on the way over, Gus. Let's face it, you have a few issues. Not so much with Vanessa maybe, but certainly with her life. It's pretty clear you aren't comfortable with the whole celebrity aspect of it and if you ain't, you need to face the facts, man and let her get on with it 'cause that is who she is, matey . . . or at least that's what the missus thinks, anyways," concluded Hardie, playing his get-out card.

"I just don't think I can cope with the whole goldfish bowl, mate," admitted Thoroughgood. "But I'm going to have to make my mind up now, because if I don't show at the Hall for this bloody whisky and high fashion extravaganza it is over . . . that is if it isn't over already, of course." He fished out his invitation to the launch and slapped it down on the table.

Hardie hadn't finished with his interrogation, "I dunno, Gus, you sure you are telling me everything?"

"What you on about, faither?" demanded Thoroughgood, throwing him a dirty look as he replaced his pint on the table.

"I'll tell you what I mean. I mean that young Victoria Roxburgh seems to be pretty taken with you. You forget I had the pleasure of her company when I took her statement after the business with the first Boniek fecker at the Art School, made sure she was all right and generally held her hand while we waited for big brother Bobby to pick her up. I'll tell you, there was only one copper she wanted a bit of TLC from, mate, and sadly, it wasn't moi," said Hardie, raising an eyebrow.

Thoroughgood shifted uncomfortably in his seat. "What you on about, Kenny? She's almost half my age, for Chrissakes."

"Oh, I know how old she is, Gus. Twenty years and seven months, almost. I don't know how you have managed it, mate, but I'd say you will need to play that one very carefully if you are planning to mix with the hoi polloi this weekend. I mean, for crying out loud, Gus, what is all this stuff about Ivanhoe? Aren't you taking the whole knight in shining armour thing a bit far?" a smile enveloped Hardie's hangdog features.

"You sound just like Vanessa," replied Thoroughgood forlornly.

"Well, maybe she has a point, Gus. If you ask me and in fact, even if you don't, I would say if you are at all able to do it you need to front up for Vanessa this weekend, press some flesh, flash yer ivories and put her first, mucka. 'Cos if you don't, do you think she'll be short of offers? Come to think of it, old Randy Pigeon was making some pretty tasty comments about her earlier on!"

"What do you mean, faither?" snapped Thoroughgood a little too loudly.

"Come on, Gus, wake up and smell the coffee, mate. The woman is now a national treasure after that business with the mad Imam and if you fuck her about you are gonna attract a lot of very unwelcome press. It's one thing being her man, but an entirely different one being the bastard that breaks Queen Vanessa's heart. If you think the whole celebrity thing is a pain just now, how do you think it will pan out if it all turns to shit? You better watch how you play this one, pal. I had no idea just how much is involved in the launch until your little friend Victoria started to fill me in. Did you know they have Hello! magazine covering it, for instance?"

"That rings a bell," responded Thoroughgood morosely.

"Just think, a nice shot of you and Vanessa in the centre spread? Aye, that would go nice, up on the canteen wall at Stewart Street!" said Hardie, erupting into peals of laughter.

"It's no bloody laughing matter, Hardie," snapped Thoroughgood before he stood up abruptly, "I take it you want another Fursty and if you do, get that bloody brain of yours working on how I can negotiate my way through this whole mess, tout suite," said Thoroughgood. Hardie nodded sheepishly and the DS made his way over to the bar.

As he stationed himself to the left of the lawyers, Thoroughgood could feel the woman's eyes lingering on him and managed to respond with a smile that immediately sent a wave of guilt over him. Quickly, he readjusted his gaze to the overhead gantry that paralleled the bar beneath. It was fully stocked with a fascinating array of bevvy; Thoroughgood had always worried that one day the laws of gravity would kick in and it would drop on his head.

Then the voice in that same head took control, 'Right now, Gus, you need to get to the bottom line and quick.'

"That'll be £7.50, mate," said the barman and Thoroughgood realised he had been dreaming: "Jeez, you should be wearing a mask, pal. What's yer first name . . . Dick?" he responded. Shaking his head, he picked up the pint pots and made his way back to Hardie.

"Well?" asked Thoroughgood.

"Here's a different angle for you, Gus. Don't you fancy being a fly on the wall while Pigeon and Lightning Bolt are flapping around the Hall making sure no one is coming to any harm? I tell you, it's all there for you, mate. You've got Raymond Cheung, the Triad boss, all those VIP's, with your bloody bird arguably the biggest of the lot, and the gentry, all under one roof with Randy Pigeon trying to make sure everything proceeds in an orderly fashion. Christ, the potential for disaster is awesome. What a people watch," quipped Hardie.

"That is an interesting concept, my dear Hardie." said Thoroughgood allowing himself a smile for the first time since he had arrived. "But one I feel I wouldn't be able to face without you, my dear Hardie, accompanying me."

"Is that an order, Detective Sergeant?"

"Yer damn' tootin'" replied Thoroughgood and took a mouthful of his Guinness.

41

VICTORIA ROXBURGH signed off on the last delivery sheet confirming that canapés for 300 had arrived and that the chocolate fountains were installed and fully functional. It was noon and the launch was due to kick-off at 2.30, with guests beginning to arrive at 2pm and everything was perfect – including the weather, for once. The Hall shimmered in the magnificent spring sunshine while Loch Lomond sparkled with azure brilliance just beyond, and yet there still remained snow on the peak of the distant Ben Lomond.

Victoria had just completed a final run-through of the schedule for the charity fashion show with Vanessa in the clothing queen's trailer. But there was one giant shadow cast over everything. Robert Roxburgh was missing. Victoria had not seen her eldest brother since he had left her to read their grandfather's diaries on Thursday night. She had tried texting him and calling his mobile, but whereas the phone had initially rung out it now went straight to voicemail – and what had at first been concern had now turned to fear.

The strain of keeping this from her mother, was taking its toll and Victoria couldn't remain silent any longer.

"Where is he Vanessa? How can he expect me to carry this off, all on my own? I can't keep fobbing Mama off with lies," said Victoria.

Vanessa smiled warmly and placed a reassuring hand on Victoria's shoulder, "Look, Vicky, I know how important this is to your family. Maybe your big brother has gone off on a bender before he gets himself together for the big day. After all, he knows everything is in very safe hands. Always remember, Vicky, men are the weaker of the species.

"Look," she added, "how much do we need your brother? So what if Robert has taken stage fright? Between us we'll make sure the fashion show goes according to plan. I'm more than happy to help out with the launch afterwards. Surely you and your mother can do the meet-and-greet and make your excuses? Is it your fault that Robert's been confined to bed with a nasty attack of Norovirus?"

"It is not as easy as that, Vanessa," Vicky replied. "Our partner from the Gwai Lo, Raymond Cheung, will be here. Do you think he'll believe that? He's the most powerful Triad leader in Scotland, possibly Britain. Robbie's got him to bankroll the whole deal. The plans he has for The Dark Ocean launch in China are almost unbelievable – and now Robbie has disappeared and put it all in jeopardy,"

Vanessa placed both hands on Vicky's shoulders, "Look at me, Victoria Roxburgh, and listen carefully because this is the best advice you will ever get. In life, moments arise when an opportunity comes your way and if you take it with both hands it can be the making of you and, in this case, your family. I'm sure Robert will turn up in time to take all the plaudits when the Dark Ocean is being served to your guests, but if he doesn't then you make sure that no one notices his absence.

"Okay, so Raymond Cheung will be there, but do you think he will care whether it is you or your brother who make this launch a great success? The only thing that will matter to him is that it's a success, so why not get him involved? In fact, it sounds like I need to meet Mr Cheung!"

Victoria smiled weakly as Vanessa continued, "I will give you all the support you need Victoria. As you will see, our whole fashion show has a theme in keeping with the launch. At the end I will stand up and set the scene for you and you will carry everything off just fine. Why? Because you must."

"But I don't know what to say, Vanessa. I am not prepared and Cheung will be sitting in the front row watching me and wondering where the hell Robbie is. Mama has been taking sedatives to cope with the grief of losing Alex, God knows how she will be. It's going to be just like the Titanic, a once in a lifetime disaster." said Victoria as tears began to roll down her cheek.

"It will, if you let it," said Vanessa. "Put that all to one side and let's just focus on what is good. This is a fantastic opportunity for your family and it looks like only you can make it happen. We have both pulled in a lot of favours. You've used the Roxburgh name to make sure the guest list is A-list, and I have called in a few debts. We will get Cheung involved, I'm sure he'd love the chance to bullshit the glitterati about these 'unbelievable' plans he has for the Asian launch. I'm sure that will give your guests something to talk about for years. After all, it's not everyday a notorious Triad leader gives you his chat! Now is your chance to step out from behind the shadows and show exactly what you are made of. You worry about Robert later, but correct me if I am wrong, the police are here, what with everything that happened with Alexander?"

"Yes," said Victoria from behind a handkerchief.

"Well, after we finish here, you find them and tell them exactly why we are telling everyone Robert has come down with Norovirus. Let them do what they are paid to do, Victoria," and Vanessa took Victoria's hands and clasped them warmly once more.

"What you need to learn from this experience, Vicky, is that in this life you trust no-one, especially men. I have come through failed marriages, to a pop star and an industrialist, and I would have saved myself a whole lot of grief if I'd married neither. And now it seems I am on my own again," said Vanessa.

"What about Detective Sergeant Thoroughgood, Vanessa? You seem like the perfect couple," asked Victoria.

"He's not cool with my life and it looks like his feelings for me are not strong enough to overcome those reservations and his own . . . issues, shall I say. But that is what makes you strong, Victoria. You must learn that you don't always need to be attached to a man. That has become crystal clear to me."

Victoria's discomfort at Vanessa's words of wisdom was clear, as she looked down at her hands and fidgeted with the handkerchief.

"Look, Vicky I know that you are quite taken with the Detective Sergeant and I know that he got you out of a very nasty experience at the Art School, but he is not Mr Perfect by any manner of means. Gus Thoroughgood carries an awful lot of baggage around with him, Vicky, and it is baggage you don't want to become attached to. Trust me."

"What do you mean?" asked Victoria, her face screened by her long chestnut tresses.

"I mean that the Detective Sergeant is a man with a broken heart he doesn't seem capable of mending. His biggest problem is that he can't admit that fact to himself. Until he does . . ." Vanessa deliberately let her words taper off.

"If he has had his heart broken, Vanessa, then surely he deserves the chance to have it mended. I read what he did for you in the papers last year and he must love you to do that. It's not everyday that someone saves your life, surely it's fate that you guys are meant to be together?" asked Victoria, for the first time holding Vanessa's gaze.

"I think the price that the woman who wants to mend Gus Thoroughgood's broken heart will have to pay, is to have hers broken in the process. Because she will always find herself competing with the one thing she can not beat."

"And that is?"

"A ghost called Celine Lynott," answered Vanessa.

For the first time Victoria could see real sadness and what appeared to be almost resignation, in her features.

"So, is it over between you and Gus?"

"I think it was probably over before it ever really started, Vicky. Take my advice and stay well clear. But enough of Gus Thoroughgood, it is you and I against the world this afternoon and we will make it happen, you have my word."

A knock on the trailer door brought their chat to an end as the photographer from Hello! made his presence known and in turn made it clear that Vanessa's presence was very much in demand . . . immediately. The female reporter accompanying him identified herself as Jackie Marquis and asked if she could interview Victoria.

Vanessa smiled reassuringly once more, "This is it, Vicky, showtime. If you need me, you know where to find me, but remember what I said about you-know-who and Robert. Make sure they're your next call."

With that, Vanessa was gone. Victoria offered her hand to the immaculate, raven-haired middle-aged reporter and played the part Vanessa had told her she must.

42

THOROUGHGOOD ENGAGED third gear and listened to the response from his newly-acquired Mini Cooper, "Listen to that, faither, throaty ain't she? So what do you make of the whole Mini experience, then?"

Hardie sat in the passenger seat, his arms folded across his chest, showing as much emotion as a sphinx.

"Slap the Deep Purple CD in for me, mate, and flick it to number nine. I think you'll find Speed King is more than appropriate and features the greatest ever keyboard rock solo by the great Jon Lord."

"Wasn't he a porn star?" Hardie quipped and added, "Naw bad I suppose, Gus. It's bloody well a long way down though, you're gonnae need a crowbar or a crane to get me out of this. In fact, I would say it's even lower slung than the RX-8 and I'll tell you something for nothing, I'd prefer to be firing up the drive way to Roxburgh Hall in the latter. In the name of the wee man, Gus, we are gonnae be looking a bit out of place in a red Mini Cooper with a black and white chequered flag on the lid, to say the least."

"I never had you down for a snob, faither, never in all my days. Well, the boys at Arnold Clark were good enough to have it delivered to me this morn' and I'm afraid when it comes to a nearly new motor I just had to drive the thing. Who cares what the toffs think?"

As they continued through the countryside the rustle of newspaper shook Thoroughgood from his thoughts and he saw to his amazement that Hardie was actually scanning the sports pages of his Daily Telegraph.

"Jeez, why do you read this guff, Gus? This boy Forsyth, aye Roddy Forsyth, he's a day behind the Record – and the Sun, for that matter, with this guff about her Britannic Majesty's XI being after the Israeli striker," snorted Hardie in triumph at the final proof Thoroughgood's favourite read had been exposed as second rate to his preferred tabloid fodder.

"Have you checked the date, faither?" asked Thoroughgood as sarcastically as possible.

"Oh," said Hardie, suitably chastised.

"I think you'll find the weekly Forsyth saga is every bit as up to date as your tabloid friends, but with damn more insight and gravitas attached to it," Thoroughgood laughed long and loud.

"Up ye, with respect, Detective Sergeant," said Hardie grudgingly.

Moments later the discreet sign warning them that Roxburgh Hall was a quarter of a mile away loomed at the side of the road.

"14.15hrs. Not bad timing, Gus. I dunno about you but I am beginning to feel like an extra arriving for an episode of Downton Abbey," quipped Hardie.

"At least your suit doesn't have any stains on it, faither. Nice of you to make an effort, or was it the missus?"

"The missus," admitted Hardie, "Trust me to be wearing a black suit on the warmest day of the year so far. Anyway, that's rich coming from the walking clothes horse that is Gus Thoroughgood. What's with the jacket, mate?"

"This is a Charles Tyrwhitt, 100 percent cool wool, Air Force Stripe, classic fit jacket, faither. With the emphasis being on classic, old fella," laughed Thoroughgood. "What's wrong, you a bit nervous there, faither? How do you think I'm feeling?"

"I wouldn't be worrying about Vanessa, mate. After all, she'll be up to her neck in it. Your worries aren't likely to start until after the launch and by then you'll know which way the wind is blowing all right, mate," advised Hardie.

"You're quite the amateur psychologist, faither. Anyway, here we are, the turn off for the Hall. By the way, you fancy driving us back, old son, and putting Miss Mini Cooper here through her paces?" enquired Thoroughgood.

"Aye, very good. I knew there had to be a reason you wanted me along on your jolly. I take it that means that the sponsor's product will be liberally partaken of by the Detective Sergeant?" asked Hardie.

"As I always say at these moments, Hardie, or correction, as you always say at these moments, faither, privileges of rank, my dear Detective Constable," smirked the DS.

They found themselves in a rapidly growing queue of traffic, directed by a middle-aged man, into a field to their right. To their left was a marquee-laden lawn, while slightly beyond lay a man-made lake with quaint wooden bridges inviting admirers to inspect the exotic vegetation surrounding the brilliantly glimmering water. But it was the gothic magnificence of Roxburgh Hall that really took Hardie's breath away.

His eyes devouring the scene that was unfolding in front of him, the DC couldn't help himself, "How about we go halfers on a taxi, Gus?" and they both roared with laughter.

Moments later they made their way on foot from the field to the entrance – a quaint stone-framed gateway with a slated roof. Producing his invitation Thoroughgood smiled weakly as a male in a gingham-checked shirt looked up from the reception table. It was Macintosh, the butler and estate manager.

"Detective Sergeant Thoroughgood, and . . . partner?" he asked with a sly smile at Hardie.

The DC could not help himself, "That's right, sonny. Just here to make sure you know how to wipe your arse."

Thoroughgood couldn't help showing his agitation, "Listen, Macintosh, can you tell me where I can find . . ." but before he could finish the sentence he heard his name being called.

"Hi, Detective Sergeant, glad you could make it, welcome to Roxburgh Hall," shouted Victoria Roxburgh.

She was standing just yards in front of the huge marquee that was rapidly filling with champagne-swilling guests. Right there, right then, Victoria Roxburgh looked to the manor born.

Thoroughgood heard Hardie mutter, "Holy Moses," in appreciation of the svelte curves that the warm spring sunshine was outlining through her silk leopard print dress.

The detectives headed through the gateway and

Thoroughgood received a welcoming kiss on either cheek from Victoria. Hardie had to make do with a brief handshake.

"There are refreshments and canapés being served in the marquee before the charity show begins, Detective Constable Hardie. You might want to make the most of these and make sure of two good seats for yourself and . . ." Victoria stalled at her over-familiarity towards Thoroughgood, but couldn't help herself, "Gus. You might even want to introduce yourself to my mother, DC Hardie. I have told her all about your kindness at the Art School and she wants to extend her thanks. Oh, and her bark is not as bad as her bite I promise you! I just need to borrow your colleague to tell him about a book I have for him."

Hardie frowned, but quickly replied, "Don't mind if I do, miss," before heading for the marquee.

Thoroughgood found himself ushered towards what looked like stables, and as they entered a corridor just outside the horse stalls, a white stallion poked his nose over a door.

"Pegasus, meet Detective Sergeant Gus Thoroughgood," said Victoria.

"How we doin', boy?" asked Thoroughgood and stroked its nose gently.

He turned to face Victoria, sensing her anxiety. "What's wrong, Vicky?"

"It's Robert," she said. "He has disappeared."

"What do you mean?"

"I haven't heard from him or been able to contact him since Thursday night, when he left me to go down to the boathouse to read over some war diaries belonging to our grandfather. Now his mobile is going straight to voicemail and there's just no way Robbie would miss the day he has worked so hard to bring about."

"Before you go any further, Vicky, let's just hold on a minute. Obviously, I know there's a police investigation into what happened to Alexander. I believe there are police officers in the grounds, including a Detective Inspector Pigeon and his colleague DS Bolt?"

Victoria nodded

"Thank God for that. Well, before you go any further, we need to find DI Pigeon and you need to share your concerns with him. I assume you've not done so already? Have you spoken to anyone else about this?"

"Just Vanessa, but I haven't gone into any details," replied Victoria, feeling very much out of her depth.

"Okay, we need to hook up with DI Pigeon immediately."

"There's more I need to tell you, Gus."

"You should be saving this for the DI, Vicky. He's the OIC. Sorry, he is the officer in charge of the case."

"I don't like him and neither did Robert. I just want to speak to you, Gus."

"All right, fire away, but you are still going to have to speak to the Detective Inspector."

"Before Robert went missing he told me all about a set of war-time diaries he'd found that belonged to our grandfather. What he read in them backed up the stuff in the copy of Ivanhoe you came across, but one of them was missing. Robbie also showed me a threatening letter someone had sent him. All it said was, 'THE OLDEST SIN CASTS THE LONGEST SHADOW'. He believed the message was linked to whatever was in the missing diary. As I said, the last time I saw him was on Thursday night when he was going down to the boathouse to try and work out what was in the missing diary. I haven't seen him since."

"Have you been down to the boathouse?"

"No. I've been flat out 24/7 for the last three or four days, Gus."

"Jeez, Vicky, you should have informed DI Pigeon as soon as you became worried about your brother, and he certainly needs to know about it now. What about the diaries and the threatening letter – had Robbie told the DI about them?"

"Robbie had shown him the letter, but he said he wanted to read the diaries before he handed them over to the Detective Inspector."

"Do you know how Robbie came by the threat? Was it posted or hand delivered?" asked Thoroughgood, his curiosity getting the better of him.

"I'm sorry Gus – all he showed me was a photocopy of the original and it looked like it had been computer printed – it was an A4 sheet of paper. I don't know any more than that."

"Has Robbie done a disappearing act before?"

"Yeah, he has been known to go off on a bender and hit the casinos. Plus, he knew that I had everything under control with the help of your . . ." Victoria hesitated before adding, "Vanessa."

Thoroughgood shifted uncomfortably, aware that he was becoming intoxicated by Victoria's delicious proximity, but he was quickly jolted back to the reality of his own domestic problems.

"I don't think Vanessa sees herself as mine or anyone else's, Vicky. But that's not important. What is important is that we get you to DI Pigeon and give him all the facts. We need to get to the bottom of this before anything else happens and we need to find your brother." Thoroughgood placed a hand on Victoria's elbow and guided her out of the stables.

They found the Detective Inspector inside one of the giant entrances to the marquee. It was clear that he was taking a keen interest in the guests and Thoroughgood's inquisitive glance soon found DS Harry Bolt located almost exactly opposite his gaffer, "Very imaginative," muttered Thoroughgood, drawing a questioning look from Victoria.

"Ah, Thoroughgood, good of you to introduce Miss Roxburgh, but really, it's Robert Roxburgh I need to speak to," said the DI.

"I'm afraid that will be difficult, DI Pigeon, because as Vicky will tell you, he has gone missing."

Pigeon's irritation showed as he snapped, "Very good, Thoroughgood. You can leave this to me now and go and enjoy the fashion show. You must be keen to see your lady friend in her full glory?"

Thoroughgood turned to Victoria, "Just make sure you tell DI Pigeon everything and don't leave the smallest detail out, Vicky. If you need me I'll be in the marquee but don't worry, you will get through this."

Victoria Roxburgh said nothing although the warmth in her eyes spoke volumes and Thoroughgood left them with his emotions back in the blender.

He found Hardie leaning lazily on a high drinks table, halfway between one of the chocolate fountains and a refreshment table that was groaning under the weight of massed ranks of champagne glasses.

"Feck me, it's like a Who's Who in here. Footballers, politicians and the aristocracy. Plus a photographer from one of those posh mags, jumping aboot like a kangaroo on fire! Fancy a game of I spy, Gus, son? Anyway, what's new, mate? I hope you haven't been messing with Miss Victoria's heart again?"

"We've got a problem – or rather, Randy Pigeon has. It looks like someone, almost certainly the same someone who took out Alexander Roxburgh, has now completed the family double on his big brother Robert who went missing just 48hours before his defining moment. Now ask yourself why, Hardie?" said Thoroughgood.

"It's pretty bloody clear. Someone who doesn't want the Roxburghs saved, someone who is nursing some kind of grievance towards them. Christ, it must be a helluva grievance right enough."

"A grievance that I believe has its answers in a 70-year-old set of war-time diaries. Journals that reveal Ludovic, grand-daddy Roxburgh, the celebrated war-time hero and member of Churchill's war-time government, was a philanderer who was involved in some sort of affair that may well provide the answer to this whole mess."

"All of which Pigeon is currently being made aware of by Miss Victoria? Right?" enquired Hardie and was met by a curt nod from Thoroughgood. "Aye, like I said a while back, Gus, thank Gawd this is his enquiry and not ours, mate. Plus, if you go getting involved at this stage, old Randy will blow a gasket and rightly so. I think we just need to take our seats at the side of the catwalk, enjoy the scenery and let DI Pigeon show us what a top cop he is."

"That's all very well, faither, but Vicky is in danger

and so is the Dowager Lady Elizabeth. I would put good money on there being someone under this bloody tent who wants them dead."

"So who stands to make the most of it if this deal falls through? It's gotta be Cheung, I would imagine. If he is bankrolling the whole thing and the Roxburghs are just its respectable front, default on the terms would put him and his, what are they called again?"

"Gwai Lo – Ghost Men in English," answered Thoroughgood helpfully.

"Exactly, them, in complete control. So it's gotta be Cheung who's behind this, although it's a bit bleedin' obvious. Plus, Pigeon has already had him questioned."

Thoroughgood's features were a study in bafflement, "What if someone had discovered dirt on the Roxburghs and informed Cheung for a tidy sum? Victoria told me that the last time she saw Robert he showed her some threatening letter with the phrase: 'THE OLDEST SIN CASTS THE LONGEST SHADOW' on it. I think the secret is in these bloody diaries," said Thoroughgood.

"So where are they?"

"That's just it. Robert Roxburgh only had three of them – the fourth one was missing and is presumably in the hands of our unknown assassin, or assassins."

"So find the diaries and we find our killer," said Hardie.

Before Thoroughgood could answer, a familiar female voice could be heard behind him. As he turned round his eyes immediately locked on the sight of Vanessa Velvet in full 1930's cocktail dress magnificence, standing on the temporary stage at the end of the catwalk.

"Ladies and gentlemen, please take your seats. The

show will start in precisely five minutes," she said into a microphone. Her gaze found the DS and Thoroughgood went comfortably numb.

"By Christ, she scrubs up well!" said Hardie.

43

THOROUGHGOOD NODDED to Hardie to make his way to the exit and was impaled on a scowl for his trouble.

Heading outside, the duo found they were walking against the tide as the guests headed for the seats surrounding the catwalk. As Thoroughgood glanced back he saw that Hardie was still clutching his champagne glass and attempting to drain its contents on the move.

"Put that down man, we have work to do. Get a move on, Hardie."

As they headed over the lush lawn Thoroughgood found his arm gripped tight and turned to find Hardie had clamped a hand on him. "Listen, Gus, I can guess what you are up to. It ain't right and it's gonnae land us in the soup good and proper with DI Pigeon."

"For cryin' out loud, Hardie, you know as well as I do that Pigeon couldn't catch a cold. He's been dragging his feet with this whole enquiry like he does with every bloody investigation that comes his way. We need to get down to that boathouse and give it the once over. Now are you in or out on this? Because we don't have time to fuck about."

Hardie folded his arms and dug his heels in, "Look, Gus, this isn't your fight. You're probably still exhausted from all that shit with the Poles. Why don't you come back into the marquee, sample the champers and enjoy the show?"

"No can do," snapped the DS, his green eyes blazing anger.

"I'm sorry, Gus, but you're on your own on this one. For Chrissakes – never mind cutting Pigeon's grass, we ain't even on duty," said Hardie flatly.

"All right, Hardie, have it your way, but if you are going to sit on your arse you can at least make yourself useful. Promise me you won't let Vicky Roxburgh out of your sight."

"You have my word," said Hardie and with an air of resignation he turned and marched back into the marquee.

Thoroughgood walked down the dirt lane that led to the boathouse, and as he turned right he took in the view. A single storey building with a clock tower positioned centrally, which had an archway acting as the entrance to a courtyard through which lay a shingled beach and a jetty.

Thoroughgood's anger from his spat with Hardie still burned and the DS took a deep breath as he tried to regain his focus on the job in hand. He knew he was breaking all the rules and was possibly about to contaminate a potential crime scene, but equally he knew he didn't have time to play by the usual rules of police procedure. The bottom line was that whoever was behind the terrorising of the Roxburgh family would do everything in their power to wreak their havoc before the crowning glory of the launch and, with it, the Roxburgh's salvation.

Thoroughgood clocked what appeared to be the office to his left. He placed his hand inside a handkerchief and tried the handle of a rickety door with its faded blue paintwork barely visible. Although locked, three dunts from his shoulder sprung it open.

Thoroughgood strode in and scanned the office and its contents. A splintered desk which had certainly seen better days, but it was what was on the desk's surface that grabbed his attention. A bottle of 18-year-old The Roxburgh single malt with maybe one glass, perhaps two, missing from it; an old jug, half-full of water, at an odd angle on the desk top. A shoogly waste paper bin held the whisky bottle's black peel.

Something else caught his eye, on the cold flagstone floor. Bending down, Thoroughgood pulled a pen from his inside pocket and lifted the object gently, making sure he avoided contaminating a potential piece of evidence. It was a strip of blue silk ribbon. He replaced it where it had been.

He tried the drawers and found them empty. "Damn!" said Thoroughgood, his hope that the diaries lay inside proving a forlorn one.

An old dresser to the left of the desk also proved useless. He observed a set of hooks holding various keys and noticed the one named 'Boat Store' was missing its key.

Thoroughgood stared through the window at the beauty of Loch Lomond while he summed up his thoughts, 'So, Roxburgh comes in for a dram and a butchers at the diaries and then what? No sign of a struggle, but then no sign of the diaries? Blue ribbon must have been used to bind them, so why leave the ribbon but not the diaries? Where is the whisky glass?' Boat store key gone.'

He thought aloud, "Outside."

He ran out of the office and made his way down on to the shingle beach looking left and right for anything that may help him. Staring down at the water, its calm irritated him and he put that down to the exhaustion of the preceding days catching up with him, 'Maybe Hardie was right, Gus, there's nothing here for you, mate, time to head back to the marquee and play the game.'

At that moment a glint of brilliant light flashed its reflection out of the tiny wavelets that were breaking on the shingle. It was a whisky glass. Thoroughgood picked it up by its rim with the help of his hanky and sniffed for content. The trace of whisky, washed out as it had been by the water, was slight but still discernible. He replaced the glass where he had found it.

'The diaries must have stayed inside the office. So Roxburgh came out here to enjoy his dram and maybe digest what he had just been reading, leaving the diaries in the office and then . . .' the voice inside his head once again escaped, "Whack," said Thoroughgood.

He began to check the shingle for any signs of a struggle. To his left a log sat on a raised part of the beach and there, impaled on a splinter, was a torn shred of navy blue wool.

Thoroughgood ran his eyes across the log and noticed a dark-coloured patch at the thicker of its two ends. The conclusion he leapt to was the obvious one – the log had either been used to assault Roxburgh or had in fact been the murder weapon.

'So where is Roxburgh's body if he's bought it?' he asked himself as a seagull squawked overhead.

He continued along the shingle, searching for he knew not what. He headed for a clump of trees, all the time seeking for any signs that a body had been dragged along the shingle. Nothing. As his attention fixed on a small island about 100 metres out, it dawned on him he had been going in the wrong direction.

"Put two and two together for once, Thoroughgood," he chastised himself before retracing his steps, back past the log and towards the small jetty, which he now realised was directly opposite the island.

Quickly, he walked out to the edge of the jetty and, as he hunkered down, observed small dark rivulets that had congealed onto the wood.

That was it, Thoroughgood reasoned, Roxburgh had been attacked from behind then dragged to the jetty, and was most probably dead, before being rowed out in the missing boat to the island where his body was probably concealed.

As he gazed out to the island the DS had no doubt it would prove to be the final resting place of Robert Roxburgh. But Thoroughgood couldn't help himself shaking his head. 'Something ain't right, pal,' said the voice in his head.

The sound of footsteps snapped the DS back to the here and now. Turning round he saw the grey-bearded, shiny-domed presence of Detective Inspector Randolph Pigeon marching down the jetty with DS Harry Bolt in his wake. Pigeon stopped a foot short of Thoroughgood and smashed his right hand off the DS' jaw.

44

THOROUGHGOOD RAISED himself on his elbows and looked up into Pigeon's livid features then ran his right hand across his throbbing jaw; tasted blood.

"Just what the fuck do you think you're doin', Thoroughgood? In fact, don't bother answering that because we both know what you're up to, don't we Detective Sergeant?"

"You're cuttin' my bleedin' grass, you son of a bitch, and tryin' to play the hero again in front of Miss Victoria and your Velvet tart. 'Thoroughgood the hero copper saves the day at Roxburgh Hall' – you just can't get enough of the headlines, can you Thoroughgood? You've become as much a fame junkie as your celebrity girlfriend. That's it though, Thoroughgood, you want a piece of the limelight and you've been tryin' to hog it ever since that business with that crazy fuck Tariq, the Imam. Every high-profile case that comes up you've got to get your fingers into it, you snivellin' arsewipe. But not this one, Thoroughgood. Not my case, not my investigation. You will swing for this and I'll make sure of it. You are finished."

Thoroughgood shakily hauled himself to his feet and

grabbed hold of one of the wooden stanchions at the side of the jetty. He took a deep breath. "Hold on a minute, Pigeon, you are way wide of the mark," but before he could plead his case for the defence Pigeon lunged at him and grabbed his lapels.

Their faces millimetres away from each other, Pigeon let the DS have it with both barrels, "Don't even try and bullshit me, Thoroughgood. Even your own man has refused to back you up on this one. You grilled Victoria Roxburgh before I had the chance and left me to take her statement knowing it was going to take time to get the job done properly and knowing that would give you enough space to snoop around the crime scene and steal a march on me. You treacherous bastard, this job is hard enough without you trying to trip up your own side."

Thoroughgood had had enough. He brought his fists up in a violent motion that knocked Pigeon's hands free, then rammed a right hand into the DI's midriff. Pigeon staggered back clutching his guts while Bolt quickly propped him up. Wiping the blood away from the side of his mouth, Thoroughgood decided there was no point in observing the niceties, "Why don't you get a grip, Pigeon? The truth is, you're out your depth and if you hadn't been dragging your feet as usual then Robert Roxburgh would never have gone missing. You're right about what you said, but I only wanted to get down here and get things moving as quickly as possible because we don't have time to pussyfoot about. This is a crime scene all right, and one that will probably lead you to Robert Roxburgh's body out there."

Thoroughgood stopped in full flow, turned and pointed to the tree-covered island in the loch and added, "Because

I am confident somewhere on that island is the sixth Viscount Roxburgh, most certainly dead rather than alive. You know what that will mean, Pigeon?"

The Detective Inspector had straightened up, but a hate-filled scowl was his only response.

"It will mean that whoever is behind these killings will then be trying to take out Lady Elizabeth and Victoria Roxburgh, and most probably before the launch reaches its climax. So, can you see why I might have been doing your dirty work for you, Pigeon? Time, man, is the answer. Or is that just too much to ask of you . . . Detective Inspector?" Thoroughgood drawled out the last two words with as much sarcasm as he could muster.

As the winded Pigeon continued to gasp for breath it was Bolt who asked the obvious question, "So what have you found, Thoroughgood?"

"Almost certainly the scene of Robert Roxburgh's murder. In the boathouse office you'll find a piece of ribbon most probably used to bind the diaries Roxburgh was reading. Next is the whisky glass glistening out from the tide, down there on the beach, where you will also find a piece of navy blue wool impaled on a log, which happens to be blood-splattered, just like the jetty. Then there is the missing key from the boat store, and most likely one of the boats with it . . . do you think you can join up the numbers? But I'm done doin' your donkey work for you, Lightning. Somewhere on that island you'll find Robert Roxburgh's body. Now, if you don't mind, I'm gonna catch the rest of the fashion show, safe in the knowledge that StrathPol's two finest detectives are on the job." With that, Thoroughgood walked straight past Pigeon and Bolt.

As he reached the end of the jetty Pigeon called out, "For fuck's sake, Thoroughgood, come back here."

Thoroughgood raised the index finger of his right hand, stuck it in the air and kept walking.

Thoroughgood strode into the boathouse courtyard, his mind a maelstrom of emotion. Had he been wrong? If he put himself in Pigeon's shoes, would he have reacted the same way? But then, what mattered most was time. The killer would strike again and there were only two targets left. It had to be Cheung. But Thoroughgood could not square the crime scene he had just seen with one that the Triad boss or his minions would have left, certainly not after doing something he guessed would be old hat to them.

Thoroughgood knew that something wasn't right; something jarred, and the problem was that he couldn't trust Pigeon to pick up on it. Then again, if Roxburgh's body was found on the island, surely there would be something of evidential value that could point the DI in the direction of his murderer.

"Clumsy, too bloody clumsy," said Thoroughgood out loud and then realised that he was no longer alone.

Standing under the clock tower arch, leaning against one of its stone walls, was Macintosh. His body reclined at an angle against the curving wall that arched into the roof.

"Please don't take this the wrong way, Detective Sergeant, but is there something wrong? Can I help in any way?" he asked.

"Yeah, probably a whole lot, mate. You will need to hold it there, Macintosh. This boathouse and the beach have become a crime scene. Do you mind if I ask you a couple of questions, pal?"

Macintosh nodded.

"When was the last time you saw Viscount Roxburgh – and did he mention anything out of the ordinary to you, indicate anything had been troubling him?"

Macintosh took his time, allowing the pause to draw out and finally answered, "You mean his grandfather's diaries?"

"That is exactly what I mean, Macintosh. Can you elaborate a bit on that? Did the Viscount show you them at any time, or go into any detail about what they contained?"

"I believe they revealed evidence of Lord Roxburgh's marital infidelity, Detective Sergeant. The problem was that Viscount Robert did not have possession of the full set and one of the diaries was missing. Beyond that I can't help you."

"By the way, how long have you been here on the estate, Macintosh?"

"All my life, man and boy. It is my home."

"That is very helpful, Macintosh, thank you. Has DI Pigeon spoken to you yet?"

Macintosh shook his head

"Then I'm afraid I'm going to have to ask you to make the Detective Inspector aware of all of this, but also to forget we had this little chat. Comprendez?"

"What chat?" smiled Macintosh.

Thoroughgood offered his hand to Macintosh. "Cheers."

Moments later Thoroughgood slipped into the empty chair situated next to Hardie's generous proportions.

The DC took a sideways glance at his mate and said in a barely audible voice, "Well, was it worth it?"

"We'll know soon enough, mate," replied Thoroughgood.

45

THE SOUND of applause from either side of the catwalk provided proof, if any were needed, that the fashion show had been an outstanding success.

The presentation of Vanessa's 'Siren' spring collection, augmented by a secondary 1930's themed show had proven the perfect mix between the provocative, slightly shocking and timeless elegant classics that were the epitome of high pre-war chic. When the fashion queen took to the stage in a gold and red lamé dress that reached to the ankle, and also boasted a plunging v-shaped back line, Vanessa' s audience were enraptured.

"Thank you, everyone, and can I just record my appreciation for your generosity. All proceeds from the tops and tails collection which will go towards Macmillan Cancer Care. I hope you have enjoyed both the exclusive modelling of my new Siren range for spring and also our peek back at 1930's glamour. We will now have a 30 minute comfort break while the marquee is refigured for the main event of the day – the launch of The Dark Ocean Roxburgh signature whisky liqueur."

Another warm round of appreciation swept through the marquee which gradually gave way to the hum of expectant conversation.

Hardie turned to Thoroughgood, "Look, before you have a go at me, Gus, I went backstage to try and keep tabs on Victoria, but there were women everywhere with hee haw on. I've never been so embarrassed in my life."

Despite himself, Thoroughgood laughed, "God, I'd love to have been a fly on the tent canvas for that one, faither. You and a bunch of scantily-clad models, all nice and cosy. Priceless. Anyway, there's probably no safer place for her right now. So don't sweat it, mate."

Hardie smiled with relief, "Why don't you join me at the bar, Gus? I figure we have plenty to talk about before the 'main event', as Vanessa called it, gets under way and . . ."

Before he could finish his sentence Vanessa's eye-catching figure materialised at his side. "My two favourite detectives," she smiled. "It's great that you decided to come. Why don't you treat me to a glass of fizz before they get the stage turned around for the launch? I'm absolutely parched."

Hardie seized his opportunity, "I'll get them in, Vanessa, and give you two time for a quick catch-up. I'll find us a table at the back of the marquee and you can join me there," with that the DC ambled off.

Vanessa slipped her fingers around Thoroughgood's left hand and gave it a slight squeeze, "I'm glad you came, Gus, really glad," she said.

"It was the least I could do, Vanessa," said Thoroughgood, then added with an apologetic smile, "I'm sorry about what happened back at the flat, I said some things I regret, things that weren't true, words you didn't deserve to hear."

"It's okay, Gus, all that matters is that you've come

along today. Now let's go and get that drink. I promised I'd help Vicky out backstage before she makes her big speech."

Moments later they joined Hardie at one of the tall tables at the back of the marquee, but before the conversation could flow it was interrupted by an uninvited guest.

"Miss Velvet, may I introduce myself? Raymond Cheung, at your service. Your pardon gentlemen, if you please, for my interruption, but permit me to congratulate you, Miss Velvet, on your fashion show. May I also say how stunning you look. As is evidenced by your dress, the males of our 1930s species were far luckier than ourselves, gentlemen. I'm sure you will agree," said the Triad boss.

Thoroughgood smiled awkwardly and Hardie stared at his black penny loafers.

Vanessa took Cheung's proffered hand and quickly found a kiss bestowed on the back of her own, "Enchanté, Miss Velvet, I am sure," said Cheung bowing courteously. However as he rose, his dark eyes gave both Thoroughgood and Hardie a frank assessment.

"Again, forgive me for being so bold, but would I be correct in assuming that you two gentlemen are Detective Sergeant Thoroughgood and DC Hardie?"

"You would be correct, Mr Cheung," replied Thoroughgood, noting Cheung's failure to extend a warm hand of friendship to either Hardie or himself.

"Alas, it is such a shame that Viscount Roxburgh has been taken ill. But just as well for the Roxburghs that Miss Victoria is proving a more than capable deputy. Now, though, I must prepare to play my part. Excuse

266

me, Miss Velvet, gentlemen," said Cheung as his gaze returned to rest on Vanessa. "I am sure we will meet again, Miss Velvet," he said, and with a nod, Cheung headed towards the curtain at the rear of the temporary stage, his every movement shadowed by his bodyguard Lam.

"Jesus H Christ, he's got some neck on him," Hardie said with an impish smile. "Looks like you've got another admirer there though, Vanessa. Big time,"

"Yeah, you better watch him behind the curtain, Vanessa, he might find himself unable to resist your little lamé number, there," added Thoroughgood.

Vanessa laughed in an endearingly girlish way, but as she placed her champagne glass to her lips, Thoroughgood quickly turned and muttered to Hardie, "We need to speak, pronto, faither."

Vanessa's ears pricked up. "I heard that Gus, I know there is a lot going on behind the scenes with the Roxburghs – but can we just enjoy a moment before I have to go? After all, isn't this DI Pigeon's bird?" she added, laughing at her own joke.

"Hi-lar-ious, darling," smiled Thoroughgood.

Before Vanessa could take her leave, Lady Elizabeth swept up to the table, escorted by the now blazered figure of Macintosh. "My dear Miss Velvet, I think we can safely call your little diversion a triumph. Let us hope it has not stolen the show ahead of the launch. Thank God that loathesome little man has gone," said the dowager, referring to Cheung. "My interruption was two-fold, Miss Velvet," she added." I also wanted to take the opportunity to thank your two policemen friends for helping Victoria out at the School of Art – that dreadful business with the Pole. Thank you indeed, Detective Sergeant and colleague," Lady Elizabeth smiled.

"I believe Mr Thoroughgood's colleague is Detective Constable Hardie, Lady Elizabeth," volunteered Macintosh without prompting, before smiling thinly.

Lady Elizabeth adjusted her position slightly, fingering the pearls that habitually adorned her neck and were currently framed in the high collar of a crisp silk Parisian blouse, "Thank you, Thomas, I don't know what I would do without you," she said with surprising warmth.

The dowager added, "We had better not keep you, Miss Velvet – I gather you are assisting Victoria for the launch. Again, my grateful thanks, it is just rotten luck that Robert is in quarantine." With that, she continued her regal progress over to a group of similarly elegant ladies, with Macintosh still in tow.

"Wow!" said Vanessa before checking her Cartier. "I better go, boys," and she ran her fingers down Thoroughgood's shoulder before smiling brilliantly and heading for the stage.

"I'm speechless," was all Hardie could manage.

Thoroughgood laughed in reply and signalled to his mate to move closer. As they huddled round the drinks table he said, "Just as well, because we need to speak and we need to speak quickly. I take it that despite your little ethical fit you want to hear what went down at the boathouse?"

"I'm all ears," said Hardie.

"Roxburgh's dead, all right. I'm convinced of it, and everything down at the boathouse points to it being the murder locus."

"Body?"

"Nowhere to be seen, but I would wager your pension on it being discovered some time very soon on a little island about 100 metres off shore. When it is, the shit will well and truly hit the fan."

"How you mean, mon gaffeur?"

"Because there is only one suspect and Pigeon will jump at the opportunity to make a grandstand arrest," replied Thoroughgood.

"So I was right all along, it's gotta be Cheung."

"That's just it, Cheung may be the only suspect, but I don't like it. The boathouse was like an amateur night out, it was just too messy, the clues too helpful."

"So what did you come across at the boathouse, Gus?" asked Hardie.

"The bottom line is that Roxburgh has been in the office reading the diaries and trying to put together their jigsaw. I think he's come across something that has finally made it all add up. Then he takes his dram outside while he stares into the loch, the moon, the wide blue yonder, or whatever else he had to do to comprehend it and whack, he's taken out. On the beach we have his empty whisky glass, a bloodstained log which helpfully has a piece of blue wool from whatever he was wearing attached to it. To round it all off, the jetty just along the shingle also has bloodstains on it and the keys to the boat store and most probably one of the boats are also gone. That doesn't just add up – it goes off the bleedin' Richter scale."

46

"SO WHAT do we do next?" asked Hardie before throwing the rest of the champagne down his throat.

"It's a waiting game and as DI Pigeon so succinctly pointed out, it ain't our game."

The music that had been piped through the discreetly located speakers stationed throughout the marquee faded and a slightly clipped voice announced, "Ladies and gentlemen, we have five minutes left before the launch of The Dark Ocean, please take your seats."

"That bleedin' Macintosh gets everywhere," said Hardie before continuing, "What did you make of him and Lady Elizabeth, mate? Thomas, eh? All a bit cosy, but to be fair to the Dowager, as the saying goes, she'd still get it," concluded the DC smugly.

"I'll make sure your missus is aware of your admiration for Lady Elizabeth, asap, faither. Aye, it is all a bit familiar. Did you notice he was cradling her arm in his paw when she was over talking to the vintage birds at the big table in the corner? Nope, I'd say there is something going on there and maybe it's just as well, Kenny, 'cos she clearly doesn't have the slightest clue about the shit that is about to hit the fan over her eldest son's likely departure from his mortal coil."

"Fair enough, governor. So what now? You want to hang fire up here and maintain a watching brief from a discreet distance? Or get down the front row and make sure we are in pole position for the first drop of sponsor's product coming our way?"

"Let's just stay where we are, and let's also take it easy on the laughing juice, DC Hardie. I don't know how this is all going to play out."

Hardie responded with a sigh and a glum nod before staring balefully at the champagne glass he had just drained.

The silence between them was soon broken as the refrains of Highland Cathedral piped out from the speakers and the curtains opened to reveal Victoria Roxburgh sweeping onto the stage, her silken leopard-print number having been replaced by a gold and silver mandarin-collared creation with a thigh length split that was obviously a nod to Cheung, and equally clearly from Vanessa's Siren collection.

"Holy mother of Kazan," said Thoroughgood.

"You never told me you knew her, mate," Hardie quipped.

As Victoria reached the podium to the right of the stage the huge screen behind her began to replay scenes from the history and geography of the Roxburgh's story as the family's long association with the whisky industry flashed in front of the enthralled audience. Then the lighting was killed and up through the floor, three stands wreathed in dry ice mist rose, all carrying elegantly shaped liqueur bottles. The screen flashed a close-up of a bottle of The Dark Ocean with a backdrop that matched its name.

Victoria swept the audience with a serene gaze and cleared her throat, her nerves showing for the first time, "The Roxburgh family is proud of its unique 200 year association with the whisky industry, proud of our reputation for the production of the best malt whisky in Scotland. But I am here today to create a new chapter in our proud history. We have never been scared to innovate and diversify in our search for excellence that will add to the Roxburgh brand and today, ladies and gentlemen, it is time for you to meet the new addition to the Roxburgh family." She paused. A man garbed in the Glen Lomond distillery livery and apron wheeled out a leather trunk towards Victoria. He opened the trunk and removed a bottle of the liqueur and placed it on the cask.

"I am proud to present to you, The Dark Ocean," said Victoria. "A new and unique whisky liqueur developed for the discerning modern palate. But before we let you savour the delights of The Dark Ocean I would like to introduce you to someone, without whom this new chapter in our history would never have been written," Victoria took a deep breath, before continuing, "Ladies and gentlemen, I would like you to meet Mr Raymond Cheung, the head of the Gwai Lo consortium, our partners in this unique development, which is, I am sure, about to take the whisky world by storm."

It was just as well that Victoria led the applause because the impact of her introduction had clearly sent a tremor of shock through the stunned audience.

As Cheung took to the stage Hardie muttered, "Here we go," but before Thoroughgood had time to respond there was a commotion at the marquee entrance just behind them and Detective Inspector Randolph Pigeon entered, accompanied by DS Harry Bolt.

Pigeon unsuccessfully attempted to catch Thoroughgood's gaze and after a short pause the DI covered the ten yards between them to arrive at their table. "Glad to see you have taken my advice, Thoroughgood, and started to enjoy yourself," said Pigeon, purposely eyeing the empty champagne glasses on the table.

Thoroughgood ignored the jibe and deliberately stared at the stage, where Cheung's nasal tones could be heard addressing the audience, "Ladies and gentlemen, did you know that 80 percent of Chinese millionaires are under 45? Further, that they love brands with history, heritage and provenance. I am proud that the Gwai Lo have been invited to help burnish the Roxburgh brand, extol its long tradition and present exclusive opportunities to enjoy and associate with the excitement of the new Dark Ocean liqueur, to a market that will, I am confident, make the Dark Ocean the top selling whisky liqueur in the world," said Cheung flashing a sickly smile.

He continued, "Let me tell you how proud I am of our partnership, and just how confident we are of its ensuing success. In Beijing right now we have a 15,000 square foot, four-storey building in the process of being branded and liveried as the Ludovic Roxburgh House, in honour of Victoria's grandfather, the great war-time hero." Cheung paused for effect and turned back towards the giant screen that had now flashed up a huge shot of the building with an image of Ludovic Roxburgh's leonine features projected onto it.

He returned to the audience, "This building will house a club for discerning Chinese whisky lovers and it stands in a quiet courtyard, just a stone's throw from Tiananmen

273

Square," Cheung stopped to sample the impact of his words.

He was not disappointed by the gasps escaping from the audience now seated around tables that were set to a 1930's Parisian night club theme. As Cheung let his silence draw out for effect, the waiting staff began to move around the tables, garbed in outfits that were the epitome of pre-war Paris, making sure that each table had a bottle of the Dark Ocean, glasses and bottles of water, lemonade and ginger ale.

"And now you know how confident we are about the unique quality of the Dark Ocean it is time, ladies and gentlemen, that you sampled it." Cheung called out, "Miss Victoria," and Victoria Roxburgh glided onto the stage to take up position at the other side of the sherry cask.

Holding his hand out Cheung took Victoria's and placed a kiss on the back of it then uttered one word, "Enchanté."

"Bet the smarmy bastard does that to every bird he meets," muttered Hardie to Thoroughgood as the duo looked on, spellbound.

Cheung stepped across to the bottle of Dark Ocean on the upturned sherry cask, poured a generous measure into the two glasses sitting on the table and lifted them, handing one to Victoria.

"Ladies and gentlemen, may you be the first to enjoy the pleasures of the Dark Ocean. Enjoy," and with that Cheung toasted Victoria and turned to the guests, "Slianthe" said the Triad boss triumphantly. No sooner had he replaced his empty glass on the sherry cask than the watching detectives' attention was drawn to the side of the stage where Pigeon and Bolt had arrived.

"Please, no," muttered Thoroughgood. But his worst fears were about to be realised and Pigeon mounted the stage with Bolt behind him and strode across to the Triad boss whose expression reflected his total disbelief at the scene unfolding in front of him.

"Raymond Cheung," boomed Pigeon, "I am arresting you for the murders of Alexander and Robert Roxburgh. I must inform you that you do not need to say anything but anything you do say maybe taken down and used in evidence against you. Have you anything to say?" demanded Pigeon, basking in his moment of supreme triumph.

"This is ridiculous . . ." began Cheung before he regained his composure and clamped his lips firmly shut.

"I thought not. DS Bolt, do the needful," ordered Pigeon. Bolt slapped the cuffs on Cheung as the press photographers snapped away in a frenzy.

Bolt and Pigeon escorted Cheung briskly offstage as his bodyguard, Lam, attempted to bar their path. He slid his hand inside his jacket, stopping when Cheung quickly nodded a warning that he was to go no further.

Before Lam could move, two uniformed cops materialised at his side and grabbed an arm each. Both men were frogmarched through the marquee as bedlam erupted amongst the great and the good all around them.

47

CHEUNG WAS propelled towards the exit, with his bodyguard roughhoused along in his wake by his two uniform attendants and Pigeon strolling triumphantly, yards behind them.

A flash lit up the marquee with a whole battery following it as the Hello! magazine photographer filled his boots with pics of what was sure to be the biggest scandal in the Scottish social calendar of that year, or many another. Jackie Marquis caught up with Pigeon and rammed her dictaphone in front of his face,

"DI Pigeon, what can you tell us?"

Pigeon played the straight bat, "Absolutely no comment."

"Can you confirm you have just arrested Raymond Cheung on suspicion of murdering both the Roxburgh brothers?" persisted Marquis, panting with excitement at her unexpected scoop.

Pigeon turned to face the reporter full on and with her photographer hovering behind her, the DI smiled benignly and said, "Correct."

Detective Inspector Randolph Pigeon had just made the biggest arrest of his career – one he knew would take him a massive step towards achieving his lifelong ambition of one day becoming Assistant Chief Constable, Crime. The photographer's flash lit up his face. Then the DI marched off as he sought to battle his way through the melee of disbelieving guests.

Ahead of him Cheung had almost reached the marquee entrance when he spotted Thoroughgood, just yards away. The Triad leader muttered something to Bolt and the DS obligingly drew to a halt, allowing Cheung to shout across to Thoroughgood,

"Please, Detective Sergeant, assure Lady Roxburgh and Miss Victoria I am innocent and will prove myself so. Tell them the Dark Ocean will not be ruined by this ludicrous . . ."

Bolt snapped, "Enough," and dragged Cheung out the tent.

"Cheung an innocent man, eh! Methinks he doth protest too much," said Hardie.

Pigeon diverted from the slipstream of his prisoners and strode over to Thoroughgood and Hardie, a broad smile on his face. "Is there anything you want to say to me, Detective Sergeant Thoroughgood?" asked Pigeon, almost glowing with triumph.

"Are you sure you've got the right man?" asked Thoroughgood, his voice emotionless.

"Never surer, Thoroughgood, but no surprise that you could doubt the ability of any copper to close a case of this profile other than yourself. We have Cheung and his underling Lam bang to rights," crowed Pigeon.

"Based on what, Detective Inspector? The evidence down at the boathouse, or what you located on the island opposite it?" asked Thoroughgood, examining the bottom of an empty champagne glass in an attempt to mask his fascination.

"Oh, that and a whole lot more, Thoroughgood. I'm afraid you were right about Robert Roxburgh. We discovered his body on the island. He had been garrotted to death. An imaginative MO, and one used regularly by the Triads, funnily enough," said Pigeon, his smugness obvious.

"It's hardly enough to slap the cuffs on Cheung, with respect, of course, Detective Inspector," said Hardie.

"You're right, DC Hardie, but thankfully some new evidence has come to light that has made the case for the prosecution overwhelming." Pigeon stopped abruptly, forcing Thoroughgood to ask the inevitable.

"Which is?"

Pigeon stroked the grey goatee that enveloped his chin and was in stark contrast to his shiny dome, as if in a severe dilemma over whether to spill. He smiled, "Under normal circumstances I couldn't possibly share information from a case with an officer not on the enquiry team, but you have been helpful, Thoroughgood, eventually. I'll give you that."

"Kind of you to say so," responded Thoroughgood, "and here I was, thinking all I was going to have to show for that help was a sore jaw and a burst mouth."

"Indeed. Heat of the moment stuff. Actually, we have two new pieces of evidence that are damning in the extreme as far as Cheung is concerned. I have managed to get hold of the contracts for the deal between the Roxburghs and the Gwai Lo and there is a very imaginative penalty clause within it. Not one but two, in fact. The first was that if the Roxburghs failed to meet 80 percent of their sales and production targets they would forfeit any power on the board and lose control of their distillery. Both Robert and Alexander Roxburgh were aware of this." Pigeon took a breather.

"And the second?" asked Hardie.

"The second penalty clause was cleverly camouflaged in the T's and C's, as they call them. This specified that if Robert, or both he and Alexander predeceased the completion of the deal, marked by the launch, then Cheung would assume complete and personal control of the Roxburgh whisky empire. I know for a fact that Alexander had no knowledge of this clause and I have grave doubts, although no proof, that Robert knew either. But I believe he missed the second clause, probably because he was too busy celebrating the seven figure bail-out he had negotiated. Now both are conveniently dead and Cheung is the last man standing. Things look very bleak for Lady Elizabeth and Victoria Roxburgh," concluded Pigeon.

"Nasty. The Roxburghs have been done up like proverbial kippers," said Hardie while Thoroughgood remained stone-faced.

Pigeon held his hand up just as Hardie made to speak again, "But there's more, and this is game, set and match. The set of three diaries that Robert Roxburgh was reading on the night of his murder were recovered by uniform officers from the glove compartment of Cheung's underling's car, just over half an hour ago."

Hardie's eyebrows shot up in amazement, "I guess it's like you said, DI Pigeon, game, set and match to the StrathPol."

Thoroughgood remained unconvinced, "What about the other diary?"

Irritation swept over Pigeon's features, "Damnation, Thoroughgood – the weight of evidence is overwhelming yet it is still not good enough for you. Anyone would think you were on Cheung's payroll, you bastard."

Thoroughgood lunged across the table, grabbing the DI by his coat and pulling him across the wooden surface between them, "Now you listen to me, Pigeon. You've just shattered the Roxburghs' lives in one fell swoop by announcing, in front of both Lady Elizabeth and Victoria and an audience of hundreds, that Robert Roxburgh has been murdered, with not a thought for either of them. All you care about is making the big arrest and climbing the next rung and it doesn't matter what the fallout is as long as your ambition is sated, you prick. But I remember your friend DCI Henry Farrell and his cosy little arrangement with Declan Meechan, and I think to myself just how close were you to friend Henry . . . so if you want to make aspersions like that be prepared for return fire, Pigeon. Now if you don't mind, someone better go and pick up the pieces because you have just blown the Roxburgh's world to smithereens." Thoroughgood launched the DI backwards and permitted himself a smile as Pigeon tripped and fell flat on his backside just inside the marquee entrance.

Turning to Hardie, Thoroughgood asked, "Are you coming?" and stormed through the gathering crowd of disbelieving guests without waiting for an answer.

In his wake Hardie quickly made his way round the table and helped the raging Pigeon to his feet. "Aye, I've seen death messages delivered with a bit more sensitivity, to say the least, Detective Inspector. With respect, of course" said Hardie, and walked off.

By the time Thoroughgood had arrived at the front of the stage Victoria was nowhere to be seen and Lady Elizabeth had also been ushered away. Just as Hardie caught up with him Vanessa called out, "Gus, over here!"

The two detectives made their way over to Vanessa. "How are they?" Thoroughgood asked.

"Vicky is backstage in a bit of a mess. But the Dowager has vanished. I'm doing my best with Vicky but we need to get her out of here and up to the Hall, away from the audience. I'd be obliged if you could find the Dowager, Gus. To have lost both her sons is something any woman would struggle to cope with, even a woman as formidable as the Lady Elizabeth."

"My guess is that Macintosh will be doing his best to comfort her, Vanessa. We picked up on a couple of signs that they were close, earlier on."

Vanessa ran her hand through her blonde tresses and her agitation was clear, "I can't believe that imbecile Pigeon did that, right there in front of everyone. What difference would a few minutes have made? Shouldn't Lady Roxburgh and Victoria have been informed of what happened to Robert before he arrested anyone? I mean, he could have arrested Cheung discreetly outside the marquee."

"Of course he could, Vanessa, but it wouldn't matter where he arrested Cheung, he is still going to have jailed the wrong man," said Thoroughgood.

48

THOROUGHGOOD AND Hardie walked out of the rear of the marquee and headed for one of the wooden bridges spanning the ornamental lake.

"Christ, it's beautiful out here on a day like this," said Hardie.

Thoroughgood pointed to a wooden bench located on the other side of the bridge and the duo took a seat, far from the madding crowd.

"What now?" asked Hardie, "I don't see what your problem is with the arrest of Cheung, other than the way it was executed."

"You didn't see the crime scene down at the boathouse. It was like a chimp's tea party," retorted Thoroughgood. "Everything was just too . . . too bloody obvious. Did you notice the way Pigeon blanked me on the missing diary?"

"Yeah, old Randy wasn't having it. He's got his man and that's it, but to be fair, Gus, although he's used Cheung's arrest to showboat and put himself right in the limelight, I think you're clutching at straws, mate. I mean one brother is poisoned with cyanide and the other garrotted? They're not exactly your bog-standard MOs, Gus. He's got Cheung, hook, line and sinker and there ain't nothing you can do about it other than say 'Good job, Randy Pigeon,' then grin and bear it," concluded Hardie.

"Wrong," snapped Thoroughgood.

"Come on, Gus, it's clear that Pigeon is going to let your little altercation down at the boathouse go, so just let it be and enjoy the rest of your sick leave," advised Hardie.

"Not before I find the third diary. If I am right then Victoria, and maybe even her mother, is still in danger. Do you want to help me on this or am I on my own?"

"In danger from whom, Gus?" demanded Hardie, his exasperation becoming increasingly clear.

"Macintosh. He is behind all this. I don't know what his motive is, but I believe he has the third diary and has framed Cheung. The answer to that and the murders of Alexander and Robert are in that bloody diary and I am going to find it, come hell or high water."

"And just how are you gonna do that, mate?" asked Hardie sceptically.

"It's time to take a butchers at Macintosh's gatehouse pad down at the edge of the estate. I need you to keep him under surveillance for me from here on in, faither, until I get to the bottom of this. You saw how close he has become to Lady Elizabeth and I will guarantee he's up at the Hall now, comforting her. Take Victoria up there and keep your eye on her, but while you are there make sure that the other one is firmly on that slimy bastard Macintosh."

"For cryin' out loud, Gus, where is this all coming from? So what if he has managed to shoehorn himself into Lady Elizabeth's affections? Christ, she deserves someone to make her happy, and they looked pretty close earlier. Right now Macintosh has a job to do, because that poor woman will be in a helluva state. Are you sure this isn't more about Pigeon getting his big arrest than Cheung being the wrong man?"

"When I was leaving the boathouse Macintosh appeared as if by magic and he said something to me that didn't add up," said Thoroughgood. "I asked him if Robert Roxburgh had revealed to him if anything had been troubling him and Macintosh knew all about the diaries, the fact that one was missing and the infidelity of Ludovic Roxburgh."

"So what, Gus? Macintosh is a trusted employee and obviously one who is close to the family, so why wouldn't Robert Roxburgh confide in him? You're on a wild goose chase, mate," said Hardie flatly.

"But that is where you are wrong, Hardie. Victoria Roxburgh told me Robert had found out about Macintosh's recent liaison with Lady Elizabeth and was determined to boot him out of his job as butler, estate manager or whatever the hell he is. So why in the name of the wee man would Robert Roxburgh share anything confidential with a weasel like Macintosh, who was trying to warm his old girl's bed for her?" demanded Thoroughgood.

"An interesting concept," said Hardie rubbing his chin before adding, "But hardly compelling evidence that Macintosh is a criminal mastermind and has just successfully set up Glasgow's answer to Fu Man Chu."

"Precisely, and also exactly why, my old friend, I need you to play the role of babysitter-in-chief up at the big hoose while I have a little clandestine inspection of Macintosh's des res. Comprendez?"

"Maybes aye, maybes naw. Okay, I'll do it, but be careful Gus. If this all blows up then we want a way out," said Hardie.

"Just trust me on this one Kenny."

"Do I have an option?" asked Hardie.

Thoroughgood smiled grimly and walked off.

It took Thoroughgood fifteen minutes to walk to the gatehouse, thanks to the flow of traffic streaming out of Roxburgh Hall after an afternoon's entertainment that none of the guests were ever likely to forget. About 100 yards before the gatehouse Thoroughgood diverted round behind a large privet hedge and approached the gatehouse from the rear.

As he did so, doubts began to surface in his mind. Was he wrong after all? Hardie had a point. The murders of both the Roxburgh brothers bore all the hallmarks of Triad killings while Pigeon's revelation over the second clause in the contract between the Gwai Lo and the Roxburghs was another powerful nail in the coffin of his argument.

But then, what of Cheung's impassioned plea of innocence and his desire to make Victoria aware that the deal wouldn't fold? It didn't add up and Thoroughgood was sure the only way he was going to work things out was to locate the third diary. Would Macintosh be foolish enough to leave it in his own home? There was something else, too. He replayed his accidental meeting with the estate manager at the boathouse and somehow it was all too premeditated. Either way, Thoroughgood was determined that if the diary was in the building he would find it. But time, he was very much aware, was not on his side.

He emerged from behind the hedge and saw that the rear door was 15 feet away. With Macintosh ensconced at the Hall there was no need for caution and he quickly approached it. The top of the door was panelled with individual glass panes. Looking around for something useful to help him make his entrance he noticed a spade, conveniently leaning against an outhouse. Peering through the outhouse windows he saw something else that interested him. Picking up the spade he went to work on the outhouse door and eventually it gave way.

Inside, under a brown dust sheet, was the clear outline of a motor bike. As Thoroughgood ripped the covers off, he saw it was no ordinary machine. There, sitting in pristine metallic magnificence, was a motorbike Thoroughgood recognised to be of huge value. Closer inspection of the vintage bike revealed it to be a Brough SS-100, made famous by the great war-time hero, TE Lawrence of Arabia. But it was the inscription on the silver tank which took Thoroughgood's breath away. Three letters were inscribed on it: "LVR".

The voice in his head spoke, 'Robert Roxburgh was shot at down by the distillery office and how did the perp make his getaway?'

"Get in there!" answered Thoroughgood out loud.

Questions fired off in his head. Not least, how had Macintosh come by the hugely valuable Roxburgh family heirloom. Why had he chosen to use it to escape his failed attempt to blow Robert Roxburgh's brains out? But the DS did not have time to let the magnificent machine prove a time-consuming diversion from his real quarry.

Moments later, having reluctantly left the Brough, Thoroughgood smashed the back door open with a combination of spade work and several boots from his size tens.

'Where do I begin?' asked the voice in his head helpfully. 'Think man, think,' he told himself, surveying the front room. 'Come on, Gus, he's the estate manager so he must have an office in his place.'

"Upstairs," said the DS aloud and took the steps two at a time.

Sure enough there was an office nestled under the eaves. A paper-strewn desk had a laptop peeking out from under a pile of correspondence. However, despite rifling his way through all the paperwork and desk drawers, and searching for any secret compartments, Thoroughgood drew a blank. The rest of the office was similarly disappointing.

He made his way into the main bedroom and continued to systematically rifle his way through Macintosh's wardrobes and cupboards. Nothing.

'What about the toilet cistern?' he asked himself. It was a favourite with drug dealers and if the diary was kept secure and watertight in a plastic container then it was as good a hiding place as any.

Thoroughgood charged into the bathroom, his anticipation growing by the minute. He snatched at the cistern lid and almost dropped it in his haste. He needn't have bothered, it was empty. The spare bedroom also yielded nothing and Thoroughgood bounded back down the stairs and stood in the hall, running his hand through his hair as his frustration grew by the minute.

Looking through the glass door into the lounge, he observed a shotgun cabinet. Quickly, Thoroughgood retrieved the spade from the kitchen and returned to the locked cabinet. He swung the spade in a precise arc and the doors burst open.

Behind three padlocked and secure shotguns lay a canvas shoulder bag. Thoroughgood grabbed it by the strap and removed it from the cabinet. As he ran his hands over it he could feel a rectangular outline emerge. 'Probably a sandwich box,' said the voice in his head. Thoroughgood sat down on a large armchair and unbuckled the bag, emptying the contents onto the carpet in front of him. With a thud a faded, navy blue book fell out. He flipped it over and read its title aloud, "LVR War Diary Vol III: 1942/43. Gotcha!" said Thoroughgood triumphantly.

But before he could scrutinise its contents the DS noticed the letters 'TLM' stitched on the inside of the canvas bag's flap.

"Thomas Ludovic Macintosh," he said out loud.

Leafing through the diary, Thoroughgood took a deep breath and tried to slow himself down and introduce some methodology to his search. He knew that what he was looking for was the revelation of what had happened to Ludovic's paramour, Jill, but he was in no doubt that the outcome would prove to be her murder. What he didn't understand was why the contents of those pages would resonate with such lethal effect some 70 years or so later?

Thoroughgood began thumbing his way through the pages and it was clear that some strain was evident in Ludovic's relationship.

Have just had word that we will be leaving for Dieppe in May. Must get things patched up with J if I am to be able to think clearly and focus on the job in hand, LVR, Feb 18/42.

Thoroughgood fingered his way through the next few pages taking care to miss nothing of import. His eyes locked on the entry for April 22, 1942:

Now the truth is out I still cannot believe it. J is with child. I have been made a laughing stock and have no one to blame but myself, LVR.

"Bloody hell!" said Thoroughgood.

Checking his watch he realised he had now been away from the Hall for almost 45 minutes. He pulled his mobile out of his pocket and picked out Hardie's number. Pressed call. It went straight to voicemail.

Concern swept through Thoroughgood. The one thing that could be guaranteed about Hardie was that his mobile was on and attached to him as if by an umbilical cord. He picked up the landline, called directory enquiries and tried to reach the Hall, but the number rang out.

"Shit," said Thoroughgood, and clutching the diary tight, he ran out of the back door and made straight for the outhouse. Flicking the bike stand up with his right foot, he wheeled it out into the open. It was then that the words spoken by the immortal Lawrence about the machine he would meet his death upon came back to Thoroughgood.

"A skittish motor-bike with a touch of blood in it is better than all the riding animals on earth," repeated Thoroughgood. Offering a silent prayer, he applied an easy swing to the kick-starter and fired the low-compression motor without drama. His relief palpable, the DS swung Ludovic Roxburgh's pride and joy onto the estate road.

Moments later, having enjoyed the ride of his life, he approached the Hall. Lacking rear drive to steady the machine, Thoroughgood dabbed at the spongy rear footbrake for stability, as he came to a halt outside Roxburgh Hall. Exhilarated by his union with history, his resolve to face whatever the immediate future would throw at him strengthened.

49

THOROUGHGOOD CHARGED up the steps and ran under the stone archway, grabbed the wrought iron door handle, turning it with a vicious yank, and was relieved to see the oak door open invitingly. Standing in the entrance foyer, feeling the chill of the flagstones seeping through his brogues, he saw no point in restraint, "Hardie!" shouted the DS.

Silence.

"Here we go again," he muttered and made his way into the Scott lounge, but there was no sign of life there. Retracing his steps he came back out into the entrance hall and this time strode into the library. As he entered he saw the back of a greying head he would recognise anywhere, peeking up above the back of a massive leather settee.

"Hardie, for crying out loud, are you asleep on the job?" asked Thoroughgood as he walked round to face his friend. Hardie's eyes were indeed shut, and the DS gripped his mate by the shoulders and gave him a shake, but the only response was a groan. Hardie's breathing was short and shallow and Thoroughgood glanced over at the coffee table to the left of the settee and spotted a half-empty whisky glass.

"Bastard's poisoned him," said Thoroughgood as a panic swept over him that his mate would meet a similar fate to Alexander Roxburgh.

Quickly he ran through a mental checklist of the key indicators of cyanide poisoning, 'cherry-red lips, almond breath, nope – neither of them.'

Immediately the DS grabbed the jug of water next to the whisky glass and slung some of it over his colleague. Hardie's eyes opened drowsily and Thoroughgood gave him two mild slaps on either cheek to try and speed his return to consciousness.

"What the feck . . .?" muttered Hardie as he began to register who stood in front of him.

"It's me, faither. You've been drugged, old mate. I don't have time to help you shake it off. I've got the diary and although I haven't had time to read it, the fact it was locked inside Macintosh's shotgun cabinet is all the proof I need that he is behind this. The whys and wherefores of the diary's contents can wait. What can't wait is, where are the Dowager and Vicky?"

"I dunno," said Hardie, wiping the water away from his world-weary coupon, "Last I remember was Macintosh bringing me the whisky, and that's it."

"Where did you last see them? Is Vanessa with them?"

"Nope. Vanessa stayed down at the marquee to supervise the cleanup. When we came up here the Dowager headed for her bedroom and Victoria went up with her to make sure she was fine. When she came back downstairs she said something about wanting to visit her old man's grave at the bluebell wood, wherever that is. I told her she should stay put and then . . . the whisky and I'm caput," summed up Hardie.

"Can you make it onto your feet, Kenny?" asked Thoroughgood and as Hardie attempted to stand up the DS was forced to grab his arms as his friend almost buckled at the knees.

"Look, Kenny, I need you to check on the Dowager while I go and find Victoria. By the way, where's your mobile?" asked Thoroughgood.

The DC stuck a hand in his suit jacket and fished it out, "Feck, I put it off when we were in the marquee for the launch."

"Well, get it on, call Tomachek and get us back-up as soon as you can, old fella. The bluebell wood's halfway towards the boathouse and a left fork. So once you have checked up on the Dowager, get your arse down there, pronto. I might need help."

"What do you mean, Gus?"

"I mean, that bastard Macintosh has murdered two of the Roxburghs already, so what is to stop whatever is motivating him making it a hat-trick? Just make sure the Dowager is okay and text me to confirm. I would help you have a scout about the hall for Macintosh, but I don't think there is much doubt where he is now. Okay, I'm off, mate."

"Take care, Gus," said Hardie as the DS walked out of the library.

Victoria Roxburgh had barely been aware of her surroundings as she walked from the Hall to the bluebell wood where her father was buried. She had made sure her mother, already self-sedated, had gone to bed and left.

Victoria wanted to be alone with her grief. Wanted time to try and work it all out, to understand what this all meant for her family and where they went from here. Cheung's arrest must surely mean that the whole deal with the Gwai Lo would collapse. If that happened, financial ruin awaited the Roxburghs.

As she reached the footpath that would take her down to the heart of the wood and her father's grave, the tears began to well up in her eyes and pour down her cheeks, just when she thought she had no more left. It was the end of the Roxburghs – the end of everything that she knew, loved and cherished. Robbie and Alex had lost their lives for nothing. But why? She felt anger burn inside her although she knew it was futile.

Stopping just short of the clearing where her father was buried she picked some fresh bluebells, as she always did, before replacing the withered flowers at her father's grave as more tears ran down her face.

Finally, she reached the bench her mother had erected at the grave. She sat down and stared at the headstone, reading the words embossed on it: "Here lies William 5th Viscount Lomond, beloved father of Robert, Alexander and Victoria, much loved husband of Elizabeth. He maybe gone but he will never be forgotten."

In the distance she heard what she thought was the sound of a motor bike engine although it seemed to lack the abrasiveness she would normally associate with one.

She spoke into the silence, "What now, Papa?"

The crack of a twig snapping sent a shiver of fear down her spine. She looked up, startled, but was immediately reassured by Thoroughgood's presence. Sitting down next to her he looked into her molten brown eyes, "Hey, Vicky, how you holdin' up?"

Despite her determination not to cry any more Victoria

was helpless to stop a huge sob escaping her and buried her head in Thoroughgood's jacket. He quickly fished out a handkerchief and after a couple of minutes she managed to regain enough composure to smile her gratitude and said, "Ever get a feeling of déjà vu, Gus?"

As he looked into her eyes Thoroughgood could feel his self-control deserting him. He managed an awkward smile, but just as he was about to open his mouth Victoria kissed him and Thoroughgood gave in to the moment.

They parted seconds later and Thoroughgood couldn't help himself, "Jeez," he said.

"I've been wanting to do that for a while now and I guess, what with everything that has happened today, my inhibitions left me. I could say I'm sorry, Gus, but that would be a lie."

"Snap," said Thoroughgood.

An awkward silence enveloped them as a tremor of guilt rippled through their minds.

Thoroughgood took the bull by the horns. "I'm sorry, Vicky. The timing is not great, but I have found your grandfather's missing diary and I'm beginning to put together who is behind the murder of your brothers and the framing of Raymond Cheung." With that, he pulled the diary from his pocket and placed it on his knees as Victoria's eyes widened in disbelief.

"Where did you find it?"

"It was in a canvas satchel hidden behind shotguns which were snugly locked up in a cabinet at Macintosh's place," said the DS.

"Dear God," said Victoria.

"There's more, Vicky. Under a dustsheet in his outhouse, I found a Brough SS-100 motorbike."

"Grandfather's pride and joy. Did it have . . .?"

"LVR engraved on the silver chrome petrol tank? Yes it did. I'm afraid I've taken the liberty of riding it up here and it's parked at the start of the way through the wood. You told me that Robert had been shot at and his assailant had escaped on a motorbike. I suspect that can mean only one thing, and that is that Macintosh is behind all of this, the threatening letter, the murders of your brothers and Cheung's wrongful arrest. But now, at last, I have a good idea why."

"Please go on."

"Macintosh's newfound affections for your mother – how long have they been evident?" asked the DS.

"Robbie found out when he walked in on them in the stable. I don't blame Mama, she's been so lonely and she has not been short of suitors, but for some reason she rejected them all in favour of Macintosh's advances. Maybe it was a case of better the devil you know," said Victoria, clearly struggling to come to terms with the unfolding scenario.

"I think Macintosh is using his growing place in your mother's affections to manoeuvre himself into a position that will not stop at mere estate manager. He wants to be lord of the bloody manor. The best way for him to achieve that is by wooing your mother, Vicky. The bad news is that I watched them earlier in the marquee and they were fairly public in their show of affection for each other. With what has happened to Alexander and Robert, and Cheung's arrest, the way is clear for Macintosh to play the strong man at your mother's side in her hour of need. I would wager that the ultimate reward for all of that will be marriage to Lady Elizabeth," said Thoroughgood, staring balefully at William Roxburgh's grave.

296

"But if my mother's feelings for him are growing like that, then why murder my brothers?" asked Victoria.

"In Robert's case that's an obvious one, Vicky, as you know. As for Alex, I'm afraid he just happened to be in the wrong place at the wrong time. The cyanide in the whisky was intended for Robert. He had discovered Macintosh's liaison with your mother and, as we know, had already warned him his days at the hall were numbered. Unfortunately, Alex got in the way. With Macintosh's original plan for Robert thwarted, the perfect way to get rid of him was to frame Cheung for his murder, making it look like Robert had been the target all along and thus kill two birds with one stone. Leaving Macintosh indispensable to your mother. But there is more Victoria – it's all here in the diary."

"What do you mean? How can there be more?" asked Victoria.

"Macintosh wanted revenge on your family. I couldn't quite comprehend the meaning of the threatening letter but ask yourself – what is the oldest sin or sins? And why would it cast the longest shadow?"

Victoria's face went blank.

"Try infidelity. It haunts your grandfather throughout his war diaries. It's ironic, because the investigation I have just completed was sparked by a similar case of infidelity, just not one that's 70 years old. Vicky, ask yourself, why does it cast the longest shadow?"

"I'm sorry, Gus, I can't work it out," said Vicky.

"Because there was a child produced from Ludovic's affair with this woman Jill. Macintosh may well be the illegitimate grandson of Ludovic, Lord Roxburgh, and his mistress Jill. I have no doubt he is of your blood, just from the wrong side of the covers. I haven't had the time to read through the third diary as thoroughly as I need to discover all the answers, but something happened between them. Most probably it was her pregnancy, which I chanced upon in an entry in April, and Ludovic's refusal to accept it. I reckon that some sort of nasty little blackmail situation developed, leading to Jill's demise. I just need time to fit the rest of the pieces together, but I believe that Macintosh has, and is, the answer to all this," said Thoroughgood.

"Dear God!" blurted out Victoria.

Thoroughgood grimaced, "I'm afraid there were three letters stitched inside the flap of the bag that contained the diary: 'TLM'. Thomas Ludovic Macintosh is the longest shadow cast by the oldest sin."

"No, it can't be true," said Victoria, her agitation obvious.

"Oh, but it is true, cousin," growled a voice from the other side of the grave.

Out of the birches and the shadow of the fading light strode Macintosh.

In his right hand a revolver was levelled at them.

50

MACINTOSH WALKED around the grave and stood five feet away to their right, keeping Thoroughgood nearest to the handgun.

"So, you have it all worked out Thoroughgood, almost."

The DS forced himself to remain calm, "Maybe not all of it. Part of me is wondering just how you thought you would get away with it? But now that we are finally getting to the bottom, let me introduce you properly."

"Be my guest," said Macintosh, the revolver now at waist height.

"Victoria, I would like you to meet Thomas Ludovic Macintosh . . ." Thoroughgood let the silence at the end of the sentence draw out deliberately.

"Buchan was my grandmother's maiden name. It was her name when Ludovic Roxburgh murdered her to avoid losing his place in Churchill's government and bringing disgrace on the House of Roxburgh. You got it right. I was given his name as a reminder of him," snapped Macintosh, the revolver wavering slightly as emotion surged through him.

"But Roxburgh didn't abandon his daughter, did he

Macintosh? Your middle name is surely proof of that. For God's sake. Surely your presence 'boy and man' was down to the fact that you were raised here, just like your mother before you, I'd guess, in an estate worker's cottage, or even raised in service at Roxburgh Hall? Born in '42, sometime between April and May, before Ludovic left on the disastrous Dieppe raid. She would be 66 now, if she was still alive. What about your father?" asked Thoroughgood.

Suddenly Macintosh took a step forward and smashed the butt of the pistol off Thoroughgood's jaw, sending the DS flying off the bench onto the grass beside it.

Victoria screamed as Macintosh gripped her throat with his left hand and placed the point of the barrel to her head, "Thanks to your blundering detective friend, you must both die, but you at least deserve the truth, my sweet little Victoria."

Macintosh spotted that Thoroughgood was trying to haul himself up with the help of the bench, "Stay where you are, Thoroughgood."

In Thoroughgood's right hand was the diary. Raising it, he taunted Macintosh, "Here it is Macintosh. Let's read all about it."

Macintosh shoved Victoria back onto the bench. "There's no need. I'll tell you what happened to Jill Buchan. My grandmother fell pregnant to Roxburgh, but he didn't want to know. The monster tried to force a termination on her. Jill wouldn't give in to him and went into hiding to have the baby. My mother Clare was born two weeks prematurely, at the beginning of May, 1942. Roxburgh found out about the birth and lured my grandmother with a pack of lies to a trysting point, not far from where he was stationed with the SOE, at Inverorchy," Macintosh took a breath and steadied the revolver, which had begun to waver again.

"Why didn't you tell any of us this, Thomas?" Victoria interrupted. "Have we all been so horrible and cruel to you? What of my mother? Surely you are aware she has feelings for you, yet . . ." Victoria broke off as the implications of what she had just said brought a wave of nausea over her.

"Be quiet, you pampered bitch, and you'll find out why." Macintosh spat. "They met and argued, and your dear grandfather's revolver went off, injuring Jill in the arm. After patching it up they quarrelled again, but this time Ludovic murdered her in cold blood and dumped her body like a piece of shit. Within 48 hours he was on his way to Dieppe while it took three days before my grandmother's body was discovered in her shallow grave." Once again Macintosh was interrupted by Victoria.

"You lying bastard! There is no way grandfather would have done that," she screamed at him.

"He admitted as much in his own hand, in that bloody diary your boyfriend is clutching. But it didn't end there. He was forced to enlist the services of the great and the good to cover up her murder, reaching as far up as Churchill. Two witnesses had seen Jill head for the 'Lovers Tree', but they also saw a man of military appearance pass them on the same route ten minutes later. Yet, despite providing descriptions of him they were never used to bring Ludovic Roxburgh to justice."

"How could that be?" demanded Thoroughgood.

"Shut up!" snapped Macintosh, as he took a step

301

closer to the DS, the gun now trained on Thoroughgood's head. "The top detective of the day was dispatched from Glasgow to solve the murder which involved four bullet wounds in Jill's body from a .38 calibre military revolver, and you know what this arsehole did? He spent the rest of the war trying to track down each and every member of the base and firing their revolvers into a barrel to match the calibre with the murder weapon," said Macintosh, his anger mounting.

"Come on, man, surely an artist's impression of the witnesses' description could be easily matched to the mugshots of every member of the base? The only problem being that most of the base were wiped out when the Dieppe landing went tits up," offered Thoroughgood.

"Exactly! Detective Chief Superintendent William F Smith, of the City of Glasgow Police, in the absence of a ballistics match, and in the aftermath of the death of most of the invasion force, opted for the convenient truth that the killer perished on the beaches of Dieppe," concluded Thomas Ludovic Macintosh.

"But why has that led you to murder my brothers, your own flesh and blood, for God's sake?" asked Victoria.

"Because your boyfriend was wrong. There is an even older sin than that of infidelity within marriage, and one that casts a far longer shadow, one I have had to live with all my life," said Macintosh, his face masked in the shade caused by the dying of the day, the emotion in his voice raw.

"What would that be, for Chrissakes, man? You've proved that you're a cold-blooded killer just like your grandfather? But murdering your own flesh and blood? You twisted fucker . . ." raged Thoroughgood.

"You're wrong. Ludovic Roxburgh was not my grandfather. He was my father," said Macintosh and advanced towards Thoroughgood.

51

VICTORIA THREW herself in front of the DS, "So you kill us both, Thomas, but what will that leave you with? Do you think it will wipe out the shadow that you have lived your life under?"

Struggling to his feet Thoroughgood added his voice to Victoria's defiance, "Ask yourself this, Macintosh. Do you think the Gwai Lo are going to walk away and just let you piss all over their Dark Ocean investment? Come on, man, why do this to the family that have given you a life? Do you think your mother, your grandmother, your fuckin' father, even, would have wanted it to end this way? With one Roxburgh, illegitimate or not, murdering all three of his cousins, and for what? Because there will be nothing left for you, or of you, by the time the Gwai Lo get through with you."

Macintosh stopped just short of them and smiled, "Believe me, Cheung will remain happily incarcerated and my secret safe with your colleague, DI Pigeon. I'm sure he will continue to remain a great help to me in my new role as head of the Roxburgh dynasty for hereafter," he erupted into a cruel laugh.

"You're fuckin' jokin'! There is no way that arse

Pigeon would be bright enough to get involved with you and your master plan to create a new Roxburgh dynasty without managing to blurt out something to someone," raged Thoroughgood.

"He's done well up until now, Thoroughgood. Do you think that the promise of a six figure job as head of security for Glen Lomond Distilleries, after he takes early retirement, isn't a powerful inducement for silence? Even for a man of the Inspector's limited intellect? It also provides a delicious parallel to the murder of my grandmother by my dear father, who clearly bought off the investigating officer with a similar promise that ended in a knighthood for services rendered . . . to Ludovic Roxburgh of course," said Macintosh resonating menace.

He continued, "But enough of your outrage, Thoroughgood. It is unfortunate for you, and even more so for my cousin, that you have demonstrated a limited level of intelligence that has allowed you to unravel my riddle, even if you got the detail wrong. But then, even 66 years later, there seems to be no change in the quality of Scottish detective work. All this time I have had to watch and endure as the Roxburgh brothers have ruined an inheritance that was rightly mine. Now the time is here for my dynasty to be created, but first you must both die."

Thoroughgood pushed in front of Victoria and once again Macintosh laughed out loud, "How very heroic of you, Thoroughgood. You may indeed be a true Ivanhoe, but it is I who am the disinherited one. Unfortunately, the time has come for you to meet your maker."

"How the hell do you propose to do that, Macintosh? Or should I call you Roxburgh? Whatever happens here, you will never walk free as an innocent man, never escape your fate, I promise you. Your dynasty is a fantasy, man! Surely you can see that?" spat Thoroughgood, desperately trying to figure out an exit strategy.

"I will put a bullet through your head and then one in dear Victoria's, both from the same gun, and covered in your prints, Detective Sergeant. More pleasing symmetry between the tragedy that happened all these years back between my father and my grandmother, and now about to befall you and my cousin. Two lovers, tormented and then killed by the heat of their passions. A pity," said Macintosh and fingered the trigger on the Colt.

"No, Thomas! I beg you!" cried Victoria.

"I'm sorry cousin, it is too late," said Macintosh.

Thoroughgood launched the diary at Macintosh with all the power he could muster and the sudden impact jerked his trigger finger. The bullet shot into the foliage a yard to Thoroughgood's left and then the DS was on Macintosh. Wrapping both arms around the estate manager's midriff, Thoroughgood rammed him back and dumped him on the ground in a spear tackle that took the breath out of Macintosh.

As Thoroughgood came down on top of his would-be killer, Macintosh once more aimed the Colt at his head and only a desperate swerve to his left caused the second bullet to miss him by an inch.

Victoria screamed. "Stop it! Stop it!"

Macintosh smashed his fist off the side of Thoroughgood's head and he reeled back against the fencing surrounding the grave. As Macintosh attempted to disengage and give himself the room to finish Thoroughgood off, Victoria threw herself on his back, gripping his neck with both hands and forcing the Colt skywards.

Thoroughgood heard Macintosh shouting, "You little bitch!" as he began to regain his scrambled senses and he saw that Macintosh had sent her flying after ramming an elbow into her stomach. With his back to Thoroughgood, the bastard of Roxburgh Hall began his murderous advance on Victoria.

"Goodbye," said Macintosh.

Thoroughgood launched himself at Macintosh. Grabbing Macintosh's right arm with both hands, he tried to manoeuvre himself between the Colt and Victoria, but the gun remained trained on her. All the hours he had spent engaged on estate husbandry had given Macintosh muscle and sinew that were too strong for Thoroughgood to overcome.

The Colt was just a foot in front of him, still aimed at Victoria. Thoroughgood could see Macintosh's trigger finger twitch. With one final surge of all the energy he still possessed, Thoroughgood wrestled the gun around towards himself and Macintosh.

His last reserves of energy almost spent, Thoroughgood knew what he had to do to save her. He had no other option.

Standing three feet away from him Victoria saw what Thoroughgood was attempting and screamed, "I love you!"

The desperation in his eyes and the exhaustion that emanated from his features seared Victoria with helplessness. With the Colt pointing his way, Thoroughgood clamped his fingers around Macintosh's hand, and applied all the strength he still retained into one desperate squeeze.

The trigger jolted back.

The shot rang out and its lethal bullet scythed right through Thoroughgood and then Macintosh, on its deadly trajectory, throwing both men backwards.

Looking on in wretched disbelief Victoria Roxburgh's tormented scream shattered the night, "Nooooooo!"

Parallel Lines:

The Glasgow Supremacy

R.J Mitchell's debut outing for Detective Inspector Gus Thoroughgood is an edgy, fast-paced crime thriller set in the streets of Glasgow that tells the story of the deadly rivalry between Detective Sergeant Gus Thoroughgood and his criminal nemesis, Declan Meechan. With Meechan on the verge of complete control of Glasgow's lucrative drug trade after bludgeoning his rivals into bloody submission, Thoroughgood vows to be the cop that will bring the crime lord down. The lethal intensity of their conflict is heightened by the presence of Celine Lynott, the woman who broke Thoroughgood's heart ten years earlier, and looks set to do so all over again when she agrees to be Meechan's wife. Parallel Lines is a powerful and compelling story with a real sting in the tail.

"They call Scottish crime fiction 'tartan noir' - and if that's the case, then the thread of red that runs through Parallel Lines is a river of blood, and the blacks and greens are the bruises on a battered corpse. This book doesn't pull any punches in its depiction of a deadly cops-and-robbers feud that strays far beyond the procedural into the personal. At the core of the story is a traditional love triangle - the hero, the villain and the girl that gets between them - but it's Mitchell's first-hand knowledge of what goes on behind the police station's closed doors that sets the book apart. This is a real page-turner: once that plot is set in motion, like a car with its brake pipes cut hurtling down a steep Glasgow street - and that's an image from the book you won't forget - it carries the reader right through to its bullet-strewn climax."

ALAN MORRISON
Group Arts Editor, Herald & Times

"RJ Mitchell has joined the ranks of Scottish crime writers with a stunning debut thriller, 'Parallel Lines: The Glasgow Supremacy'. It packs a punch that Mike Tyson would have been proud of.

"The action rages relentlessly through the streets of Glasgow with bent coppers, double-crossing gang members, brutal action and more twists than a downhill slalom race, leading to a tension-filled climax that paves the way for a sequel the reader will surely demand."

RUSSELL LEADBETTER
Evening Times.

The Hurting:

The Glasgow Terror

In R.J Mitchell's second crime novel, we find Gus Thoroughgood recovering from injuries received in his adventures in 'Parallel Lines: The Glasgow Supremacy' and wondering whether to continue his career in the Glasgow Police force. Having handed in his resignation, he finds himself rejoining the force under duress on leaving the police convalescence home, Castlebrae. Thoroughgood and Hardie find themselves embroiled in a world of terrorism, shaking the foundations of the city they love. Terrorist attacks in and around Glasgow see the duo return to action, working with MI5 in a race against time to discover the source of these attacks.

The Hurting: The Glasgow Terror is a fast-paced, rollercoaster ride through Glasgow's seedy underworld and that of international terrorism. Drawing experience from his 12 year career as a police officer, R.J. Mitchell provides an accurate portrayal of police procedure while guiding the reader through an intricate plot of lies and subterfuge.

Join the conversation

Tweet the author **@spitfiremedia** and
tag it with **#Thoroughgood**

Or tweet **@FledglingPress** using the tag
#Thoroughgood

You can also find out more about R.J Mitchell
and what he's up to by visiting his blog:
www.rjmitchellauthor.co.uk